THE SCENT OF RAIN

A NOVEL

ANNE MONTGOMERY

Treehouse Publishing Group | St. Louis, MO

Treehouse Publishing Group
Saint Louis, MO 63116

For information, contact:
Treehouse Publishing Group
4168 Hartford Street, Saint Louis, MO 63116
www.blankslatepress.com

Treehouse is an imprint of Amphorae Publishing Group, LLC
www.amphoraepublishing.com

Manufactured in the United States of America
Cover Design by Elena Makansi
Cover photography: Shutterstock / IStock
Set in Adobe Caslon Pro and Avenir Next

Library of Congress Control Number: 2017900715
ISBN: 9780996390149

Dedicated to my three sons, Brandon, Ziggy, and Troy, all of whom spent time in the foster care system. They constantly surprise me with their resiliency. I'm proud they call me Mom.

And inspired by Flora Jessop, who twice escaped the cult in the twin cities of Colorado City, Arizona, and Hildale, Utah, and has spent her life rescuing other girls and women from the Fundamentalist Church of Jesus Christ of Latter-Day Saints.

Petrichor: an earthy scent that often accompanies the
first rain after a long period of warm, dry weather . . .
constructed from Greek, *petros*, meaning stone or
rock + *ichor*, the fluid that flows in the veins of the Gods.

1

Rose Madsen couldn't risk staying out much longer. She still felt the paddle blows—what her mother called "appropriate corrective measures"—from the last time she'd disappeared for too long. But the chill of the spring morning had eased following sun-up, a full two hours after Rose had risen to do her pre-breakfast chores, and now the high desert sky was a cloudless blue. When she got back, she'd have to bathe, dress, and feed Becky, a chore she didn't mind doing, but right now all she wanted was to wade in the creek and feel the sun on her face. Becky could wait a little while longer.

"Recalcitrant," her mother often said, referring to her seventh daughter. Rose rolled the word around in her mouth, but the term had too many sharp edges. Other folks in town didn't use words like recalcitrant. Children were either good or bad. She'd overheard people say Mother's vocabulary was too prideful, a sin that needed correcting, and struggled with the thought of Mother as a sinner.

Rose dipped a hand into the stream and marveled that just a day earlier it had been dry as a bone, nothing but fine sand and loose rock. But then the snow high in the mountains had melted, delivering a clear, cold flow that Rose knew would quickly disappear.

She dabbed at the milk splotches on the hem of her ankle-length cotton dress. She'd been milking cows for over ten years, but no matter how often she squeezed those velvety teats, she could never avoid splashing her clothes. Rose scrubbed at the almost invisible stains on the sky-blue fabric knowing that Mother would probably spot them no matter how hard she worked. She'd be shut up in that tiny room in the barn, forced to study her dog-eared book of scriptures and go without food because "dirty clothes proved one harbored dirty thoughts." No matter how often Mother said that, Rose had no idea what it meant.

She removed her Nikes and socks and stepped into the current, bunching her skirt with one hand, lest the garment trail in the water providing proof she'd sneaked away. The water rushed around her legs, numbing them to mid-calf. She shivered. It was exhilarating. She closed her eyes and lifted her face to the sky. If only she could stay here as long as she wanted.

She drew in a deep breath of cool, desert air and started to step back out onto the creek bank when a rock beneath the sparkling surface caught her eye and drew her hand into the flow. The stone was egg-shaped, spotted with the remains of multi-colored pebbles. She remembered learning in science class that stones like this were made up of smaller rocks that had been forced deep into the earth, melted, and fused together, only to reemerge countless years later to be washed and tumbled by the river, edges softened, rounded. She held the stone in her palm and ran her thumb over its smooth surface.

How long had this transformation taken? Mr. Wayland, who had proudly passed his rock samples around the classroom, might have known the answer. But he was gone, and the school was closed. Large goats had eaten away the greenery that once surrounded the building that housed the classrooms. A sign above the doorway still read Colorado City Unified School District #14. Trash littered the grounds that were hemmed in by a chain link fence. The Prophet had decreed that all children should be home schooled. And so they were.

Rose wanted to keep the stone, but that was impossible. The telltale smoothness of the rock would surely shout out that its life had been spent tumbling in the riverbed, one of the many places Rose was never allowed to go. Mother had warned her repeatedly about the terrible flash floods that could barrel down the mountain without warning, sweeping away everything near Short Creek. Rose wriggled her toes in the frigid stream, then sighed and dropped the stone back into the water where it landed with a plunk.

2

The sun tormented Adan Reyes.

The road he traveled cut through almost two million acres of northwestern Arizona, a remote and unforgiving area north of the Grand Canyon called the Arizona Strip, a land of giant, tabletop mesas and rough red mountains with broken spines jutting into the sky.

He raised his hand, shielding dark brown eyes, wishing he still had his sunglasses, which he'd sold to a college kid in Flagstaff for five bucks. He'd purchased a small cheeseburger and a bottle of water at McDonald's— the only food he'd consumed since lunchtime the day before—then stuffed the remaining change in his pocket for emergencies. The absurdity was clear. The money was useless. He hadn't passed a business, a house, or any sign of civilization since the trucker dropped him off.

Adan had been sure another ride would come along, but only a few vehicles had passed by, and the drivers had stared, then ignored the boy with his thumb out. So, he'd started walking. How long ago? He had no idea.

The sun smoldered overhead, sucking at his skin.

What had brought him to this desolate place? Adan shook his head. What an idiot! He'd certainly not planned his escape well. His impulse had been to get away as fast as he could, before it was too late. So, he'd simply stuck out his thumb and gone wherever the drivers who picked him up were headed.

He was baking; his arms below the grimy white T-shirt sleeves burned a reddish-brown. Heat radiated beneath the Diamondbacks baseball cap, a parting gift from his mother. He wrestled with removing the hat to cool off and leaving his head covered so the bill would shade his eyes, giving him some chance to see the shimmering pavement stretching out before him.

Up ahead, a dusty unpaved road cut off to the left and snaked across the rocky ground. He squinted up the trail, hoping for some sign of life, but the track disappeared into the hills. He reached for the water bottle he'd tucked into the mesh netting on his backpack and held the container at eye level. The dark grime beneath his fingernails produced a sudden urge to wash his hands, but only an inch of water remained. He thought of the long showers he used to take back in Phoenix, then looked down at his filthy jeans and the once-dazzling white Jordan's he'd worked so hard for. He felt a sudden rush of guilt, thinking of his poor mother who gasped when she heard what he paid for the shoes. He took great care with his clothes, and his bi-monthly haircuts, always pestering the barber to make sure the razor-cuts edging his short black hair were perfectly straight. His eyes filled with tears, and he began to laugh.

Stop it! This isn't funny, he told himself. He gripped the plastic bottle, crackling the container, the sound piercing in the surrounding stillness. He'd grown up in the Sonoran

Desert, had been cautioned by his high school football and track coaches about the importance of hydration, and the damaging—and sometimes fatal—effects of heat sickness. And here he was, in the middle of nowhere with one slug of water left. What a fool.

Adan scanned the area, searching for evidence of a home or at least some shade. But only endless miles of wire fencing crisscrossing the land, spreading away from the mountains and the freshly oiled blacktop that ribboned up ahead, provided any proof of human habitation.

A sudden hot wind pelted him with debris so he shut his eyes tight. When he opened them again, he saw the dust devil dance down the road, the tiny tornado's funnel a smoky-swirl rising into the sky. He watched the gray shaft sway and twist, then placed the water bottle back in the mesh pocket and slung his pack on his shoulders. He removed his cap to wipe the sweat from his forehead and continued walking, eyes fixed to the golden yellow line that divided the road.

Sometime later, Adan lay on the rocky berm beside the pavement and reached for the bottle. The hot plastic container was empty. When had he finished the last of his water? He lay his head back and stared at the hazy sky and, for the first time, saw the pale half-moon resting overhead.

3

Trak Benally shifted the aged truck into gear, picking up speed as he hit the invisible line dividing Arizona and Utah. He glanced at the clock on the dash. He'd put in eight hours repairing a roof, sweltering in the late spring sun. Still, he couldn't complain. He enjoyed the work, which baffled most of his friends who thought he was destined for bigger things. He'd joined up right after 9/11 and served two stints as an army medic in Afghanistan, then earned a degree in Criminal Justice from Arizona State University. But he didn't stay in Phoenix long. Home had beckoned, and he'd returned to Hurricane where he'd made a name for himself as the guy who could fix anything.

Unscrewing the cap of his Gatorade, he gulped down the green liquid and chased it with an equal amount of water. He wiped his mouth with the back of his hand as the white Ford pickup roared down the empty road past the sign that read: Summit: 4310 Feet. Wind-sculpted cliffs rose through a dusty sky. Would he have retuned to this lonely stretch of land had his parents not needed him? His dad, in his mid-seventies at the time, struggled with heart problems. Mom, five years older, stubbornly refused to bother her only child with the fact that caring for her husband had become increasingly difficult. Trak's best friend, Chase Allred, was the one who made the call, summoning him from his job in Phoenix where he'd worked in the Maricopa County court system.

Trak laughed out loud when he thought of his friend. They attended grammar school together and went on to high school, where Chase turned out to be the smartest kid in the class. He went on to become a doctor, earning an MD in pediatrics at the University of Colorado and a PhD in anatomy and physiology at UCLA. But something had drawn him back to Hurricane as well. Dr. Allred now practiced family medicine in the place he always swore he couldn't wait to leave.

Just past the sign for Apple Valley, he saw a towering dust devil sweep along the desert floor, the twister a testament to the heat. Aside from the recent freaky storm that had left a late snow on the Vermillion Cliffs for a day, the weather in the Arizona Strip would soon be primarily high desert hot.

A shower and a walk down to the Main Street Café were all Trak could think about. His stomach rumbled, and he reached to the seat beside him to grab a handful of the peanut butter pretzels he always kept for the times he went too long between meals.

When Trak looked up, he gripped the steering wheel. There was something in the road, off to the side. Maybe a cow had broken through the wire fencing and been hit, but Trak saw no damaged cars. A cow strike at high speed would certainly disable or even total a car. He considered the possibility that a big truck might have hit the animal and just continued on, but then he saw that the lump in the road was not a cow. A bright orange line bisecting what appeared to be a backpack made him realize this was no animal.

Trak slowed to a stop by the prostrate form and jumped from the pickup, jolted by a sudden flash of memory. He was tending a soldier, unconscious and face down following an IED explosion, a young man who, when Trak turned him over, was so mutilated that only his dog tags could identify who he was.

But Track put that memory aside and went into Army medic mode, quickly checking for a pulse and obvious signs of trauma. He noted the dirty clothes and empty water bottle still clutched in the boy's hand, and, ominously, no obvious signs of sweating. What appeared to be a new Diamondback's baseball cap had rolled away, exposing a thick shock of dark hair, darker even than Trak's. But this boy did not appear to be of Native American descent, a heritage Trak claimed on his Navajo father's side. Trak was sure the kid was Hispanic; a rarity in the towns of Colorado City and Hurricane, where most everyone was blond headed and blue eyed.

The boy was suffering from heat sickness, a dangerous situation that could quickly lead to death, so Track gathered him in his arms and situated him on the front passenger seat. Then he grabbed the baseball cap from the dirt and pulled out his cellphone, hoping he could get a signal.

4

Rose brushed the skirt of her dress, then smoothed the loose wisps of her elaborately-styled blonde hair. It had been teased high off her forehead and fell in a thick white braid down her back. Satisfied there were no visible vestiges of her visit to the steam, she took a breath, and, though her inclination was to run just because she enjoyed the feeling, she forced herself to walk slowly back to the house.

She passed the high, white walls of the Prophet's compound, where, unless you were in exactly the right position, seeing inside was impossible. And even then, the view afforded only a glimpse of the vast three-gabled roof, dark windows, and a portion of the front door, which sat atop a long stairway, and over which the word ZION was spelled out in large black letters.

Rose had been taught that the Prophet should always be foremost in her mind, since he was the closest man to God on Earth. So the news of his arrest and imprisonment far from the beautiful land and the people he loved had been disturbing. But as Rose walked by the massive enclosure with tiny black cameras attached high on wrought iron fence posts, not a single thought of Eldon Higbee entered her mind.

A vast garden spread out before the Prophet's residence, where, on this morning—like all others—Billy Jessop worried over rows of crops, tending tomatoes, and corn, and squash, and potatoes, and the giant yellow sunflowers that completely edged one side of the field. Billy was a grown man who would, under different circumstances, have been called William. Females like Rose would have approached with deference and downcast eyes, lest they appear disrespectful. But Billy was what the people called one of God's punishments, sent to remind them that they were still not perfect enough for his Celestial Kingdom.

Billy peeked from under the crumpled cap that always threatened to fall from his overly large forehead and waved heartily at Rose. A smile creased his misshapen face presenting thick lips and heavy brows. In his mid-twenties, Billy had lived much longer than most of the others, and he'd found a place here, tending his beloved sunflowers with their golden petals and dark brown eyes. The plants grew taller than any in the community and produced fat gray and white seeds that even the Prophet was known to eat. Sunshine—Sunny—the longhaired yellow dog that never strayed far from Billy, watched as Rose walked past, then wagged her tail and settled back on the freshly turned dark earth under the row of sunflowers.

Rose waved back at Billy and continued down the road. She saw the unfinished shells of houses on lots along the way, dilapidated farm equipment, and scattered construction materials littering the landscape. Many buildings lacked doors or windows. A few months earlier, an untended three year old had wandered up the stairs in one of the half-built structures and fallen out onto an ancient rusted thresher. The child had been pierced right through. Since the toddler was a girl, her brother—who had been charged with watching her—had disappeared sometime in the night.

Rose shivered even though the day was already quite hot. She had to be very careful, as Mother always said. She feared being plucked away, becoming one of the people who vanished without warning, most of whom never came back.

Birds played in the massive pecan trees that shaded Rose's home, branches spreading into the sky with emerald leaves that whispered in the gentle breeze. She walked along the white picket fence and through the gate. The iron-framed swing sets with their green, white, pink, and blue plastic bucket seats sat empty, abandoned since only Rose and her two sisters remained in the home that had once housed sixteen children. Damp bath towels hung limp on the lines. The vegetable garden glittered, evidence that someone, probably Sister Wife Glea, had just watered.

Rose smiled as she mounted the steps. But then the screen door creaked open.

"Where have you been?" Bliss Madsen asked her daughter, guarding the entryway, arms folded across her chest.

5

Adan tried to focus on the man. He could make out a blue flannel shirt and close-cropped, white-blond hair, but his head pounded and his tongue felt like a foreign object, swollen and wedged in his mouth so he couldn't swallow. He closed his eyes and listened.

"You were right to call me." Chase readjusted the cold pack he'd placed beneath the boy's neck.

Trak shook his head and looked down at the boy.

"When I couldn't get a response out of him . . . Shit."

"What the hell do you think he was doing out there?"

"Hitching. What else?"

"You miss my point. Look at him. Kid's Hispanic. Who is he? Where's he going?"

"I searched his pack and he has no identification. No drivers license, no school ID, no name or address on anything," Trak said. "The only identifying thing I can see is that logo on his shirt."

The doctor peered at the boy's left breast. The name, 'Jaguars Football' was emblazoned over a blue cat head that bore ferocious incisors.

Adan flinched at the doctor's touch and tried to get up.

"Whoa, hold on there, cowboy," Chase said. "Grab his arm, Trak. I don't want him ripping out the IV line."

Adan struggled, but was too weak to do much good. The dark-haired man had huge hands that were now firmly pinning him to a sheet-covered table.

The cold pack placed along the boy's thigh fell to the floor. Chase reached down and laid it against his leg.

"Relax," Chase admonished him, "no one's going to hurt you. I'm a doctor."

Adan squinted at the average-size man with the bright blue eyes whose brows and lashes were almost ghost white. Despite the smile, Adan didn't believe him. If they found out, he knew they'd send him back. He wasn't about to let that happen. So he struggled again.

"Damn!" Trak placed both hands hard on the boy's shoulders and watched as the intravenous bag of salt solution swayed on the metal pole. "Can't you give him something to calm him down?"

"I don't think that's a good idea," Chase said. "I'll hold onto his legs. You keep an eye on the needle. Don't let him rip it out."

"That's it, Doctor?" Trak said. "After all your education, you don't have some kind of magic elixir to calm down a scared patient?"

"Beer."

"Really? Beer? That's what you learned at med school?" Trak watched the needle and continued restraining the boy.

"Beer can have a calming effect," Chase said. "And a beer—as in one—is kind of like a sports drink, or that IV solution there. It's got sodium and fluid. And there are carbohydrates. So, a beer will replenish glycogen energy stores, and replace salt lost through sweat. It will also quench your thirst." The doctor picked up another ice pack that had fallen to the floor.

Trak looked over at his friend. "So you're telling me you're going to give this kid a beer? He doesn't look old enough to drink."

"Hell, no!" Chase replied. "You want me to lose my license over a pet theory? Though, I have to admit, I've personally been working on the idea for years."

"I know you have. My front porch has been your laboratory."

Finally, Adan stopped fighting and relaxed. While he was clearly in a medical clinic and these men were trying to help, he still didn't trust them, but he was just too tired and miserable to care. He thought about dying. Maybe that was the only answer left. So, he closed his eyes and soon fell into a troubled sleep where he was running, always running, and looking back to see who was behind him.

6

Rose stood at the foot of the short stairway that led into the kitchen and winced as the screen door slammed shut behind her mother.

Bliss Madsen, an ironically named, once-pretty girl, had become a coarse and bloated woman, the product of nineteen pregnancies, sixteen of which had gone full term. Her ornate hairstyle, a complex gray web of braids and rolls, made her seem much taller than she was. She favored colorless, beige, ankle-length dresses, and a constant, unforgiving expression that was intimidating to adults and children alike.

And, Bliss was one of the rare, outspoken women in the community. But because her devotion to the word of the Prophet—and to the man himself—could not be questioned, no one, not even the men of the community, ever reproached her publicly.

"I ask you again, Rose. Where were you?"

"Just walking, Mother," the girl answered, turning her blue eyes away.

Bliss sighed deeply. "I have no time for this, Rose. You

know you are not to leave without permission. You are not to go about at your age unattended. Am I right?"

"Yes, Mother. I'm sorry Mother. I won't—"

"Enough! Go tend your sister. Then get your book." Rose's mother turned and opened the screen door. The smell of hot, freshly-baked bread wafted from the kitchen. "And I'm sure you won't have time to eat first," she said, reading her daughter's mind.

An hour later, Rose finished styling Daisy's hair. Nothing fancy for the sister who was four years her junior, just a long, straight blond braid down the back. Rose placed her hand behind Daisy's head and leaned the girl into the wheelchair.

Most people who saw Daisy assumed she couldn't possibly comprehend anything, but Rose believed they were wrong. Rose knew, for example, that Daisy loved water. The girl almost always had the faintest of smiles on her damaged face when Rose gently splashed her in the tub. Sometimes Daisy tried to slap at the water herself.

Rose's mother claimed that while Daisy was, like Billy Jessop, a glorious and challenging gift from God, the girl understood nothing, felt nothing, had no thoughts or hopes or wishes. Her presence was merely a test for the rest of them.

Rose had stopped arguing about Daisy and now even refrained from sharing her sister's small triumphs. Like her ability to follow the antics of the blue and white parakeet with her eyes, as the creature flitted about the cage in the corner of the room, or the apparent delight she took in wriggling out of her shoes, which forced Rose to put them back on the girl's crooked feet again and again.

Rose secured the straps that kept Daisy upright in

the wheelchair. Then she rolled her closer to the little bird, kissed her sister on the forehead, and departed.

Caring for her sister was becoming more difficult, especially since Joseph was gone. Rose's parents had explained that her brother, a good-natured, strong boy who had always helped lift and move Daisy whenever Rose asked, had been sent to visit a sister city in Canada. While Rose believed what her parents told her, she still found it strange that her brother had simply vanished one night. Not too long after he had been found holding hands with one of the Barlow girls.

She frowned and glanced down at her own hands. She wondered what holding hands with a boy might feel like, but was pretty sure this was one of those dirty thoughts she'd been warned about. Still, the idea of grasping fingers with Jacob Babbitt, who always smiled at her when no one was looking, made her insides flutter.

"Rose," her mother yelled from downstairs. "Get your book!"

She winced and stifled a groan, knowing what was ahead.

7

The boy slept on the single bed in Trak's workroom. The small, detached building at the end of a white-pebbled drive had been built as a residence in 1908. The main house, which had been erected the following year, settled nearby on a tree-covered lot just west of Main Street in the old part of Hurricane. Trak had inherited the property—it was the house he grew up in—when his mother passed away, just four months after his father died.

Trak pushed open the door to the bathroom, which offered a toilet, a small sink, and an out-of-place mirror framed in ornately carved wood. The wood had once been painted gold, and small specks still glittered when the morning light shone though the four-paned window. He straightened the heirloom and smiled, remembering how his mother had treasured the object because it had belonged to his great-grandmother Pearl, one of the first of the pioneer women to live in Hurricane Valley.

After propping the bathroom door open, Trak placed a note for the boy on the table beside the bed. The letter explained that water and Gatorade were in the small, square refrigerator on the counter, and that he was welcome to make a sandwich from the ham, cheddar cheese, and bread that were also inside. He instructed the boy to rest, and explained that he and Dr. Allred would be back soon to check on him.

Before he left, Trak looked back at the sleeping boy. How could anyone be foolish enough to hitch down that particular stretch of road? The unforgiving landscape was bad enough, but one also had to consider the people of Colorado City. They certainly weren't inclined to assist a teenage boy, especially one who looked so different.

Trak was suddenly struck by the irony. He had been taunted; a brown-skinned child teased, often running home in tears to his blond, blue-eyed mother who'd stood tall beside her Navajo husband. People said his parents were an odd pair; yet their love had continued for almost sixty years, a relationship built on mutual support, the concept of never holding a grudge, the ability to laugh loud and often, and their delight at becoming parents so late in life

As he got older, the bullying gradually ceased. He'd grown bigger than all of his classmates, taller and stronger. High school coaches sought him out, handing him footballs and basketballs, and anointing him a leader in their varied quests for state titles. He hurled the shot put farther than anyone in the county, and, even on a dare, played the lead in the school production of *Damn Yankees*. His take on the conflicted Joe Hardy had stunned the community. The local newspaper had praised him for his superb acting and strong singing voice, which overshadowed the fact that he wasn't much of a dancer.

Trak flicked on the ceiling fan and opened the screen door. He took one last look at the sleeping boy whose mouth had fallen open and who was snoring softly. Then he eased the door closed without making a sound.

Trak walked to the front of the house and slapped his thigh once. The brown and white, blue-eyed cattle dog mix that had been sleeping on the porch lifted her head, pricking up a pair of spotted ears.

"Come on, girl," Trak called. "Let's go over to the café."

The animal leaped joyously down the front steps, bouncing across the white flagstone pathway that bisected the front yard, and followed her master through the opening in the picket fence, nipping at his heels.

The sun, still bright in the sky, cast a golden light that twinkled and danced on the vibrant green leaves of massive pecan trees that overhung the road, a legacy of the settlers who had been directed by Brigham Young himself to grow the trees. The Mormon leader had sent the seeds, which the pioneers had lovingly planted and tended. In turn, the seeds had produced the present-day giants that provided their fruit each fall—sweet nuts that fed the people in both good times and bad.

"Stop it, Holly!" Trak said, after the dog had grabbed his ankle a bit too hard. "I'm going to have a get you a cow."

The animal barked and licked his hand.

"OK. Two cows."

8

Rose snapped awake, realizing that her dog-eared copy of *The Pearl of Great Price* had slipped from her lap and fallen to the uneven, slatted floor. The tiny back room in the barn smelled of hay and dust and mold. Miniscule particles floated in a weak beam of light that filtered through the smudged west-facing window.

She yawned and stretched, tired of sitting in the uncomfortable wooden chair. Reaching down for the book with the broken spine, she grazed her forearm along the rough edge of the seat and yelped in pain as a fat splinter lodged just below her elbow. She turned her arm over and saw an inch of dark wood visible beneath her pale skin.

She left the book on the floor and sat back, picking at the jagged end of the sliver. Able to get a good hold with her fingernails, she gritted her teeth and eased the splinter out. Blood oozed from the wound, and Rose rubbed at the spot until the flow stopped. She couldn't risk dirtying her dress and upsetting Mother again.

When she was satisfied the bleeding had ceased, Rose leaned over and grabbed the book—one of the four official versions of the Scriptures to which the Church of Jesus Christ of Latter-Day Saints subscribed—and laid the volume in her lap. Rose's mother had assigned Articles of Faith 1:13, Being Honest, which Rose knew by heart having read the passage so often. She closed her eyes and recited the words of former church president, Spencer W. Kimball.

"It is a sin to lie. It is a tragedy to be the victim of lies. Being trapped in the snares of dishonesty and misrepresentation does not happen instantaneously. One little lie or dishonest act leads to another until the perpetrator is caught in the web of deceit. Those who become victims of this entrapment often struggle through life bearing their heavy burden because they are unwilling to acknowledge their problem and make the effort to change."

Rose sighed and opened her eyes. The book had fallen open to the rules about being chaste.

"Sexual immorality creates a barrier to the influence of the Holy Spirit with all its uplifting, enlightening, and empowering capabilities. It causes powerful physical and emotional stimulation. In time, that creates an unquenchable appetite that drives the offender to ever more serious sin. It engenders selfishness and can produce aggressive acts such as brutality, abortion, sexual abuse, and violent crime. Such stimulation can lead to acts of homosexuality, and they are evil and absolutely wrong."

Rose considered this much more interesting than her assigned reading on honesty. Her stomach grumbled. Surely, Mother didn't mean for her to miss supper as well.

She'd eaten nothing all day. Rose tried to put the thought of food out of her mind and continued reading.

> "Any sexual intimacy outside of the bonds of marriage—I mean any intentional contact with the sacred, private parts of another's body, with or without clothing—is a sin and is forbidden by God. It is also a transgression to intentionally stimulate these emotions within your own body."

Rose heard the door creak open and saw her younger sister, Iris. The diminutive, overly shy six year old wore a light-green dress, fashioned exactly like the one Rose wore, and which mirrored the style that clothed every other female in town.

"Mother says you may come out now," Iris said, placing a pink thumb in her mouth.

"Don't do that, sweetie," Rose pleaded. She walked over and gently grasped the girl's hand.

"Mother will be angry," Iris said. "I'm too old to suck my thumb."

"That's right," Rose said, smiling at her doll-like sister, who often acted half her age. Rose took the child by the hand and led her out the door and into the barn.

9

The Main Street Café was a one-story brick building that had long ago housed Hurricane's post office. The structure was now painted pink and boasted a geometrically designed band of green, turquoise, and blue that wrapped the building just below the flat roof. Tan awnings jutted over large windows, in front of which were two round wrought iron tables with matching chairs. A somewhat dilapidated sign peeled above the doorway, reading Main Street Café: A Quiet Friendly Place to Eat.

Inside, the riot of color continued. Some walls were deep purple, others light blue and green. The optimistic aphorism Determination and Positive Energy Can Overcome Anything had been stenciled on one wall, and was hemmed in by the words Believe and Hope. Orders were taken at a brick-faced counter, behind which were a sink, a tiny grill, and shelves holding cooking utensils, glassware, and dishes.

Chase retrieved his order and sat down. Trak stared at the hot patty melt. The meat and cheese were encased in slices of thick sourdough and grilled with a generous helping of butter. The sandwich butted up against a steaming pile of crisp hand-cut fries.

Trak shook his head. "Dr. Allred, how do expect to get the rest of us to eat a healthy diet when you don't set a good example?"

"It's all about allowing yourself to indulge once in a while, my friend. And let's remember, I'm not obese. I don't have high blood pressure, or high cholesterol, or out-of-control blood sugar, or any of the other plagues that are currently afflicting mankind." Chase popped the top off a bottle of catsup and drenched the fries. "How's the boy?"

"He was sleeping when I left. Out cold. By the way, thanks for your help, especially on such short notice. Just go ahead and send me the bill."

Chase stopped with the burger halfway to his mouth. "I think I can manage to spring for a little saline and a few ice packs. I'm sure the kid'll be all right in a few days. That said, I haven't seen you all week. Where've ya been?"

A strange look appeared on Trak's face. When his friend failed to respond, Chase said, "Earth to Benally. Come in."

"Oh, sorry."

"Sorry?" Chase turned around. "Oh, shit! A redhead."

"Shut up!" Trak said under his breath.

"If I recall correctly, you made me promise to drag you away the next time you so much as looked at a redhead. Remember the great carrot-top incident of aught three? Messy. Very messy. And, quite frankly, I have never understood the appeal. Though, I do admit there are things that make gingers rather interesting scientifically.

"Did you know that redheads often require up to twenty per cent more anesthesia than people with other hair colors? And that bees like redheads more than the rest of us? They get stung more than everyone else. Pretty strange, if you ask me."

He picked a fat fry out of the catsup and popped it in his mouth. After chewing, swallowing, and chasing the food with a gulp of cold beer, he continued. "Back in the fifteenth century, people believed freckles were a sign of the devil. That didn't work out too well for redheads who got burned at the stake for being witches."

Trak rolled his eyes. "Just relax and eat your burger, Chase."

The doctor smiled. "When was the last time you had a date, my friend? Been a while, hasn't it? Let me think. Um . . . that dark-haired, elementary school teacher. Cute little thing. What was her name? Becky? Betsy? I don't remember. As I recall, that was quite the torrid affair. But geez, that was what over a year ago?" Chase took another bite of his patty melt.

Trak looked hard at his friend. "Don't make me hurt you, Chase."

"Don't say I didn't try."

10

Brooke Neal thanked the girl behind the counter and followed the teen's pointing finger to an exit on the north-facing wall of the little restaurant. With her paper napkin-wrapped knife and fork in hand, she walked over, pushed the door open, and stepped onto a flagstone patio. Three umbrella-topped tables were shaded by the massive pecan trees that seemed to be everywhere on Main Street. A bright picket fence surrounded the back patio and was bordered by flowers and bushy rosemary shrubs that tinged the evening air with a piney fragrance. A hard-packed dirt lane separated the patio from a tall fence sporting thick tangles of grapevines. The garden gate before her beckoned.

Brooke had a fleeting desire to step through the passageway. Like Alice in her Wonderland—she felt out of place. Not here in Hurricane necessarily, even though she'd only been in town a few days. It was just that Brooke, like the fictional Alice, felt as if a gigantic game was being played all around her, one in which not everyone followed the rules, a condemnation of which she herself was guilty.

She eyed the garden opening for a moment, then

sat at a round wrought-iron table. She squeezed her eyes shut and pinched the bridge of her nose, hoping to ward off the coming attack. She never used to have headaches. Brooke had always been the one who never got sick. The flu could be ravaging her brothers and sisters and classmates, yet illnesses never touched her. "You're lucky," people said. Which was true. Brooke Neal had led an enchanted life. Until recently. A sudden surge of heat enveloped her, and she fought the urge to cry.

The door opened and the girl from behind the counter appeared, carrying a sweating silver pitcher and an oblong plate bearing an omelet with ham and fresh tomatoes with Swiss cheese oozing from the edges. Two fat pieces of nine-grain toast with small ramekins of soft butter and raspberry jam nestled around the eggs.

"Here you go," the blonde-haired teen said, setting the plate ceremoniously in front of Brooke and gracing her with an infectious grin. The girl poured just-brewed black iced tea into a tall glass. "Let me know if I can get you anything else."

"No, I'm fine," Brooke said.

The waitress went back into the café, letting the screen door snap shut behind her.

Brooke ate half the eggs and one piece of what in the Lone Star State was referred to as Texas toast. She had no idea what people in Utah called the thick-cut slices, but in the short time she'd been in Hurricane, it had become clear that this fat bread was the norm.

Waiting for her meal to settle, she stared out at the bit of western sky that poked through the leaves across Main Street. It was just after 9:00 p.m., and still the soft glow of the sun illuminated the sky. A gentle breeze tamped down the remaining heat of the day.

Brooke still wasn't used to the radical desert temperatures. She'd grown up in the northern part of the country's mid-section, where she was accustomed to winter snows and darkness and summer's sticky humidity. But until she moved west with what she now knew to be her idealistic fantasies; she never really understood about the dry heat of the desert where locals assured her that any temperature under one-hundred-and-ten was downright balmy.

Just then, the touch of a cold nose on her leg surprised her. Brooke looked down at the brown and white spotted dog with the strange blue eyes. The animal nestled its head on her lap and gazed up at her as if pleading.

"Don't feed her."

Brooke looked toward the voice. A tall, broad-shouldered man, maybe six-three, smiled at her from the café's open screen door. He had short dark hair and high cheekbones that marked him as being at least partly Native American. She guessed Navajo, or maybe Paiute, since she knew both had reservations in the area. But his skin was lighter than most western Indians she'd seen, and his dark brown eyes slanted slightly and seemed to be questioning her.

The dog abruptly sat down and placed one thick paw on her leg.

"Holly is on a diet."

Brooke stroked the dog's big head, and smiled for the first time in months.

11

Rose followed the warm dinner smells into the dinning room with the thick oak table that seated eighteen people. The family didn't need that much room anymore, since all of Rose's older sisters were married and lived with their husbands and sister wives. Two brothers had been sent off to college—a privilege Mother never failed to mention was a result of her own piousness and continued personal devotion to the Prophet. James and John and Joseph, her teenage brothers, were in Canada, visiting with friends and relatives in Bountiful. Rose was disappointed that the boys never wrote and didn't understand why her parents refused to talk about them.

She was upset to see that the evening meal had already been served and the dishes cleared away. She could hear Sister Wife Glea cleaning in the kitchen. The sight of her parents huddled at the head of the table, speaking in hushed, inaudible tones, suddenly filled her with an unexplained apprehension. The way her parents stopped when they saw her standing in the doorway was even more disconcerting. Then her father smiled.

"Come here, Rose. I've had a long day. Give me a hug." Logan Madsen grinned at his favorite child and Rose smiled back. She crossed the room much too quickly.

"Walk, Rose! A lady does not run like a child. Look at you. You've been old enough to be married for almost two years now." Bliss Madsen paused, testing her daughter.

Rose's stomach grumbled loudly as she hugged her father. "Mother, the girl is hungry. When did you eat last, Rose?"

"Last night. I—"

Bliss cut her off. "She disappeared this morning unattended and without permission. If she is hungry, it is her own fault!"

"Where'd you go, honey?" her father asked.

Rose simply could not lie to him. "I wanted to see the water in the creek," she said, avoiding all eye contact with her mother. "The snowmelt came rushing down. It was cold and wonderful. I found a beautiful stone that—"

"You went in the water?" Bliss Madsen placed both hands on the table and rose from the straight-backed chair. "Don't you understand what can happen? Don't you remember?"

"Yes . . . I do, but—"

Her mother grabbed the long wooden spoon from the sideboard. Rose stood rooted in place as her mother came around the table.

"Obedience, Rose. Without that you are nothing."

The spoon came down with a thwack, slicing the back of Rose's neck. She winced, but stood still and lifted her chin. Bliss hit her again and again, one blow striking Rose's cheek, raising a bright red welt.

"Not the face, Mother," Logan Madsen said sadly, unwilling to look his daughter in the eye.

Bliss Madsen paused. "Of course, you are right," she answered. "Who will want her if it is so obvious she misbehaves?"

"I don't want to get married!" Rose blurted out, surprising herself. Two sets of eyes burned into her. "I want to go to college. I want to be a science teacher."

A heavy silence compressed the cavernous dining room. Then her mother spoke slowly, her tone clipped, determined. "Swallow your pride, Rose. It will burn you. It doesn't matter what you want. Don't make trouble. Don't ask questions. Don't find fault. Don't complain. Complaining disturbs the spirit of God. You will keep sweet. That is your job, now and until the day you die."

Bliss Madsen brought the spoon down again. Rose braced herself and stared at her father, but he had already turned away.

12

"Maybe I'll see you around. Was that the best you could do? Geez! I sounded like a kid," Trak mumbled early the next morning.

He slid the eggs out of the fridge, berating himself for not, at least, asking for the woman's number. Her name was Brooke, and when he shook her hand and said goodnight, he couldn't help noticing the band of freckles spread across her nose and cheeks. He didn't want to seem too forward, since she explained she'd only been in Hurricane two days, and wouldn't even start her new job until Monday. Brooke had let go of his hand and walked off into the cool night, before he had the chance to ask her where she would be working. Still, Hurricane was a small town. He'd run into her, sooner, he hoped, rather than later.

He placed the cardboard egg carton on the countertop and grabbed a small bowl and fork. Perhaps he should wake the kid for breakfast. He'd looked in on the sleeping boy earlier, watched the healthy rise and fall of his chest. After checking his watch, Trak decided he had time for a talk before work. Maybe someone was expecting his arrival and was worried. Perhaps there were family members out looking for him. While there was certainly the possibility that the boy was over eighteen and legally on his own, Trak didn't think so. And if he was underage, he'd have to contact the police so they could locate his parents.

Trak opened the refrigerator door again, knowing the perfect way to wake a teenaged boy.

Adan's mother cried as she hugged her only child. Two guards looked on, impassive as Adan cried right along with her. His mother was speaking Spanish, though the words were not clear. She'd never adapted to English and counted on him to translate on the rare occasions when she ventured out of their tight-knit South Phoenix community of mostly Mexican immigrants. She wanted Adan to remember something important, but the words made no sense. He asked her again and again to explain, but before she could, the guards shouted that her time was up and—

Adan jerked awake, disoriented and confused by his surroundings. He tried not to think of the dream, of the guards, of his mother. Right now, he needed to figure out where he was and how he'd gotten here. He squinted up at the walls and ceiling of an unfamiliar room. He was lying on a couch between two white cotton sheets. A blue and white comforter lay crumpled on the floor beside him. Through a set of large windows, a bright ray of sunlight shone, but Adan didn't know whether they were facing east or west, and so, couldn't discern the time. He suddenly realized he didn't even know what day it was.

He lifted his head from the pillow, groaned, and dropped back, hands pressed against his temples. The screaming headache made moving torturous. Still, he forced himself to sit up, gently easing his legs from under the top sheet and placing his feet on the floor. Every inch of his body ached. On the wall opposite the makeshift bed, a myriad of tools were mounted on a pegboard; beneath that, a workbench. What appeared to be a broken brass lamp rested in pieces atop the bench, and a wide, dark green lampshade sat off to one side. A single, padded stool was pushed under the counter. Where am I? he wondered.

After gingerly pushing himself up from the couch, Adan shuffled toward the open door of a bathroom. He felt like he was ninety, even a hundred years old. Although he tried, he was unable to pee. Standing before the old wooden-framed mirror, he noted the red tinge to his skin and remembered the highway, the burning sun, the empty water bottle. He laid a hand on his face and felt the heat still radiating from his cheek. Then, stepping back from the mirror, he noticed the unfamiliar shirt; ASU adorned the front in bright red and gold print. Sparky the Sun Devil grinned from beneath the letters.

Then the smell hit him. Bacon. His mouth began to water, and he stumbled out of the bathroom, almost frantic to find where the aroma was coming from. He crossed the room, pushed open the screen door, and hurried across the neat green lawn to three stone steps leading to another screen door. He paused before taking the stairs slowly, one at a time, straining to peer through the silver mesh once he reached the porch. He reached for the door handle.

"Come on in," a voice called from inside.

Adan pulled the door open.

"Hungry?" The big man smiled and lifted a slice of bacon from a sizzling cast-iron skillet.

Adan bit his lip and stared at the basket of thick, cut bread on the table next to a container of whipped butter and a jar of what appeared to be raspberry jam. But he stayed on the stoop, just outside the kitchen.

"There's a place for you right there," Trak indicated with a nod, his big hands still occupied with the frying pan and tongs. "Have a seat. I'll have your eggs ready in just a minute. How do you like them?"

Adan opened the door and stepped inside, and took a few tentative steps toward the table. "Scrambled." He mumbled the word.

"Wet or dry?" Trak placed the bacon on a plate covered with a paper towel.

Adan couldn't take his eyes off the bacon and the fat chunks of bread and the golden swirl of butter. He collapsed into a kitchen chair and reached for the bread, but then paused, hand hanging in midair.

"Go ahead. Eat." Trak skillfully cracked four brown eggs on the lip of a bowl, using just one hand. "Cheese?" he said, turning to the table.

"Mmhuh," Adan mumbled through a mouthful of bread.

13

Brooke had slept fitfully. Again. Still, she hoped the move and new job would help her find the way back to the glorious gift of restful sleep. Surely, the sick dread of dreams and twisted sheets, and night sweats could not be a permanent part of her future. She simply couldn't face that prospect.

"One day at a time," she whispered from her seat at the tiny patio table that looked out on Carla Kimball's obscenely lush garden. Filled with flowers, vegetables, and herbs, and partly shaded by the gnarled branches of several peach trees, the view was a stark contrast to where she'd just come from.

While she watched her landlady, who, she had learned, was also Hurricane's mayor, tend her garden, Brooke sipped her coffee, savoring the sweetness on her tongue. Down on her hands and knees, Carla wore a khaki Aussie slouch hat secured with a chinstrap and which was perched jauntily on her head, one side rolled up. The scene brought back memories of Brooke's mother who had also tended a small kitchen garden back home. Davenport, Iowa, Brooke thought, was a long way from southern Utah. In more ways than one.

That morning, Carla had taken one look at Brooke, held a single finger in the air, and then disappeared. A few minutes later, she'd returned with a tray bearing slabs of homemade wholegrain bread, a jar of thick, creamy honey, a jar of peanut butter, and a small cup full of brown sugar. "You need to put some meat on those bones," Carla said with a shake of her head. "The brown sugar is for your coffee. The honey and peanut butter both go on the bread. Come to think of it, a little brown sugar on the honey and peanut butter sounds pretty good, too." Carla winked.

Brooke had nodded and complied. She'd struggled with the extra weight she put on in college. How ironic that those pounds had simply fallen away. Now she could finally say she'd reached her ideal weight—that size six she'd always dreamed of. But like many women brought up on Photoshopped images of perfection, the reality was, that now, she looked ill. "Gray," a concerned friend had commented, noting Brooke's nearly translucent skin.

Brooke dipped a finger in the honey and stuck it in her mouth. As she savored the sweetness, she wondered what her parents would say. Eventually she'd have to tell them what happened. Why she left her job. Unlike so many others, she'd been lucky. An uneventful childhood in a happy family with two loving, stable parents and five siblings—three brothers and two sisters. Her parents were both teachers at picturesque St. Ambrose University, where her mother taught nursing and her father was a history professor. Like their dedication to the college, founded originally as a Catholic school for men, they practiced their Catholicism wholeheartedly, and reveled in the

Church's teachings. Still they were pliable people, unafraid to contradict doctrines that might be outmoded. And they were willing to embrace change, if it meant a stronger Church that enhanced the community, always welcoming everyone they met in a positive way. It wasn't until college that Brooke realized she'd never questioned how her parents managed to be both highly educated and extremely religious at the same time. Somehow, they'd managed to blend these two important elements of their lives together and make them work.

And now she had failed them. Failed everyone. The bread suddenly felt heavy in her stomach, the coffee bitter. Weekly calls home had been difficult. Keeping up a cheery facade, raving about how much she loved her work, saying her job was everything she hoped it would be. Keeping up the charade was exhausting. And, oh yes, she had lots of friends. Well, that, at least, had been true. But after everything became public, and her name had been splashed all over the local papers and TV, those friends had stopped calling. The thought that her parents might find her name on the Internet was a constant torment.

"Here, love. Come give me a hand with these," Carla called out, brushing back a wisp of hair and pointing toward a small green plastic bucket. "Do you mind?" Carla smiled up at Brooke then turned her attention back to a weed, which she grabbed and pulled from the dark, almost black, soil.

Brooke retrieved the pail, then bent and gathered the weeds that lay in the trenches alongside the rows of tall, green corn and huge spreading squash plants. She couldn't help squeezing a clump of coffee-colored earth between her fingers. Dirt that looked and smelled almost like Iowa.

She sniffed the soil. The rich, clean scent brought visions of her mother's face, who would gently tuck green seedlings into precise rows in the vegetable garden behind the house. Brooke wondered if she could just go home. Forget the horrors she'd seen. Evil in which she'd ultimately played a part.

Carla smiled up at her. "Doesn't look like Southern Utah soil, does it?" The older woman beamed. "You know, before the Mormon settlers arrived, this was a land of nothing but greasewood, cockle burr, chaparral, slippery elm, and rocks. Nothing but a hot dry, waterless plain. But then the people dug the Hurricane Canal with not much more than their bare hands. When you drive up the mountain on your way to work, make sure to look down and see our beautiful green valley."

No, it doesn't" she answered, again studying the dark clump of soil, which seemed out of place in the arid desert.

"Of course, along with the water, we've added years of love." Carla brushed stray strands of silvery hair from her eyes and sat back on her heals. "And compost."

Opening her palm, Brooke let the crumbled black earth fall to the ground.

14

Rose had severely underestimated her mother's reaction.

Following the beating with the spoon and further punishment with the strap, Bliss had grabbed Rose by the hair, dragged her up the stairs, shoved open the door to her own room, and forced her daughter inside. She pushed Rose down onto a small cushioned seat before an ornate dressing table with a large mirror. Then she seized hold of a thick chunk of Rose's blond hair, close to the scalp. Rose flinched as her mother jerked her head toward the mirror.

"Look!" Bliss ordered.

Rose could feel hot breath on her cheek.

"You see what you are?"

She didn't know the answer her mother wanted to hear.

"You are a woman! You have one purpose in life. Only one! There are no options for you. Your purpose is to make children for the Lord to use in any way He sees fit."

"But . . . why can't. . . ?"

Bliss Madsen spun her daughter around in the chair and backhanded her across the face before Rose could finish.

"This has gone on way too long, daughter. You will be married. And soon."

Rose couldn't help herself. A choked sob broke free, and tears spilled down her cheeks. "Daisy!" she called out, then waited for another blow. But none came. "Who will take care of Daisy if you send me away?"

Bliss crossed her arms over her chest and appraised her daughter. Then, without saying a word, the woman disappeared into the closet. Rose knew better than to move. The sting on her cheek still a fresh reminder. So, she sat. While she waited, Rose glanced around the room that was her mother's private domain and focused on the pictures on Mother's dresser. None included any of her or her brothers and sisters, which Rose found very odd. Other homes Rose had visited had every bit of wall space and all available tabletops weighted down with generations of family members—mothers and fathers and teens and toddlers and grandparents and great-grandparents and babies in blankets. But the pictures here were entirely of Bliss Madsen, pictures of a pretty, smiling young woman. Rose was stunned, having never assumed that her Mother might have once been beautiful.

Mother's face appeared in the mirror. "Get up!"

Despite pleading and wailing, despite struggling against her steely grip, Bliss forced Rose into the closet and then into another, still darker place. The door swung closed and latched with a solid click. In the recess of the tiny room, Rose listened as her mother shuffled things—blankets maybe—to block the exit. The tiny slice of light that had slipped through the crack between the floorboards and the bottom of the door was suddenly extinguished, leaving Rose in absolute darkness. In an attempt to calm herself, she took slow, deep breaths and patted her hands on the bare wood floor of the small box encasing her. Stars danced before her eyes and she felt as if she might pass out in what felt like an airless tomb. She pulled her knees tightly and hugged them to her chest, and scrunched up against the back wall, which provided only an eighteen-inch gap between her face and the locked door.

Rose despised small, tight spaces. Did her mother know this, or was the punishment the same for all children who misbehaved so gravely? She had not heard any of her brothers or sisters speak of this place.

She took another deep breath, clapped both hands on her mouth, and stifled a scream.

15

Colorado City Town Marshal Sterling Buttars slowly put down the phone. He stared at the large calendar he used as a blotter on his desk—pristine as the day he'd removed the cellophane from it back in January—wishing the Prophet hadn't made the order. Of course, he had no choice. Perhaps that made things easier.

"I will take care of it immediately," he'd said to the man, who, above all on Earth, was closest to God.

Still, the logical part of his brain, which had only surfaced sporadically over his fifty-two years, whispered that this edict made little sense and would cause his brothers and sisters great pain. Even so, he hoped the good news—that the Prophet, having been bailed out of jail by the high-powered lawyers that served him, was returning home soon—would placate the people, giving them reason to rejoice at a time that, well, would be difficult.

Buttars sighed and heaved his rotund body out of the black swivel desk chair. "Come on, girl," he called to the little dog that rested on a lumpy pink pillow in the corner. The poodle mix, who Buttars had found ten years earlier abandoned on the road, was his constant companion. He called her Mouse because of her diminutive size and soft gray curls.

Walking passed Travis Forbush, his deputy, who was eating a thick sandwich of ham and cheese at his desk, he said, "I'm going out." When he opened the door, as if on cue, Mouse bounced from the pillow and trotted after him, her nails ticking on the linoleum floor.

"What do you want me to say if anyone calls?" Forbush asked, spitting out a full mouth of half-chewed food.

Butters paused. "Tell 'em . . . tell 'em . . . Shit! Don't tell 'em nothin."

Forbush eyed his boss, who did not elaborate as he slammed the door behind him.

In the small parking lot that butted up to the side of building, Butters opened the door of his truck. Mouse sat down, lifted her front legs, and let out a few small squeaks. With one chubby hand, Butters reached down and lifted the dog.

An hour later, Buttars paced the bank of Short Creek at a spot out behind the Isaac W. Carling Memorial Cemetery. Water from the spring thaw had quickly run through, leaving damp, white sand among the jumble of red rocks and scattered remnants of fallen trees in the streambed.

Buttars had spent his entire life in Colorado City. Been brought into the world by midwives at the town birthing clinic, raised by three mothers with twenty-seven brothers and sisters, had been steeped in the sacred doctrines of the Church. He worked hard to be one of the chosen men. He'd proven himself by following orders unquestioningly. When he was young, he feared being one of the Lost Boys—rejects, tossed from the community—a man who had no chance of ever going to heaven. Their lot was to languish in hell, both in the living world and the next, separated from home and family and church.

Buttars shuddered. He didn't want to think about life on the outside. The ugliness of that world was incomprehensible. Here, he was adored by his three wives and a houseful of children and grandchildren. A sudden nagging thought pricked him, making Buttars wonder if it was love his family felt for him, or something else. But what they thought about him was, ultimately, unimportant. What mattered was Buttars had three wives, which guaranteed that he would rise up into Paradise. Who could want more? Still . . . the marshal wished he'd asked the Prophet, "Why?" But that word simply wasn't spoken.

He sat down heavily on the bank of the dry streambed beneath the shade of a massive cottonwood. Mouse jumped into his lap, leapt up, and licked his face as Buttars began to cry. He jerked his head from side to side, hoping no one was nearby to see the big man bawling like a newborn babe.

"That's my girl," he said, scratching the little dog behind the ears. "You love Daddy, don't you?"

Mouse squeaked out a few happy barks, wagging her tail as Buttars held her face in his meaty hands. After a while, the marshal lifted the dog from his lap and placed her on the ground beside him. Then, Buttars rose and unlatched his service weapon resting on his hip. He froze, just for a moment, allowing his gaze to climb up along the massive sheer red rock face that soared upward into the heavens.

Tears ran down Sterling Buttars face as he raised the weapon to eye level. Then, he lowered the gun and put a bullet through Mouse's head.

16

Trak observed the boy for a moment. The kid's wide brown eyes searched the sunny kitchen as he lathered another piece of bread with butter and jam. Obviously, he'd been without a good meal for a while. Trak was reminded of some of the kids he'd encountered in Afghanistan—children with hollow checks and empty eyes. What did their grownup selves look like now? Did the spark that starvation robbed from them ever return? Were they happy, healthy people now, despite the hunger and despair they encountered during the war? Or was their war still raging? Were they even still alive?

He pushed the thought away. He mixed the eggs with a fork and poured them into the skillet. A few minutes later, he dumped the eggs into a steaming, golden pile next to six strips of bacon and set the plate in front of the boy. He wanted to question him, but instead, told himself to let the child eat.

Turning back to the stove, he cracked two eggs for himself. He liked his over-easy, with the whites solid and the yokes runny. When the eggs were done, he slid them onto a plate, along with two pieces of bacon and took a seat at the rectangular kitchen table where he'd eaten when he was a boy. Only happy memories in this house enveloped him. Loving parents, who, despite their cultural differences, had provided a nurturing environment focused on their only child. He missed them everyday.

As he reached for a slice of the bread and the raspberry preserves, both homemade; both gifts from Carla, he stopped. He envisioned Brooke, sweeping loose strands of bright red hair behind her ear, exposing the fine line of her jaw. He gazed down at his stomach, which currently carried ten extra pounds. He drew back his hand. Perhaps a run was in order.

Trak sighed and looked over at the boy. "What's your name, son?"

The boy swallowed and met his gaze. "A . . . Andy," he said, then quickly looked away.

17

Eldon Higbee waited for the door of his limousine to be opened by the head of his security team. Even though the car was now parked inside the locked gates, and surrounded by the high, white, protective walls of his personal compound, the Prophet enjoyed being served. And who would deny him the right?

A small smile played on Higbee's fleshy, almost feminine lips as he smoothed the receding gray hairline that exposed a large expanse of forehead. Hard brown eyes and a prominent nose, combined with pockmarked skin—the result of adolescent acne—and yellowing teeth, marked him as a wholly unattractive man. But Higbee had learned, much to his delight, that looks simply didn't matter when one was the Prophet.

As he stepped from the vehicle, stretching out his bony, six-foot-four frame, a chorus of voices sounded above him.

"Welcome Home!" the women and children of his household cried in unison. They waved enthusiastically from the steps of his personal residence. Close to one hundred people stood on the wide stairs leading to the front door—not counting the infants held proudly in their mothers' arms, nor all his many wives and offspring. Higbee smiled, scanning his brood, noting that he really had no idea how many children and grandchildren he had. As he approached the steps, he glanced up at the prominently displayed word in large, bold black letters: ZION.

Higbee had been in jail almost four months, longer than he'd ever been imprisoned before. The authorities had once again tried to get him on child abuse charges, but of course, none of his young brides would ever testify against him. So, the state's case fell apart. A sudden spasm in his stomach gave him pause. There was no doubt the government—the Beast—was trying harder to bring him down. He longed for the days when his people had been left in peace, when governors and senators and the FBI and state police had simply turned their backs, ignoring Higbee's paradise on Earth. His Eden.

The Prophet proceeded up the stairway amid the din of well wishers, and considered the still-pending case involving child labor. He soured at the thought that his community leaders were accused of removing children, some as young as twelve, from school, and conscripting them to employers who forced them to work up to twelve-hour shifts and even confiscated their pay, which prosecutors said amounted to nothing more than slavery. But right now, just happy to be home, Higbee banished those thoughts.

He acknowledged his wives and children with almost imperceptible nods as they reached out to touch him. He met the eyes of some of the women. They watched him adoringly, but even though he'd been away so long, Higbee had no interest in any of them. From the time they were bound to him in spiritual marriage, all of his wives had been permanently pregnant. Which, of course, was their purpose. In fact, Higbee reveled in the fact that Belle, his third wife, had produced nineteen living children over the course of their marriage. She was held up as the perfect example of womanhood, touted in church, and practically worshipped by the other women in the community. He knew, too, she longed for that twentieth child. But his interest in each of his wives was gone.

Higbee mounted the stairs and stood before Belle, who had positioned herself just under the word ZION. She wrapped her gnarled fingers around his arm. Higbee stifled a shudder. Belle was fat, and even though he had insisted, she did not always follow house orders and shave herself completely. Touching body hair made him want to retch. She smiled up at him, revealing brownish teeth wrapped in a doughy face that not even the elaborately braided, upswept hair could improve. Having sex with her was revolting. But, he quickly regained his composure and smiled, then patted the woman's shoulder.

He moved past her without a word, never noticing the sour expression that creased Belle's prematurely aged features. Then he disappeared into the building that housed his family and offices.

A thickly muscled, dark-suited man stepped forward. "Nice to have you home, sir."

Higbee nodded. "Oran."

"Your quarters are arranged, as per your request. When would you like your meal sent up?"

"Give me a chance to bathe and relax a bit."

"Yes, sir. Is there anything special you'd like me to arrange?"

Higbee glanced at Oran Coombs, his second-in-command, and whose eyes betrayed not the slightest hint of judgment.

"I think I will concentrate on getting a good night's sleep," Higbee said. "After you have the meal sent up, please lock my apartment. I want no visitors."

"Yes, sir," Coombs answered, bowing his head. "I will take care of it."

18

All that was left from breakfast was a single piece of bread with some butter. Rose tried to chew and swallow slowly so she wouldn't anger her mother, but her hands shook; she was weak and light-headed from her night in the closet. Rose scanned the dining room, saw no one, and jammed the bread into her mouth.

Sister Wife Glea, only a few years older than Rose, entered the room holding a glass of milk and a small plate of oatmeal cookies. She sat at the table. "Oh my, child. You are so pale."

"Thank you." Rose reached for a cookie.

The kitchen door opened and snapped shut. They stared at one another, frozen. Rose dropped her head and waited. When no one appeared, she quickly put the whole cookie in her mouth. She'd probably take another beating, but at least she'd have food in her stomach.

"Isn't it wonderful?" Rose's mother called from the entryway to the dining room. Glea clasped her hands tightly. Rose swiped the back of her hand across her mouth in an effort to wipe away imaginary crumbs.

"Oh! But of course you wouldn't know," Bliss said, appearing in the doorway with a smile splitting her usually somber face. "He's home!"

Rose looked around for her father, but realized that his appearance usually did not elicit such a joyful response from her mother.

Glea was equally confused. "Who is home, Sister Bliss?"

"Who? Why the Prophet. He has returned to us. Certainly we should pray and give our thanks to the Lord. Our world has been a dark and miserable place since he was taken from us."

Bliss seemed ready to twirl right there in the doorway like a little girl getting her first taste of ice cream. Mother's behavior was quite shocking. For just a moment, Rose glimpsed the teenager in the photographs.

A loud rumbling came from Rose's stomach and she braced for a blow. Mother insisted that no sounds should ever emanate from a person's body, such noise a telltale sign of an apostate—a wicked one who has turned from the Prophet and fallen away from the Gospel teachings—Those who reject the light and truth and are left to wallow alone in darkness and filth.

Rose waited, aching for the remaining cookies on the plate. When would her mother strike? But Bliss didn't seem to notice the cookies, or her daughter's noisy belly.

"I think I will pray alone in my room and thank God for our good fortune," Bliss said, before practically dancing up the stairs.

Rose and Glea gaped at one another, then they both giggled. Rose's hand shot out for a cookie.

"Girls," Bliss called midway up the staircase.

Rose tensed.

"There will be a church service tonight. So please make sure everyone has clean clothes. The Prophet has a special announcement."

Rose palmed the cookie and slipped the treat into her lap. "What about Daisy?"

"What about her?"

"Will she be going to church as well?" Glea asked.

"Do you think there's any reason to parade Daisy around in church? Think, girl! What man would want that slobbering cripple? The best thing that can happen is that the child dies. There is no purpose for her in this world. Ah, but in the next, the day of healing will come. 'Bodies which are deformed and minds that are warped will be made perfect'," Bliss quoted from the scriptures. "Pray Daisy dies soon." Then she disappeared up the stairs.

Rose just stared at her plate.

19

Trak cleared the table, placed the dirty dishes in the sink, and turned on the faucet. Hot water, combined with a splash of dish soap formed a thick layer of white bubbles. He grabbed a sponge and glanced at the boy. With the exception of identifying himself as Andy, he had said nothing during the meal.

"Andy, come here and dry," Trak said, sinking both hands into the suds.

Adan didn't move. Instead, his first thought was of his best friend, Andy, the giant offensive lineman he met freshman year when they sat next to each other in English class. Andy was smart and told anyone who listened that the brightest players in football were offensive lineman. As proof, he challenged anyone who argued to check with the NFL, where the big guys in front of the quarterback routinely averaged a higher score on the Wonderlic intelligence test than any other players. Adan smiled. Andy had been impossible once he ferreted out that detail.

It was Andy, who, after watching Adan work out on

the school track one afternoon, tossed a football at his friend. Adan had reached out and snatched the long throw effortlessly. Thereafter, Andy had practically carried him to the coach's office, insisting that he'd found the team's new wide receiver. The fact that Adan had never even seen a football game—not what Americans called football—hadn't bothered Andy one bit. The coach, to Adan's surprise, was as enthusiastic as his friend.

"Andy, come on, give me a hand." Trak tossed a blue and white dishtowel toward the boy.

Adan's hand jerked up and he snatched the cloth from the air. Then he rose slowly. Despite the full belly, he still didn't feel well.

Trak held out a wet dish. "Just dry them and put them in the rack on the counter."

When the last plate was washed and dried, Adan turned and wobbled. Then everything started to go black, and he felt Trak grab him as he fell, easing him to the kitchen floor.

A short time later, Trak sat cross-legged on the green and white linoleum, holding Adan's head in his lap. He felt the boy stir and asked, "You okay?"

"I . . . I think so. I just got light-headed." Trak helped Adan to a sitting position, and leaned him against the counter.

"Light-headed? You flat out fainted dead away. We'll wait here until your feel better."

Adan did as he was told.

"You know it can take several days to recover from heat sickness. When I was in Afghanistan, soldiers keeled over all the time. All that gear and the desert heat."

"You were in the war?"

"Two tours. I was a medic, so I know all about heat sickness. So listen, you need to take it easy."

Adan nodded.

"Isn't there someone we should call? Someone who might be worried about you?"

Adan glanced at the man with the kind brown eyes staring at him with legitimate concern. He shook his head and looked away. "No. There's no one looking for me."

20

Dr. Chase Allred sat behind the desk in his office at the Hurricane Medical Clinic where he'd practiced family medicine since returning home. Before him sat two parents who'd come from Colorado City with the young boy in the wheelchair.

The term dysmorphic—malformed or misshapen—defined the boy's appearance: overly large head, thick lips, and heavy brows. The teen also suffered from severe mental retardation. Chase estimated that he might have an IQ somewhere around twenty-five. In speaking to the parents, he struggled to keep his voice neutral, his manner professional. How many were on the list now?

Before him sat an extremely gaunt man and his wife, who wore one of the signature floor-length dresses favored by the women of the Fundamentalist Church of Jesus Christ of Latter-Day Saints. "Are there any more children in your family like John here?"

"Our daughter has cerebral palsy," Bill Barlow answered.

His wife nodded, but said nothing. Chase appraised

the woman and noted in the boy's file that his mother suffered from severe exotropia. One of her eyes pointed so far to the right that her eyeball appeared to be almost entirely white.

Chase looked down at the paperwork on his desk, not because he expected to see anything new, but because he was momentarily at a loss for something to say. Why had they waited so long to bring the boy to a doctor? There were not many options for the child with regard to extending his life. The boy, strapped in the wheelchair, head lolling to one side, drool running from a mouth filled with cavity-filled teeth pointing in all the wrong directions, would not live much longer. There was not a single thing Chase could do about it. As a doctor, this thought infuriated him, but the fact that these cases were preventable angered him more than anything.

The woman shifted in her seat and Chase looked up at her. "Can't you help him?" she pleaded in a tiny voice.

Chase placed his hands flat on the desk. "I will send the blood and urine samples off to the lab. When they come back, perhaps we can find something to, um, make John more comfortable."

Neither parent responded. They seemed to be waiting for more.

Chase had a hunch. "I think maybe you should bring your daughter in for testing as well."

"But she has cerebral palsy," Bill Barlow repeated. "The nurses at our clinic were perfectly clear."

Chase forced himself not to speak out of anger. He had a great deal of respect for the midwives who toiled at the birthing center in Colorado City. He had worked with some of them over the years and admired their always-practical approaches to medical care. Generally, the women were competent with common illnesses and injuries, as well as uncomplicated childbirth, but they were not doctors or nurses. And making diagnoses was outside their purview— and beyond their training. Chase knew full well that in medicine, many things were far from "perfectly clear." He wanted to chide the people before him for not getting help for their horribly damaged son years ago. There was no cure for this type of birth defect, but there were resources that would certainly have helped in the feeding and care of the boy, and that would have alleviated some of the suffering that surely tormented him.

"Your daughter—"

"Elsa," the woman said.

"Elsa. Bring her to see me as soon as you can." Perhaps, Chase thought, he could at least help make that child's life a little less of a living hell.

The husband and wife looked at one another.

"We don't have much money," Bill Barlow admitted. "We can't afford to bring her." He got up to leave.

Chase pushed his chair back and stood behind his desk. There was something they were not telling him. He looked at the woman who put her head down and stared at the floor.

"Please, don't worry about money," the doctor insisted. "We'll find a way."

Barlow stared at Chase, then turned on his heel, and walked out of the office. His wife gripped the handles on the back of their son's wheelchair, maneuvered it toward the door, and followed her husband out without another word.

21

Marshal Sterling Buttars walked amid the throng of people making their way to the meetinghouse—men, women, and children excited at the prospect of seeing the Prophet after his four months in prison. Buttars' three wives walked demurely behind him; he knew they were all silently wondering what was wrong with their husband. They'd seen him crying, but he refused to answer their questions.

Not one of them seemed to notice that he'd come home alone, without the dog. His little Mouse. They fawned over him, as they always did, but did they really see him? He'd always believed his wives lavished him with praise and attention because they loved him, but recently he'd overheard them talking amongst themselves and discovered that, to the extent they cared for him at all, it was only as their key to heaven. Without his permission, any one of them—or all of them, for that matter—could be denied access to the Celestial Kingdom. The Prophet himself had given Buttars that power.

Each time he'd married, he'd hoped his new wife would love him, or at least like him. Especially his third wife, Bonnie, now a lovely sixteen year old, who he yearned for in ways he couldn't explain. He stopped short and gazed at the giant doors that yawned open leading into the meetinghouse. After what he'd done that afternoon, he should not be thinking of Bonnie like that, especially as he was mounting these steps. In fact, if anyone discovered that he actually made Bonnie remove all her clothes when they had sex and that he looked at her—all over, even in the bright light of day—well, that was simply not allowed, even with one's wife. One was just supposed to enter a woman through the slit in her garments. And, certainly, enjoyment wasn't supposed to be part of the ritual. The Prophet had made that quite clear. Sex was for procreation only. If one was enjoying the process, one was not having sex properly.

But Bonnie, with her beautiful body and glowing, flawless pink skin unmarred by continual childbirth, stirred something in him his other wives couldn't. Of course, the fact that Bonnie had not produced a child was problematic. Her failure to conceive was not for lack of trying on his part. He spent more time with her than with his other two wives combined, and even though he knew it caused friction in the household, he didn't care. The almost yearly ritual of pregnancy and birth and breastfeeding had taken a mighty toll on his other two wives and now their breasts sagged down to meet great mounds of flab around their middles.

What was odd was that Bonnie didn't seem to care that she had not produced a child. It was a strange attitude that Buttars had not encountered in any other woman in the community. Others unable to conceive had been forced to become nothing more than servants in their own homes. Some had committed suicide. Since Buttars was the marshal, he had been called upon in several cases to quietly remove the bodies of despondent women who had given up when their husbands had abandoned them because of their inability to reproduce. Like so many of the young men in the community, some of the barren wives had been sent to live "with relatives." He had no idea where the boys or the women had really gone, but to his knowledge, none of them had been heard from again.

He stumbled on the first step, but the pressing crowd moving toward the meetinghouse helped to keep his corpulent body upright. For the first time in his life, he dreaded walking through those doors. A vision of his little Mouse floated before him and forced any thoughts of Bonnie from his mind. He was glad his cap, brim low on his wide forehead, shielded his face and obscured his red, puffy eyes. When he entered the meetinghouse and had to remove his hat, all eyes would be focused on the Prophet, so hopefully, no one would ask him what was wrong. His throat tightened with a stifled a sob. He thought of Mouse's adorable brown eyes gazing up at him, wagging her curly tail, eager to show how much she loved him. He looked down at his hands as if he couldn't quite imagine how his finger had pulled the trigger. Then a fat tear slid down his cheek, and he quickly wiped the back of his meaty hand across his face, hoping no one had noticed.

22

Rose deliberately let herself get caught up in the crowd, and so was separated from her family. Since the seats in the meetinghouse were filled when she finally made her way through the massive doors, she slipped to the back wall of the room that accommodated several thousand worshippers. She wedged herself into the corner. So taken with the excitement of the congregation, she didn't notice when Jacob Babbitt squeezed into the spot right next to her.

Like most of the teenage boys in town, Jacob wore baggy jeans coated with layers of grime, and his head of thick blond hair was cut just like all the other boys, too. A navy blue, hooded sweatshirt was zipped halfway up his chest and revealed a once white T-shirt that was now a dingy gray. Girls were always expected to wear spotless clothes and be impeccably groomed, but there was no dress code for boys. While her brothers, when they lived at home, were up and out of the house doing their chores in no time flat, Rose had to spend extra time not only getting herself ready, but also helping Daisy, even though she never went anywhere. She didn't think it was fair, but she'd never dared say so.

Jacob leaned down, his lips almost touching Rose's ear. "Hey," he whispered.

She jumped and felt his hot breath on her neck. A strange tingle ran up and down the length of her spine.

And then Jacob reached around her back, slid his hand down to her bottom, and gave it a squeeze, right through her dress. She yelped and tried to move away. But her cry went unheard in the cacophony of the crowd, and she was pressed in by bodies in front of her and by the corner behind her. She had nowhere to go. Rose grabbed at his wrist and tried to push him away.

A satisfied smile played at Jacob's thin lips. "You can't stop me, Rose. It's my right, and you have no choice. I am a member of the priesthood."

Rose stiffened and turned to look at him. Dark brown eyes raked over her. His mouth, turned up at one corner, taunted her. She once believed she might happily marry Jacob Babbitt. She would never feel that way again.

"You know what the priesthood means, don't you?" Jacob placed a large warm hand on her neck, his fingers playing at the edge of her collar. "It means I can have any female I want. Anytime I want. I don't even have to ask." He smiled and Rose wondered why she had never before noticed how crooked his teeth were.

Then a voice boomed from the microphone, silencing the crowd. Jacob released his hold, and, with a burst of strength, Rose pushed her way through the crowd and away from him.

Eldon Higbee looked out over what he considered to be his worshippers. As the Prophet, was he not much like God himself and worthy of their unbridled devotion? He liked to think so, though, of course, he would not ever say this to any other human being.

He stared down at the adoring parishioners and began his sermon about the trials he'd survived in prison and how his confinement had strengthened his commitment to God. It was a speech reinforcing his belief—and, of course, that of his adoring flock—that there was not a single man on Earth who was his equal.

But halfway through the discourse, Higbee suddenly stopped. A wave of exhaustion threatened to overwhelm him. Despite thousands of faces gazing up in expectation, and, yes, adoration and wonder, Higbee could not continue. He pulled at the collar of his starched shirt and loosened his silk Armani tie. He was drained. Perhaps it was too soon to resume the mantle of leadership after four months languishing in the state prison.

There was no sound in the meetinghouse. Even the tiniest children were silent, having been instilled with the virtues of tranquility. Infants had their mouths filled with water whenever they whimpered, a lesson to make them understand that God finds crying babies offensive.

Higbee inadvertently let out a sigh that expressed his boredom. Then he flipped through his speech and placed the last page on the top. "I am glad to be home," he adlibbed. "While in prison, forced to live among sinners and devil worshippers, I had a revelation."

The crowd moved toward him in anticipation. He went back to his script. "God is upset with us." He paused and gazed out on his people. "God is concerned that we are not doing as we've been asked." He could see the fear in their faces. "God told Adam and Eve to multiply and replenish the Earth. This is our highest calling. This is our reason for being." Almost in unison, the members of the congregation nodded their heads in affirmation. He paused for effect again, searching out particular faces, looking over the crowd as if he personally addressed each man, woman, and child in the room. "We are not having enough children!" His voice bellowed through the room, amplified by giant speakers and an obscenely expensive sound system. "How do I know? Many, perhaps most of you, are guilty. Look at yourselves. Look at your neighbors."

The people gazed at one another, confused.

"How many of you harbor animals in your homes and yards? Not the creatures God has given us dominion over for our sustenance, but those animals you call pets. Dogs and cats that we lavish with attention when we should be attending to the business of the Lord. Animals that do nothing but consume resources that could be used for another child born for the glory of God!"

Higbee saw fear on the faces throughout the crowd and only a smattering of nods, still he did not deviate.

"You will go to your homes. You will dispatch the beasts that serve no purpose other than to use up our resources. You will redouble your efforts, and you will produce more children so we may fulfill our calling to honor God."

No one in the meetinghouse moved.

"And to prove your devotion to God and to me"—he added the last with a small smile—"I command that the owner of the pet must kill the beast. No one is exempt. Neither man, nor woman, nor child." He waited another moment and then raised his arm like a prophet of old and jabbed a finger toward the door. "Go and do the Lord's bidding!"

The congregation stood still, stunned at the revelation.

"Now!" the Prophet shrieked, and the doors flew open as everyone began moving at once.

23

The next morning, Adan and Trak again faced one another across the breakfast table in the bright kitchen of the hundred-year-old house. While Trak had no trouble getting the boy to eat, having a conversation with the kid was nearly impossible. Andy, if that was really his name, was monosyllabic, uttering yes and no and little else.

All Trak knew was that the boy claimed to be eighteen and that he had no family or anyone who was searching for him. And the kid had produced no ID or driver's license as evidence, which made the former Maricopa County Court system employee and devoted police TV drama watcher more than a little suspicious. But since Trak could not read minds, and didn't want to be held accountable for harboring an underage runaway, he planned to contact some friends in the police department to find out what he could. But right now he needed to go to work.

"You feeling better today?" he asked as the boy downed a sixth piece of fat, crispy bacon.

Adan nodded.

"Good! I need some help; so let's mount up." Trak

rose from the table, gathered the plates, and placed them in the sink. Adan hesitated as Trak pushed open the screen door, but before it could slam shut, he rose and headed outside and down the steps.

Half an hour later, the truck was flying south down SR389 on what was another unseasonably hot day along the Arizona Strip. A gauzy haze nearly obscured the distant mountains as the truck followed the road, twisting and turning through cuts exposing tan dirt mixed with rocks. Wind-sculpted cliffs loomed in the distance. Creosote bushes topped with pussy willow-like flower puffs massed along the roadside and across the flatlands to the south. Wire fencing crisscrossed the empty land where clouds of dust rose from the ground and hung in the air.

They passed the sign that read "Summit: 4,310 feet." Trak gestured toward the vista. "Do you remember any of this?"

Adan looked at the parched land and sandstone layered cliffs. "No."

They continued past huge metal-rimmed irrigation wheels and rusted farm equipment that appeared ancient and abandoned. Black and brown cows rested in the dirt and flicked their tails at flies, while others congregated around water troughs.

"Where are we going?"

Trak almost jumped out of his seat. "Nice to know you can string words together," he said in an effort to lighten the mood. But the boy didn't smile. "We're going to Colorado City. I have a roofing job. You afraid of heights?"

Adan shook his head. "No."

Out of the corner of his eye, Trak saw the boy exhale as if relieved. He could feel some of the tension dissipate as the boy scratched his chin and gazed out the window. "Good." Trak smiled. "I was hoping you could help."

As they approached Hildale—Colorado City's Utah sister—they past a giant semi-truck perched on a low hill. On the side of the rig, someone had painted a huge yellow smiley face. Trak saw the boy staring as they whizzed past.

"This is supposed to be the happiest place on Earth," Trak explained.

"I thought that was Disneyland."

"Good point. Still, the folks that live here in Hildale and Colorado City up ahead believe they live in a kind of Eden. Like in the Bible," Trak explained. "They're Fundamentalist Mormons, and this, for them, is Paradise."

When the truck turned off the road and down into the town of Colorado City, Adan found little that was appealing in this modern-day Eden. Old cars and trucks sat corroding in lots next to houses that were in various states of construction. Some had only a few walls. Others displayed two floors, but no doors or windows. And these were not buildings that appeared to be undergoing active construction. It seemed that they had been sitting, perhaps for years, incomplete and empty.

Incongruously, sometimes right next to these bone houses, huge multi-story, walled-in complexes, shining white in the bright, high desert light, proved some folks in Colorado City did, perhaps, live in Eden. Vast green vegetable gardens spread out from the mansions, some of which were ringed with giant golden sunflowers nodding happily in the morning breeze. Black and white cows dotted fenced-in pastures.

Then Adan saw a strange site. A girl, probably close to his own age, running along the road in an odd, long-sleeved, ankle-length dress of light blue. Her white-blonde hair was swept up in an elaborate design of braids and rolls. He noted the athletic shoes on her feet and thought they seemed out of place. The girl faced the truck, and, though she quickly looked away, Adan could see she was crying.

24

Brooke was nervous now and not only because this was her first day on a new job. The woman across the desk knew.

Evelyn Garner peered over the top of a pair of reading glasses attached to a loop of multi-colored beads. Brooke was reminded of her sixth-grade teacher, Mrs. Ross, who always appeared tired. Considering her recent battle with insomnia, Brooke, for the first time, sensed a kinship with her former elementary-school teacher.

"Of course, I know what happened," Evelyn said, leafing through the sheaf of papers. "Still, since I'm leaving at the end of the week, and I'm the only one here, at this point, we are in desperate need of help."

Brooke twined her fingers together and folded her hands in her lap. She realized she was shaking. She couldn't remember the last time she'd a good night's sleep, and her appetite had been nearly nonexistent for weeks.

"I see here that the charges were dropped, in the end."

"Yes, ma'am," Brooke answered. A pain, like she was being eaten from the inside by a small angry rodent, gnawed at her stomach.

"And up until that . . . um . . . unfortunate event, you had performed exemplary work with Child Protective Services."

All Brooke could do was nod.

Evelyn closed the folder and removed her reading glasses. "While what happened was horrific—" Brooke winced at the word, causing Evelyn to pause and take a breath. Her voice softened. "You are obviously good at what you do, Brooke, and you are needed here. Someone must help these children. I arrived just six months ago, and, if it weren't for the fact that my sister is ill and her family needs me, I would stay. From what I've seen in your file, I know you can do some good here."

Brooke stared at the earnest Evelyn Garner and felt the tears prick at her eyes. Could she ever do enough good to atone for her mistake? She looked around the Spartan single-wide trailer, noting the fake-wood paneled walls, and the two gray metal desks, each with matching four-drawer filing cabinets. There was a small kitchenette and an even smaller bathroom, all squeezed into the eighteen-by-sixty-foot mobile home turned CPS office.

"There's a culture of abuse in this community, and what's happening here has been going on a long time. Too long. Now, finally, the Attorney General's office wants to do something about it." Garner handed over a press release. "This is from six months ago." Brooke took the document and read it silently.

> "The issue in Colorado City is first and foremost the protection of children. It is not religion or culture or lifestyle. I want to assure the people of Arizona that I will not tolerate

child abuse. No matter where it occurs, no matter who the abuser might be, I will use the resources of the AG's office to investigate and prosecute reports of child abuse and neglect to the full extent of the law.

No corner of Arizona, however remote, is beyond reach. But neither is any corner to be singled out for prosecution. Every child in Arizona has the right to be safe and secure, whether in Colorado City or in Tucson. We have and will continue to look into every allegation of misconduct out of Colorado City, and will act on those we can substantiate in court.

Finally, to secure criminal prosecutions, to protect children, we need FACTS. I encourage anyone with a report of criminal activity to contact law enforcement or to call our office. And if anyone sees a child being abused or neglected, or if you are a child fleeing an abusive environment, please call the Child Protective Services hotline at 1-888-SOS-CHILD."

Brooke let the page fall to her lap.

25

Rose had been so upset she'd thrown the vitamins on the floor and fled. She still heard Mother screaming after her, insisting that she collect the scattered pills from the floor and take them right this minute! The vitamins were not an option. Everyone consumed them following the morning meal. The Prophet insisted. After all, the capsules were meant to keep them well.

But right then, Rose didn't care about vitamins. Didn't care about her health. She played the conversation over and over again in her head.

"Of course, Daisy will have to kill the creature," her mother had casually mentioned as she slathered yellow butter on her slab of homemade whole-wheat toast.

"What?" Rose had said, noting that no one else, not even her father, had responded to her mother's statement.

Bliss rolled her eyes. "Did you not hear the Prophet speak, girl?" Bliss dropped the knife onto her plate. The harsh clang made all heads rise at the table. Everyone stared at Rose.

"No more pets!" Bliss said. "Which, of course,

doesn't bother me. When I was growing up, we only had animals meant for the table. Pets were a luxury we could ill afford, and I'm not surprised at the Prophet's revelation at all."

Rose had long ago stopped asking for a dog or cat, since Mother did not abide an animal in, or even near the house, unless the creature had already been slaughtered for a meal. In retrospect, that she had accepted the little blue parakeet into the house had been rather astonishing. Then again, the Prophet was the one who had asked Bliss to take the bird. Mother had instantly agreed, but had then stuck the cage on the third floor where Daisy spent her days, and she had grown attached to the creature, while Rose had tended to the parakeet's needs.

"We have been ordered to kill all non-essential animals and we shall. It's as simple as that," Bliss said, taking a small bite of her toast, chewing demurely.

Rose thought of her friends who had pets. She pictured Billy, his crooked face, tending the big sunflowers, the long-haired yellow dog, Sunny, always nearby. Surely, the Prophet didn't mean Sunny should die, or that Billy had to kill the animal himself. She had stifled a shudder. Simple, gentle Billy would never be able to hurt Sunny.

"What harm are they doing?" Rose had asked in a defiant tone she would certainly pay for.

Bliss eyed her child from across the table. Then her hand darted out and grabbed the wooden spoon. But before she could act, Logan Madsen stopped her. He met his wife's furious gaze; slowly, she placed the spoon back on the table.

"Rose," her father said with a sigh. "The Prophet believes that pets cost us too much in resources. This food and attention is better spent on other human beings. Can you not see that?"

"Yes, sir. But why must Daisy kill the bird?" Tears had begun to spill over her golden lashes and roll down her cheeks.

"I understand that this might seem cruel to you, Rose," her father explained. "But it is important that we show complete devotion to both God and the Prophet. It is the only way. I want you—all of you—in the Celestial Kingdom with me when the time comes. If we do not do what we are asked, that might not happen."

Rose had dropped her head and stared at her lap, thinking there might be another reason for the Prophet's proclamation. The two Belnap boys once told her a secret. They had witnessed Eldon Higbee run in fear from an old, almost blind, cattle dog that had barked and backed the Prophet into a corner one afternoon near his home, right before he'd been taken back to prison. He had fallen on his rump into a pile of cow dung.

"You do want Daisy in heaven with us, don't you Rose?" her father asked.

But before she could answer, her mother pushed her chair noisily over the floorboards. "Come with me, Rose." Bliss Madsen stood. "Perhaps some time in the closet will help you see things more clearly."

Rose pictured the tiny black space and felt like she was suffocating. "No! I won't go in there again!" She didn't know what had made her grab the small dish of vitamins and hurl them to the floor. Or what had made her defy her mother and run. All she knew was that fifteen minutes later she was running down the side of the road when she locked eyes for an instant with a dark boy in the passenger seat of a white pickup. Then she turned off the road and ran toward a thick stand of cottonwood trees at the base of Canaan Mountain.

26

Trak pulled the pickup onto a gravel drive where a man and two teenage boys were lifting boxes of shingles onto the roof. Rolls of black tarpaper had been placed strategically across the top of what appeared to be a barn. The thickset man dropped a heavy box of shingles and waved a hand at Trak.

"Morning, Clay," Trak called and opened the door. "Come on, Andy."

Adan exited the truck and stood gazing at the half-finished building—a concrete pad with a skeletal structure of framing and trusses and plywood. He heard a crash, and turned toward Trak, who had just dropped the Ford's tailgate.

"Buckle up," the big man said, tossing over a leather tool belt. "And don't forget the water," he added, indicating a cooler that contained two chilled stainless steel bottles, as well as several gallons of water in plastic jugs. "When you're empty, get a refill. And don't wait until you're thirsty. Keep sipping all the time."

Although Adan was unfamiliar with roofing, he found

the simplicity and repetition of placing and nailing the shingles strangely soothing. The spot where he was working was overhung by a giant tree, which provided shade from the morning sun. Trak had placed him there, saying he was still concerned about the boy's bout with heat sickness.

Adan sat back on his heels and reached for the water bottle, but paused when a horrible wailing sound rose up on the breeze. The five men on the roof stared at one another, then toward the direction of the cries, which were coming from a nearby garden bordered by huge yellow sunflowers.

"Just do it!"

"No! No! No! No! No!"

While Clay and his sons turned away from the sound and continued working, Trak laid down his tools, and though he motioned for Adan to stay where he was, the boy dropped his hammer and followed him down the ladder. They ran toward the field and through the wall of towering flowers.

Billy Jessop, his damaged faced scrunched up and wet with tears, held a shotgun pointed at the ground.

"Go ahead! We ain't got all day," his father Frank said.

Great gobs of snot ran down Billy's chin. "Why?"

"No reason your pathetic brain would understand, boy. Just do as you're told."

Frank whirled around when two men appeared at the edge of the field. He squinted into the sun. "That you, Trak? My eyes ain't that great."

"Hey, Frank, Billy. We thought maybe someone needed help."

"Don't need nothin'."

Billy tossed the gun on the ground and rushed over to Sunny. The old dog sat up on her haunches, as Billy wrapped his arms around her neck and buried his face in her golden fur.

Frank sighed, walked over, and picked up the weapon. Then he grabbed Billy by the back of his overalls and jerked him to his feet. Three times he slapped Billy hard in the face.

Trak's first instinct was to grab Frank Jessop and slam him to the ground. But he remembered where he was. "Frank," he said as casually as he could, "are you sure there isn't—"

A blast and keening wails shattered the dry desert air. Billy fell next to the dog whose golden coat was now nothing but a wet, red crater. The animal twitched a few times as Billy caressed her, blood covering his hands and forming a pool that seeped into the dark garden earth.

"It was your job, you great twit! Not mine." Frank Jessop waved a gnarled hand at Trak and Adan, a dismissive gesture indicating that they should move on. But they both stood frozen, staring at the deformed man who wept beside the ruin of his dog.

27

Rose bent over, hands on her knees, panting hard. While running felt good, she was simply not used to any extended physical exercise. Mother believed this sort of "display" was unseemly and wholly unattractive, especially for young ladies who should be concentrating on being demure and attracting a husband.

She stood on the rocky edge of Short Creek. The massive red cliffs of Canaan Mountain loomed behind the now dry, white sand bed. Rose stared at the multi-colored hues of the jagged rock face and smiled. In science class, Mr. Wayland always referred to the wall that towered over the town as "a fabulous layer cake of geological wonder."

"What are ya doin'?"

Rose jumped, startled by the voice. She turned toward the direction of the sound. Her eyes darted to the side of a large boulder that was shaded by one of the immense cottonwoods lining the river. A strange smell, something like wood smoke but different, tickled her nose. Rose sneezed loudly.

"Well?" the girl asked.

Rose recognized the town marshal's third wife, a girl just one year older than she was, sitting atop the rock. She watched fascinated as Bonnie Buttars took a deep drag on a cigarette and exhaled a long white plume of smoke.

"You're not gonna tell, are ya?"

Rose just stared. Bonnie's pale yellow dress was hiked up to her thighs, exposing creamy white legs to the dappled sunlight. Bright blue Nikes sat on the rock beside her. Bonnie leaned forward, brushing something away from her naked toes.

"Wanna smoke?" Bonnie asked.

Rose shook her head. "What are you doing here?"

Bonnie glared at her. "What does it look like I'm doing?"

"Smoking." Rose had only witnessed this once before. She'd come upon a few boys along the trail that snaked around the base of the mountain. She had been careful to stay hidden.

Bonnie patted a spot on the rock next to her as she exhaled another white breath into the air. "Come on up and have a seat, Rose."

Without hesitation, Rose walked to the red boulder and climbed to the top. She looked at Bonnie Buttars as the girl tapped loose ash from the end of the burning cigarette. Bonnie graced Rose with a big smile. The girl's skin was flawless, and, even though her hair was blonde, her eye lashes and brows were dark—perfect frames for her blue-green eyes. She was the most beautiful girl Rose had ever seen.

"How come you're not married, Rose? I mean, how the hell did you manage that?"

Rose was speechless. There were very strict rules

against swearing, especially for girls. Still, she found herself giggling.

"Come on and tell me, Rose. I tried everything to get out of marrying old, fat Sterling Buttars. But my father locked me in the basement for six days with only a gallon of water. Made me pee in a bucket."

Rose's eyes widened. "Really?"

"I had no choice. And being his wife is really disgusting." Bonnie stubbed out the cigarette, grinding the remains into the rock.

"What do you mean?" Rose asked.

"Well, Rose, you must certainly know what happens between men and women."

Rose shook her head.

"Oh, come on. Haven't you ever seen a bull on a cow? Or two dogs?"

Rose frowned for a moment. "Yes, but those are animals."

Bonnie burst out laughing. "People are just the same, Rose. Trust me. I know. I'm an old married woman." She paused, wrapping her arms around her knees. "But that's gonna change." Bonnie Buttars' blue eyes flashed. "I'm going to find some way to get out of here. Wanna come?"

28

Eldon Higbee paced his well-appointed private rooms. While in prison he had dreamed of the seclusion the massive suite provided. Thick hand-woven carpets, an antique walnut desk, and soft brown leather armchairs filled the office space. A dining alcove boasted a mahogany table with matching chairs, fronting a huge bay window that looked out onto Canaan Mountain. Fresh purple and white flowers filled a crystal vase atop the gleaming dark wood. The room smelled of lemony wood polish.

But Higbee, who had so loudly and often bemoaned the lack of amenities in prison, found that nothing here soothed him. He had planned his welcome home sermon from the moment the metal prison doors clanked shut behind him, a stirring speech that would awaken his people and remind them of their duties to God, and, of course, to him. But when he found himself facing the congregation— the people's mouths agape in what he was sure was profound adoration—he felt . . . nothing.

Higbee was puzzled. Perhaps he should call the kitchen and have some of his favorite foods sent up. A prime piece of Kobe beef—purchased at great expense and reserved only for his table—might perk him up. But he wasn't hungry. Had the swill he'd been forced to consume in prison permanently ruined his appetite? Or was something else causing the uneasy feeling that made him uncomfortable here in the haven of his own home?

He loosened the silver silk tie and undid the top button of his tailored shirt, then slumped into one of the leather chairs. His gaze fell on the set of carved wooden double doors at the far end of the room. Inside was the special bed. His skin prickled as he sensed the women in the rooms below. Of course, they wondered who'd be called first. He pinched the bridge of his nose.

There was a knock at the outer door.

"Come."

Oran Coombs entered, then closed the door behind him. "Is there something I can do for you, sir?"

Higbee eyed his personal bodyguard and second-in-command. "Are the people complying with my orders?"

"Many are. Though it may take a few days to finish the job. There is now a disposal problem, however."

"Disposal?"

"Yes, sir. Most families do have pets of some kind. Primarily dogs."

Higbee shuddered. "Disgusting creatures."

"Some of the people seem concerned about exactly which animals to kill. Some have small ponies for the children to ride."

"If the purpose of the animal is amusement, it must die," Higbee said. "If the animal is a goat or sheep and can produce a useful product, it may live."

"Yes, sir."

"Get a group of men together and have them dig a pit out behind the graveyard. Have the people bring the dead animals. Then order Buttars and his men to do a house-to-house search. Make sure everyone has complied."

"Yes, sir. Is there anything else?"

Higbee noticed Coombs was staring at him. The Prophet scratched the back of his neck, stretched his long skeletal legs, and stood up. He understood the man was waiting for him to choose. "No," Higbee answered, waving both hands out before him. "No, I just want to be alone."

"Yes, sir."

After Coombs left, Higbee reflected on the fact that he had no interest in any of the women who were his wives. The problem was really quite simple. When he'd married them, they were beautiful young girls. But the sweet things he bound himself to in celestial marriage changed quickly and in such awful ways. Their breasts grew large and sagged with breastfeeding. Hair grew on their once-smooth bodies, the thought of which sent a shiver of revulsion down his spine. Their perfect trim bodies plumped up as they aged.

Higbee tried to minimize this roundness that held no allure for him. He had personally designed the long pastel-colored dresses all females wore. The top panels of the garments pressed down and flattened women's breasts. The shapeless skirts concealed curved hips and bottoms. Even the elaborate hairstyles with their multiple braids reflected Higbee's desire to see them all as very young girls. The Prophet felt himself get hard at the thought.

29

Trak and Adan remounted the ladder and finished the roofing, though neither one of them could stop thinking about what had happened with the disabled man and his dog. When Clay and his sons appeared unwilling to address the subject, Trak let the issue drop, at least publicly. He'd lived most of his life around Colorado City and knew the people followed their own way of living. As a dog owner, however, the event was horribly disturbing. Yet, he'd done nothing to stop the shooting. He was raised with the idea that the Fundamentalists had a right to live the way they chose. Still. . . .

At the end of the day, Trak and Adan were silent as they drove down Central Street past the Mercantile, where women and children chatted in the parking lot as they deposited mounds of groceries into what were mostly pickup trucks and SUVs. All females, young and old, wore long dresses—single colored garments in pastel hues of purple, pink, brown, and blue—that swept close to the pavement. Heavy-soled athletic shoes peeked incongruously from underneath.

When the truck approached Mohave Avenue, several low tan buildings appeared ahead on the left side of the road. Trak turned the steering wheel to make the right turn that would lead them to SR389 and back to Hurricane, but he suddenly slammed on the breaks. The pickup rocked back and forth.

A big grin spread across Trak's face. Instead of turning, he guided the pickup through the intersection to the front of what was a tiny extension of the Mojave County Community College system. They neared the cluster of simple, one-story block structures fronted by a pole sporting an American flag and a boulder with a red sign bearing the word Mojave. Green manicured lawns seemed out of place in the otherwise arid landscape.

His eyes were now focused on a small woman with flaming red hair that was pulled into a high ponytail. Dressed in blue jeans and a light green, loose-fitting cotton blouse, she walked across the grassy area in front of a building boasting a sign that said Science Lab. She carried a stack of black folders and had a woven, multicolored Navajo-design purse slung over one shoulder.

The truck had barely pulled to a stop when Trak jumped out. "Brooke," he called out much too eagerly. He waved at the woman he'd met at the café.

Brooke stopped short and gazed at the man by the truck. Then she smiled, walked over, and extended her hand. "Nice to see you again."

Trak quickly removed his cowboy hat. He ran one hand across his scalp to slick back damp hair that was surely suffering from a serious case of hat-head. He wiped his fingers on his dirty jeans and grabbed Brooke's hand.

She squinted at him. The sun, which was dropping

toward the horizon, shined in her face, making her pupils shrink. Brooke's blue-green eyes glowed in the light.

Trak finally pulled his hand back. "What are you doing out here?" he asked, recovering his composure.

"I'll be working for CPS, um, Child Protective Services."

"Here at the school?" he said. "Aren't most of these students at least eighteen, which would be out of your purview?"

Brooke tilted her head. The gesture indicated that she realized her earlier estimation of Trak was wrong. She had taken him for an unschooled cowboy.

"Yes, eighteen year olds are generally out of my purview," she answered, repeating the word that had tipped her off that Trak had probably spent a good deal of time in a classroom. "Our office, if you want to call a trailer with a few desks and a couple of file cabinets an office, is over there, behind the Science Lab." She pointed to a path that led around the right side of the building.

"Looks like you already have a lot of work to do," Trak said, indicating the folders she carried. Again he pushed a big hand through his dark hair.

Brooke suppressed a grin, and seemed flattered that she was making Trak nervous. "This was my first day." She opened the door to an ancient metallic blue Nissan Sentra. She got in and rolled down the window.

"Maybe I'll see you at the café," he said.

"Maybe," she said, a smile spreading across her face. She gave him a small wave as she backed out and then drove away.

When he opened the door to his truck, the boy looked at him and burst out laughing.

30

Rose made her way home, walking slowly as the fear of what she would face once her mother opened the door tempered the exhilaration of talking to Bonnie. But her mother was not waiting for her on the doorstep. Instead, Rose pulled the door open to hear high-pitched screams coming from the top floor.

"WA, WA, WA!" Daisy's voice echoed through the house. Rose forgot her fear of punishment and raced up the stairs toward the room she shared with her sisters. Daisy screamed, rocking her head back and forth and flailing her weak arms out before her.

"Take it!" Bliss stood over Daisy, gripping the little blue and white parakeet that squawked in panic, twisting its tiny head one way then the other as it tried to free itself.

Logan wrapped large hands around his damaged daughter's arms, and slid them down to her thin wrists, forcing the child's hands together. "Go head, Mother. I've got her."

"What are you doing?" Rose demanded.

Daisy stopped rocking. Her head drooped to one

side, chin jutting out. One dark eye glared at Rose as if in condemnation. Saliva ran from her open mouth and tears dripped off her chin. For a moment there was silence. Both parents turned toward the doorway—Bliss with a scowl of disgust, and Logan with a resigned but determined look that Rose could hardly bear. Then Bliss and Logan Madsen turned back to their task and Daisy's screaming recommenced. She twisted in her chair all the while keeping her eye focused on Rose.

"Help us, Rose," her father called out. "Calm the girl. You can do that."

"Why?"

"You know why, Rose Madsen! The Prophet ordered this," her mother said. "Who are you to question him? You are nothing, and if you have any hope of a future, you will do as you're told."

The little bird managed to slip a wing out of Bliss's grasp and began flapping in a frantic effort to get away. The parakeet bit and pecked at Bliss's thumb and she instinctively loosened her grip. "Rose, come hold this animal!"

Rose paused in the doorway then stepped toward her mother. Out of the corner of her eye, she saw that Daisy had calmed slightly.

"Take the creature," her father pleaded. "Do it for me," he said. A sad smile creased his lips.

Rose stared at him, realizing in that instant that he was the only person in the whole world who truly loved her. She took the bird, noticing the spot of blood dotting her mother's thumb. The animal seemed to relax in Rose's hands. She brought the bird to her face and cooed softly to quiet the creature.

"I've got her," Logan said, cupping Daisy's thin-fingered hands in his own. "Now, Rose, place the bird in Daisy's hands."

Rose looked at her father, but made no move to comply.

"Do as you are ordered," her mother said in a deadly calm voice that always preceded pain and hunger.

"And what will you do when I put the bird in her hands, Father?" Rose asked in a voice uncharacteristically verging on sarcasm.

Bliss slapped her daughter in the face, but Rose neither winced, nor stepped back.

"Don't you want your sister to be with us in heaven, Rose? Where she will get up and walk and smile and be like other girls? For that to happen she must be obedient," Logan said. "We will help Daisy crush the bird until it dies. It is the Prophet's command and so we must obey."

The wailing began anew, and Rose realized for the first time that her sister really did understand everything going on around her.

"Come, Rose. It is God's work we are doing. Don't you see?" her father pleaded. "We are directed to have unquestioning obedience to the Lord and his prophets in all things."

"What kind of God would ask this?" Rose said, motioning toward Daisy with the tiny bird still enclosed in her palm.

This time the slap almost knocked Rose to the floor. She staggered, but managed to right herself.

"Rose Madsen! I ask you again, who are you to question the Prophet?" Then Bliss's eyes opened wide. "You smell like . . . like tobacco! You see, Father," she said whirling to face to her husband. "I told you what would happen to this one."

Her father let go of Daisy's hands and stood. Would he hit her? Rose wondered . . . something he had never done.

"Give me the bird," Logan said quietly.

Rose stared at her father, then took one step toward the window, pushed her arms through the fluttering curtains, opened her hands, and released the tiny bird. She watched it fly toward one of the pecan trees in the yard.

Fly away, fly far, far away.

31

"What's so funny?" Trak eyed the boy who had a smile on his face for the first time since they'd met.

"Who is she?" Adan countered.

"A very nice woman I met recently. Her name is Brooke." Trak turned his attention back to the road. "Why do you ask?"

"You reminded me of some of my friends in school when they ask a girl to the prom."

"Really?"

"Yep. And what's with that? My mom used to tell me that it gets easier to ask girls for dates when you get older."

"Did she now?"

"Are you saying it's not? Easier, I mean." Adan remembered the sweaty palms and incessant wondering about how he should react if a girl said no. How he and his friends urged one another on, watching, torturing those who were spurned, and endlessly questioning those who actually went on a date, wanting to know everything that happened.

"I'm afraid, at least in this case, Mom is not completely right." Trak reached for his water bottle, the other hand on the wheel, as they sped down the SR389 back toward Hurricane. "It's always a little uncomfortable, especially if you really like someone."

"So you really like the redhead?"

Trak pursed his lips. "Maybe. We just met."

"Well, you were certainly looking a little uncomfortable for a guy who isn't sure if he likes a girl or not."

"You're a funny kid. Drink some more water. And, since you brought it up, where did you go to school?"

Adan frowned. "Phoenix."

"Hey! I used to live in Phoenix. I went to ASU, but maybe you figured that out from the shirt you're wearing. Good old Sparky."

Adan didn't respond. The boy scratched his chin again and turned to look out the window. They passed a group of black cows huddled by a gold water truck. Fields of light green grass were dotted here and there by what looked like small conical Christmas trees rolled away from the road.

They drove down into Hurricane in silence. Once they pulled onto the concrete pad that fronted the detached garage, Trak reached into his pocket and extracted a wad of bills. He counted out half the money and held the cash out to Adan.

"Thanks for your help today."

He waved the man's hand away. "You don't need to do that. You probably have a doctor bill because of me."

Trak paused. "No, I don't. Chase is my oldest and best friend. He wouldn't let me pay him."

Adan looked at the bills. Who knew where he might end up? The thought of being hungry again knotted a tight fist in his gut.

"Go ahead and take it. Maybe I'll let you buy me a burger tonight at the café. Does that work for you?"

"Yeah, that works," Adan said as he took the money.

32

Carla Kimball heard the teacup shatter on the flagstone patio and looked up. Generally, an unflappable sort, she dropped her gardening bucket and gloves amid a row of massive yellow squash blossoms and hurried toward her new boarder who lay sprawled, half in and half out of the chair where she'd been looking over the contents of a pile of black folders. Carla fished her cellphone from her jeans and punched a button, the fingers of her other hand reaching for the girl's neck, in the hope of finding a pulse.

A voice reached out of the haze. "Ms. Neal, how are you feeling?" A white-haired man with pale blue eyes stared down at her. She had seen him somewhere before, but had no idea who he was.

"How's she doing?" Another man's voice. Also vaguely familiar.

"Well now, my friend, there is that patient confidentiality thing, and as far as I can tell, you're not next of kin or anything, so maybe you shouldn't just barge in here."

"Oh, come on, Chase." Trak stepped into the examining room.

Brooke's eyes fluttered. She realized she was looking up at a doctor, who, despite the almost white hair, was maybe in his mid-thirties. Then she turned her head and saw the man she'd met at the café, and then again outside her office. "Trak?"

"OK. Ms. Neal. Do you mind if my friend, who completely lacks any sense of decorum, is here in the room?"

Brooke shook her head weakly. "What happened?"

"Carla brought you in. You passed out on the patio. She brought you around with some smoking creosote. Says it woke you up long enough to get you into her truck, but then you passed out again."

"Creosote has many therapeutic uses," Trak said with a kind smile, "but please don't blame the Native Americans for that bit of homeopathic medicine."

"Yeah," the doctor added, "I'm pretty sure Carla made it up."

Trak pulled up a chair and leaned both elbows on the examination table. "How do you feel?"

Dark eyes that turned up at the corners stared intently at Brooke. The look of concern on the man's face made her want to cry. In fact, tears welled in her eyes and threatened to spill down her cheeks.

"Do you want me to throw this great lout out of here, Ms. Neal?"

"No." She smiled wearily and closed her eyes. Her head pounded, she was slightly nauseous, and completely exhausted.

"You rest now," Chase said.

"So what happened?" Trak asked, once they shut the door to the examining room and walked into Chase's office.

"I don't know."

Trak stared at his friend, obviously not satisfied.

Chase sighed. "Her vitals are fine, so I'll have to give you an educated guess." He leaned back in his chair and put his feet on the desk. "I'm going with dehydration and exhaustion. Her face is drawn and it looks like she hasn't been getting much sleep."

Trak nodded.

"Or . . . she's pregnant."

Trak's head shot up. "Really?"

"I don't know. It's always possible with young women. I'm sure you're not the only one who finds redheads attractive. Maybe she's running away from a torrid love affair. Maybe a love triangle." He arched his white brows.

"Shut up."

"You asked my opinion."

"So what do we do now?"

"We? I will let her rest and get some more fluids into her. Then I will get her back to Carla's. You will do nothing."

Trak narrowed his eyes.

Chase chuckled. "Not my type, Trak. This will not be a repeat of Suzy Peterson from tenth grade biology. I promise."

33

Three days later, still suffering from the death of his beloved little Mouse, Sterling Buttars wasn't sure he was up to dealing with anyone or anything. Things were tense at home; he wasn't used to having people question one of the Prophet's orders, and disposing of the growing number of dead pets was a nightmare. But his deputy had sounded frantic on the phone, and when Buttars pushed his bulk through the door of the Colorado City Marshal's Office, the look on Travis Forbush's face made him stop short.

Buttars removed a black cowboy hat and swiped at his moist brow with the back of his hand. "What's wrong?"

The deputy's eyes were wide. "There's a body."

Buttars heaved a sigh. It wasn't uncommon for bodies to turn up in the desert, but it was never pleasant, especially if it was a member of the community. He didn't think he'd ever get used to it, and always tried to hide his discomfort behind a façade of professional bravado. "Relax, boy," he said, patting his deputy on the shoulder before heading for the coffee maker. "Who called it in?" He poured the strong black brew into a ceramic cup bearing the words, "Follow the Prophet."

Forbush just looked at him.

"Ain't ya never seen a dead body before, son?" Buttars turned and watched the deputy shake his head. "You'll get used to it after a while. Now, who called it in and where're we goin'?"

"Um ... Evans. Bill Evans. Out west of the cemetery."

Buttars scratched his head. "Bill know who it is?"

"No, but it's a woman. Probably a local. She's wearing the dress."

Twenty minutes later, Buttars and Forbush approached a wiry man chewing a long stem of grass, arms folded across his chest. He leaned against the thick, furrowed trunk of a sprawling cottonwood.

"Out back behind that rock." He pointed into the distance with his chin.

"Any idea who it is?" Buttars asked.

"Can't tell. She's face down. Didn't wanna move her till you got here."

"Thanks. That was the right way to handle it." Buttars turned to his deputy. "Let's go see what we've got before we call anybody, all right Travis?" Buttars was feeling fatherly toward his deputy, a good man who'd only been on the job a few months. He remembered his first body and knew the sight of it could stay with you. In fact, he remembered every single body he'd seen, every corpse he'd ever had to deal with. He started toward the boulder, then realized Forbush wasn't behind him. He turned and motioned toward the cottonwood. "Tell you what, you go on over and interview Bill. Write down what he saw and when he found the body, OK?"

"Thanks, Chief," Forbush muttered, looking relieved.

Buttars walked on toward the area Bill Evans indicated. The boulder, about fifty yards ahead, was nestled inside a thick clump of young cottonwood trees that butted up against the edge of the now dry streambed. He shuddered as he crossed a patch of ground, that, unlike the rest of the area, had no native vegetation and was dotted with numerous small piles of mounded dirt. He picked his way carefully, avoiding the disturbed ground, only once glancing back at the fenced-in confines of the Isaac W. Carling Memorial Park—the town cemetery. He quickened his pace, anxious to get through the area. A buzzing, like hundreds of tiny insects droned, yet he saw none nearby. The noise morphed into a myriad of tiny voices, darting low to the ground. But he knew there was nothing there. He clenched his jaw. Sweat poured profusely off his chin. I'm just tired, he told himself. He'd always hated this place, and knew he was being ridiculous. But even though logic told him there was nothing to fear, he couldn't shake the feeling of dread that made the hairs on the back of his neck stand on end.

He reached the boulder and placed his hand on the warm, red sandstone. He took a deep breath, steeling himself. You've done this before and you can do it again, he whispered. He glanced up for a moment, his eyes searching the mountains that rocketed up behind the stream and into the blue morning sky. A hawk floated lazily on the currents above. The creature screeched once before winging off, disappearing behind the jagged peaks.

Marshal Buttars walked around the boulder and froze.

34

Travis Forbush snapped his cellphone shut as he watched Sterling Buttars lumber toward him. "I phoned County. They'll be sending a coroner and asked that we remain on-site until they get here."

"What?" Buttars, out of breath, placed both hands on the patrol car. His face was flushed. He appeared confused.

"The coroner, Chief."

Buttars turned to the deputy. "Who?"

"The Mojave County Coroner. Someone will be here, but since they're coming from Lake Havasu, it'll be five hours, at least."

"Why the fuck did you call them?"

Forbush stepped back like he'd been hit.

"What if it's just natural causes, boy?" Buttars clenched his hands into thick fists and slammed the front of the truck.

"I . . . I thought that was protocol, sir."

The deputy was partially correct, and not entirely to blame. The manual did say to contact the county coroner before moving a body in which the manner of death was suspicious. However, the Prophet should have been notified first. The last thing the Eldon Higbee would want was to have county authorities involved. There was always trouble when outsiders showed up.

"Who is it?" Forbush asked.

"I don't know." Buttars heart pounded in his chest. "It's a young woman. Her head's been smashed in and she's face down. I didn't touch her."

"Are you sure she's . . . dead?" Forbush grimaced. "I mean, you didn't check?"

"I didn't have to, Travis. It's obvious."

The deputy nodded.

"Get the tarp out of the trunk. We'll need to cover her up." Buttars pinched the space between his eyes and let out a long breath. "You stay here and wait for the coroner. I'll pick up some food and drinks and come back."

"I don't need this now, Sterling!" The Prophet, dressed in a white, long-sleeved dress shirt, dark pressed slacks, and soft, black leather loafers, paced across the intricately patterned carpet that spread out before his desk.

Buttars rolled his hat in his hands. "The boy is new, sir. Down from Bountiful. I know his uncle and—"

"I don't care. It's on you. Clean it up before anyone gets here."

Buttars dropped his hands to his sides. "What do you want us to do?"

Eldon Higbee spread his hands wide. "You're the marshal, Sterling. Get rid of the body, and figure out something to say to the county people. I do not want them snooping around. We can't have them here!" His voice was shrill. "Say you were mistaken. Say she was simply injured and is being treated and will be fine." He straightened up as if the uttering of these words made it so. "I believe it was just an unfortunate misunderstanding. Tell them. Call the county people. Make it clear!"

"But what about the woman's family?" Buttars choked on the words, hoping against hope he was wrong. Why hadn't he rolled her over just to be sure, protocol be damned?

Higbee stared out the window and looked toward the striated, red wall of Canaan Mountain, his hands clasped tightly behind his back.

"The family?" He turned and glared at Buttars. "It's a woman." He spread his hands, palms up. "If she's someone's wife, I'll give him another."

35

Buttars was too late. He stood with his deputy and watched the helicopter descend, landing on a stretch of brown grass and dirt just outside the cemetery. Bold black and gold lettering on the side of the helicopter said Mojave County Sheriff.

While the rotors continued to whirl, churning up a high plume of dust, the door opened and a petite woman in a white T-shirt, blue jeans, and a baseball cap stepped out, carrying a large black case. She turned and waved to the pilot, and as soon as she cleared the landing area, the helicopter lifted of the ground, whop, whop, whopping its way in the direction of Hurricane. Buttars and Forbush walked out to meet her.

"Bev Tyler." The woman extended her free hand to Buttars. "I'm the Medical Examiner."

Buttars forced a smile. "That was fast."

"Buck was headed out here before the call came in." She nodded toward the helicopter that was already just a tiny version of itself in the cloudless blue sky. "I definitely don't have any helicopter rides in my budget. Where's the body?"

Buttars pointed.

"Has anyone moved or disturbed the scene in any way?" Bev asked as they made their way toward the small copse of trees shading the boulder.

"N-No, ma'am," Forbush said, eyes to the ground.

"Identification?"

"The subject is face down. So . . . we really don't know anything except that it appears to be a young woman."

A few minutes later, Buttars led the way around the rust-colored boulder. He and Forbush removed the tarp they'd placed over the body and stepped back. The marshal watched, arms crossed and resting on his distended belly. He tried to look away, but couldn't stop focusing on the victim's legs. Creamy smooth and almost blindingly white. So horribly familiar. He tried to swallow, but his tongue and throat wouldn't cooperate. He was lightheaded, queasy. He reached out and put a hand on the boulder to steady himself.

Bev Tyler spent over an hour taking a myriad of digital photographs of the scene. Then she bagged and tagged bits and pieces of evidence she recovered from the grass surrounding the body. "Could you both help me turn her over?" she said, hands on slim boyish hips.

Both men paused. Buttars, shirt soaked with sweat, nodded to his deputy and they both walked over. Bev passed them latex gloves, then explained where to place their hands. The three of them carefully turned the victim over.

Buttars stared. A great well of pain crushed his chest. He stumbled backwards, turned away and threw up, the office coffee stinging the back of his throat as the liquid rocketed out onto the green grass and scattered river rocks. He staggered away, unwilling to look back.

Bev watched him go, then shrugged her shoulders. It happened that way with some folks. She looked back at the smashed-in face, now a ragged bloody hole. "Do you know her?" she asked, looking up at Forbush.

He nodded slowly, his head moving up and down mechanically.

"What can you tell me about her?" Bev asked. She flipped to a clean page in the small notebook she carried in her back pocket.

"She was—"

Bev waited. The only sound was the droning of bees as they busied themselves coming and going from a dead tree that lay sideways along the bank.

Travis dropped his hands to his sides and glanced at the marshal who staggered toward the truck "Bonnie. She was the chief's wife."

Bev wrinkled her brow. "She seems awfully young, I mean, to be married to him."

The deputy did not respond.

36

A small crowd gathered, drawn to the area by the helicopter touching down to pick up the coroner. Brooke heard the commotion. Recalling the doctor's admonition that she stay hydrated, she grabbed a cold bottle of water from the tiny refrigerator that hummed in the kitchenette, then stepped out the door and descended the wooden stairs. She followed a man and two women, who also seemed intent on discovering what was going on behind the cemetery.

When Brooke reached the scene, she observed yellow tape that ringed an area by a huge red boulder and some old cottonwoods. She could see nothing except a woman who appeared to be taking notes. Every so often, the woman knelt and examined the ground. Once, she bent over, her nose almost touching the dried brush. After a moment she straightened and jotted something in her notebook.

Soon others began to congregate in the area, whispering in small groups. Brooke looked over and made eye contact with several young people in a nearby cluster. They all stared for a moment and then, almost in unison, turned away. Brooke continued perusing the crowd that was still growing. All the people stayed far away from her. There was an obvious gap—a half-circle of empty space—separating her from the other observers.

A young man in a police uniform approached the woman with the notebook. She shook her head and pointed toward a truck parked just outside the tape. The policeman turned around and walked toward the vehicle.

That was the moment Brooke caught a glimpse of something off to the right, low in the trees. A flash of blue. A young, frightened face. Then the vision was gone.

Brooke turned quickly to the nearest group. Had they witnessed the apparition? There, too, she saw the same blue hue covered several females. In one case, the baby blue dress encased a small child. Maybe five years old. A tiny doll in an ankle-length prairie costume. Long, white-blond braids cascaded down her back. The child locked eyes with Brooke, who graced the girl with a friendly smile. The doll child showed no expression. No emotion. No happiness. No fear. Nothing.

Brooke shivered.

She turned away and stared again into the trees. Almost imperceptibly, something stirred. Someone else must surely have noticed. She watched as people whispered to one another and realized that, along with the activities inside the yellow tape, she was the one being observed. Perhaps no one else had seen the person in the trees because everyone had been looking at her. What was it with these people? Clearly, they found her presence here disturbing. But why? She knew small towns were sometimes insular, but this was ... strange. Certainly, after six years of working for CPS, she should be familiar with being seen as an outsider, an intruder. How often had she been sent to homes where children had been abused and their family members were hostile? When she decided to go into social work, she had, quite foolishly, seen herself as an avenging angel. Someone who could help children. Maybe even save their lives. Her stomach turned, and, horribly, she almost laughed at the irony.

Still, the fact that she was eliciting so many stares from the assemblage kept her rooted in place. Brooke felt an affinity with the blue dress in the trees, much like the two year old she'd picked up in the squalor of a crack house—an emaciated child in a reeking diaper, squatting barefoot on broken glass, and who immediately stretched out thin arms, begging to be picked up. The child's eyes pleaded with Brooke not to let go when the police officer eased the baby from her arms. That face—those haunted eyes—never left her.

Brooke dared not move from her place outside the yellow tape. She sensed a need out there in the trees, and thought, that perhaps her presence offered the apparition some semblance of cover.

37

Brooke sipped a tall iced tea at a patio table and watched the sun set at the Main Street Café. A cool breeze puffed through the massive pecan trees riffling the leaves.

"Is this seat taken?" Trak asked.

"No, go ahead." Brooke smiled at the big man who had washed and changed into clean jeans and a white button-down shirt. His sleeves were rolled up, exposing muscular forearms and short dark hair, still wet, glistening in the fading light.

Trak nodded toward the empty table in front of her. "Just drinking your dinner?"

Brooke sighed. "I'm not hungry. I had a tough day."

He sat and listened as she recounted the events by the cemetery, though Brooke left out the part about the vision in the trees. She wanted to trust him, but she was required, as part of her job, to keep information on her cases private. Details could only be shared on a need-to-know basis. But why was she thinking of the individual in the trees as a case? The person might not even be a child. Still. . . .

Trak sat back in his chair. "Do you know who died?"

"No. Though apparently, it was a young woman."

"An accident, perhaps?"

"I don't know." She looked beyond the vine-covered fence toward the garden, already dark, the last of the light unable to penetrate the thick grove of trees.

"Is there something else bothering you?" Trak leaned back in his chair and the two sat in silence as the apricot-colored clouds faded to gray.

"The people," she said finally.

"Colorado City people?"

Brooke nodded.

He tilted his head and looked at her from underneath long, dark lashes. "Do you know anything about them?"

"Before coming up here, I knew nothing, except that they were practicing polygamy. But there seems to be more to it than that. They won't talk to me. Any of them. They stare at me like I'm some sort of evil creature. Especially the little children. I'm definitely not used to that. I'm not thin skinned. I've been a CPS caseworker for almost six years. I've had lots of people get mad when I show up at their homes to investigate possible acts of child abuse. But this is different. The open animosity. The suspicion. I don't understand it." Brooke shook her head.

Trak raised both eyebrows and stared at her.

"What?"

"I've never heard you say so much at one time."

Brooke felt her cheeks turn pink.

The screen door pushed open. A waitress appeared with a large plate of mixed greens covered with thick slabs of tomatoes, round slices of cucumber, and a pile of grilled vegetables, including asparagus, small purple potatoes, and thick wedges of onions.

Brooke eyed the food. "You seem more like a burger and fries kind of guy."

"Now don't go stereotyping us country folk. We might surprise you," he said, rising from his seat.

Brooke watched Trak walk back into the café. A few moments later, he reappeared with another plate and some utensils wrapped in a paper napkin.

"Here, he said." He put the place setting in front of her. "We'll share this one, and if you like it, maybe we'll share another."

'You mean, like a date?" Brooke smiled and watched as he scooped a pile of vegetables onto her plate.

"Try the dressing. It's homemade." He handed her a small white pitcher. Then, with a wide grin, said, "And yes, like a date."

At that moment the screen door opened and Adan appeared holding a plate with a thick burger and a huge pile of fries.

Trak eyed him for a moment. "Andy, this is Brooke."

Adan smiled and held up his hand. He waved at Brooke. "Hi."

Trak pulled out the chair next to him. "Come and sit down."

Adan chuckled and shook his head. "No, man. I'm good." He turned and went back inside the café.

38

Later that night, Trak pushed through his front screen door, holding two sweating bottles of beer. He handed one to Chase, who was rocking in a faded green, metal porch chair. Trak dropped into a similar seat next to his friend, and, for a while, they were silent, listening to a chorus of crickets singing in the darkness. Neither man saw Adan sitting out in the yard, his back against a tree, Holly curled up beside him.

"It was Bonnie Buttars," Chase said without being asked.

"The marshal's wife?"

"One of them." Chase took a long draught from the bottle. "I got a call from Bev Tyler."

Trak turned and stared.

"That was a long time ago," the doctor said. "Bev was looking for any records I might have on Bonnie, but I only treated the girl once. Her parents brought her in right before she married Butters. If I recall, she was only fifteen."

"Why you? Don't they usually take care of folks in their own clinic?"

"I get patients from Colorado City. Their clinic is good with basic medicine, but when a condition is complicated, the midwives sometimes can't handle it. Also, often families want to keep their concerns private."

Trak nodded. He pictured the disabled man and the bloody body of the dog then pushed the vision away.

"Looking back, it was rather odd," Chase said. "Her parents brought her to me because they felt she was acting strangely. That was all they would say. She'd changed her attitude and was behaving differently than what they felt was normal. I examined Bonnie and found her to be completely healthy in every way. She seemed bright and fit and had a good sense of humor, which I haven't seen very often in the young people I've treated from Colorado City. Mostly, they don't say much. But she talked. A lot. So much so that I actually noted it in my records. But she only spoke to me when her parents were out of the room."

"How'd you pull that off?" Trak asked. "You're an outsider and they left her alone with you?"

Chase sighed. "I'm a known entity. Family history in the area, local boy, you know how it is. It doesn't always work, but I can get my way more often than not."

"If anyone could, it'd be you."

"Anyway, when I was talking with Bonnie privately, she started asking me all kinds of questions about movies and TV."

"But how would she know anything about those things?"

"No idea. When I asked her why her parents had brought her in, she just smiled. She was a beautiful young girl."

Trak raised his eyebrows.

"Oh, don't be disgusting! You know me better than that. It was just an observation. What I saw was a lovely young girl, eager, excited, full of life. Now, the child is dead."

"How?"

"Bev wasn't at liberty to share much, but with an obvious investigation underway, the death was probably not by natural causes."

The silence stretched out between them. Chase took a long pull from his beer.

"Acting strangely? That's all they said?"

"Yep." Chase drained his beer and set the bottle on the porch beside him. "There was one thing, and I probably shouldn't tell you."

"Let me guess. Doctor-patient confidentiality? But since the patient is deceased . . ."

Chase pinched the bridge of his nose and took a deep breath. "Bonnie had stopped taking her vitamins. She said her parents had no idea and insisted I not tell them."

"Vitamins?"

"I've learned over the years that everyone in the community takes vitamins prescribed by Eldon Higbee. It's required."

"What kind of vitamins?

"Damned if I know. But Bonnie Butters had stopped taking them and her behavior changed."

39

Rose remained huddled inside the massive remnants of an ancient fallen cottonwood. The tree's thick limbs, long shorn of leaves, surrounded her in what had felt like a protective embrace. The soft tall grasses—still green thanks to their proximity to the riverbed—shielded her from view, while the towering wall of layered red sandstone stood as a sentinel at her back. But since the sun had vanished, darkening the sky, this nest now filled her with a sense of foreboding. She retched again, but her stomach had long since been emptied. Her mouth was raw, dry, sour. She craved water.

Rose pulled her knees to her chest, took a deep breath, and blew it out slowly. Then she drew in another and another, trying to calm herself. She flinched as something skittered in the brush, then quietly admonished herself. There is nothing out here to fear. Mr. Wayland had taught her and her classmates all about the creatures—mammals and insects and reptiles and birds—that lived in these mountains and lowlands. Though sometimes they might bite or sting a human, this was not something they wanted to do. They inflicted injury because they were afraid and had to protect themselves. "And so I will not fear you and you will not fear me and we will get along," she whispered into the night.

The movement in the leaf litter ceased. Rose lifted her head and gazed at the sky, now bathed in a swath of bright stars. She breathed in the cool air and tried to think. The scent—damp sand mixed with wet rock—indicated there was water nearby. She needed to locate the source.

Then her skin prickled. A blinding light flashed—yellow then red. In the vision, her mother was screaming. She forced Rose back into the closet. Daisy's screams filled her head as the tiny parakeet flapped and tried to free itself from their mother's long-fingered grip.

Jacob Babbitt's hard eyes bit into her. The boy bent close to her ear. "You can't stop me, Rose. It's my right, and you have no choice. I am a member of the priesthood." He planted one grubby hand on the collar of her dress and pulled, ripping the buttons open. He smiled like a reptile and transformed into a creature with yellow eyes and multiple clawed arms that assaulted every part of her.

She drew in a sharp breath and rubbed her eyes. The webs of the vision released her and were replaced by cool, soft air. What is wrong with me? Why did I run? Why am I hiding? Rose squeezed her eyes shut and again tried to think.

She had been talking to Bonnie Buttars, the strange girl on the rock who smoked cigarettes. She remembered Daisy and the little bird that had flown to freedom. Or, more likely, a quick end on the talons of a hawk. She had learned in science class that a domesticated animal rarely survived when released. They didn't know how to avoid predators or feed themselves. Still, she felt a sense of satisfaction for freeing the tiny bird and for liberating Daisy from being responsible for the creature's death. She remembered having to go outside to cut a thick switch, the blows that had fallen repeatedly on her back and neck, and the second trip to the dark, airless closet. Then came thirst and hunger and finally a strange sense of calm with which she returned to the dining room table to sit with the rest of her family—except, of course, Daisy—at breakfast. No one spoke, and no one noticed when she had only pretended to swallow her vitamins, that day and the next.

It had been a small act of rebellion, and Rose didn't even understand what had driven her to do it. She popped the pills in her mouth and appeared to swallow them with the rich fresh milk produced daily by the family cows. But when the glass touched her lips she spit the white tablets out and they slid unnoticed into the thick, foamy milk. After the meal, Rose was quick to clear the dishes and disposed of the pills unseen. It had been easy.

Then the visions started. And the nausea. While scrubbing the kitchen floor she was nearly paralyzed with a spasm of panic. Then she was running. She had passed women loading bags of groceries into identical cars, women who all looked the same, all wearing the same dresses, all with the same hair, all with her mother's face when they turned toward her. She passed men and boys digging a giant hole and saw the bodies of dogs and cats and a small dappled-gray pony gathering flies, the smell of putrefying flesh heavy in the hot air. She kept running. Then she passed the red rock where she almost tripped over Bonnie's body, her yellow dress bunched up around her waist, her religious garments removed, and her pale, bare bottom exposed.

Rose had tried to help the girl. She pulled the dress down, the idea of modesty at all times having been drilled into the deepest recesses of her brain. Then she tried to roll Bonnie over, but when she stared at the gaping hole that had been the girl's lovely face, nausea assaulted her. Then she heard people coming. So Rose left Bonnie face down in the dirt and ran.

40

Early the next morning, Trak and Adan turned left on Central Street, but not before Trak glanced at the parking spaces in front of the North Mojave County Community College main office.

Adan smiled. "Yep, that's her car."

Trak narrowed his eyes at the boy. "You gonna give me crap about this?"

Adan put his hands up in mock surrender. "No sir, just an observation."

A few minutes later, Trak approached a four-way stop. Another pickup turned in front of him, the bed filled with a mound of dead creatures, limbs sticking out from the pile in various stages of rigor mortis.

"Why are they killing all these animals?" Adan asked.

"I have no idea." Trak's voice was edged with anger.

"Can they do that? I mean, isn't it against the law?"

"Well, it depends. If an animal is attacking a person or another animal, you can kill it. Certainly, hunting an animal for food is fine. But this . . ."

Adan watched the pickup stop by a large brown and

white dog that had been dumped on the side of the street. Two raggedly dressed boys hopped out of the cab, grabbed the creature by the legs, and swung the carcass atop the pile in the pickup. A bright red collar adorned the dead animal's neck. "I don't understand. Why would anyone kill their pet?"

Trak had no answer. He thought of his Holly, safe at home, and was filled with revulsion.

Adan hadn't volunteered any additional background information beyond the fact that he'd gone to school in Phoenix, and was glad Trak hadn't pressed him. In the meantime, he was happy to help on the construction jobs, not just because he was earning a bit of money—earning his keep, he thought—but because he genuinely enjoyed Trak's company. Their current job was to build a six-foot, concrete block wall to enclose a garden at the edge of Colorado City near Short Creek. They worked all morning to dig out a footing sixteen inches deep, and Trak showed him how to use a level to make sure the trench was universally flat. They fixed corner stakes firmly into the ground to keep the angles consistent, and toted block from a neatly layered stack, arranging the gray bricks starting at one corner of the wall and working in one direction. They applied an inch deep frosting of mortar to the tops and sides of each block and pressed the pieces onto and next to one another, careful not to leave any gaps in the sealant, as this would weaken the wall.

Around noon, a dour woman in a long, tan dress arrived with a tray bearing a pitcher of water, two glasses, and several slices of thick bread with butter and slabs of white cheese. Trak thanked her and received only a nod in reply. The woman turned and walked back into her home without a word.

They ate in silence in the shade of a pecan tree. Adan was exhausted, but the physical activity felt good. He missed working out. He'd been pretty skinny that first year his buddy had convinced him to go out for football, but had ended up pumping iron alongside Andy and the rest of the lineman on the team. He'd been amazed at the changes the hard work had made in his body. By the time that next season rolled around, he'd gained almost twenty pounds of muscle. Adan chewed the sandwich—thick crusty bread and tangy cheese. What he really missed was the camaraderie. Being with the other players who liked him, and whom he liked back. He was just one of the team when they were together. Part of a unit. Nothing else mattered when they were on the field.

He'd tried explaining this new kinship to his mother, but she didn't understand his need to belong. To her, family was all that mattered, and she didn't see how these boys, some white, some black, some brown, could be considered *familia*.

"Ready to get back to it?" Trak asked.

"Yep." Adan downed the rest of the water in his glass, stood, and stretched.

"We still have a lot to do." Trak smiled. "Let's go."

It was late in the afternoon when Adan saw something strange. She was in the distance, behind a home near a bend in the stream, too far away to see her face. The girl seemed to be scavenging for something on the ground. Then she stood and ran across the dry creek bed, disappearing into the trees. Instantly, he knew. Adan had spent several years running track and knew that people's strides were like signatures. Despite the fact that a long, blue dress covered her legs, he could tell this was the same girl he'd seen the other day along the side of the road. Blonde hair and running shoes.

He glanced at Trak, who was so intent on laying blocks he hadn't noticed.

41

Brooke faced a stack of reports piled neatly in alphabetical order. The papers detailed evidence of possible child abuse in Colorado City. A purple flash drive, which held the information in electronic form, rested atop the stack. She slid the flash drive into her laptop, loaded the first file, and began to read.

An hour later, she leaned back in her chair. She squeezed her eyes shut and then opened them, gazing out the window on an open field of mixed grasses, and, in the distance, a swath of trees and the stark red mountain that rose up behind the community. She flipped the top of the computer down and made a cup of instant coffee, dumping in one packet of sugar and stirring the drink with a red plastic straw. Then she went out and sat on the wooden steps to think.

How was it possible that not a single incident of child abuse had been corroborated or prosecuted in the whole town? Statistically, in a community of this size, there should have been some cases that advanced beyond the initial report. But every file had just a single entry. A call had come in. Evidence had been recorded. And that was the end of it. Every report was exactly the same.

Adding to the mystery was the fact that there was only one person in the entire town who ever filed a report: Bob Wayland, the science teacher at Colorado City's school. That Wayland called in the incidents clearly made sense. Like those in the medical and mental health professions, law enforcement, and social work, teachers were mandated to report suspicions of child abuse. Failure to file evidence of suspected abuse could lead to thousands of dollars in fines and jail terms of up to five years. No doubt these mandated reporters could also end up booted from their professions permanently if they failed to call in and file the required information.

But what of the other Colorado City teachers? Why had they failed to make reports? More first-hand accounts would give a case additional credence.

Brooke sipped the coffee and watched two older teens walk toward the college's science building. The ankle-length dresses, long-sleeved, high-necked—one pale green and one light blue—fluttered in the breeze. Elaborately piled hair was fashioned in frozen mounds. Obviously, evidence of abuse would be difficult to spot, at least with the girls, who appeared to be completely covered at all times, with only their faces and hands exposed. The girls entered the science building. Brooke watched the door close behind them.

She downed the rest of the coffee. Over the course of her time with CPS, Brooke had discovered that, in most abuse cases, parents were guilty primarily of neglect. They did not wish to harm their children, but were simply ill equipped to deal with raising a child, let alone several. The parents might be teens—children themselves—or unable to manage financially. They might be addicts or mentally ill or homeless. The subsequent abuse was a product of their condition. This, however, did not excuse the action—morally or legally.

Brooke had checked the Internet for information about the residents of Colorado City. While she did not agree with the construct on which polygamy was based, on the surface, one would think that having multiple mothers to tend to the needs of children might be a plus. And this was a farming community, far from the dangers of city life where gangs and drugs and violence permeated some subcultures, perpetuating cycles of child abuse.

So where was the abuse coming from here? Bob Wayland had made fifty-seven reports on different students over what Brooke noted to be a two-year period. Clearly, something bad was happening to the children in Colorado City. But who were the perpetrators? And since these people seem to have food and shelter and a community based on helping one another, why were these children being targeted?

She got up, went inside the trailer, rinsed her mug, and placed the cup upside down on a folded dishcloth. Then she left, locking the door behind her. There wasn't a cloud in the sky, so Brooke decided to walk to the high school. She'd speak with Bob Wayland personally.

42

Brooke frowned.

She looked at the sign. Colorado City Unified School District #14 was emblazoned at the top of the one-story building. The school had white walls with a red stone facing around the bottom. A tall chain link fence enclosed what had once been manicured lawns and green shrubs. Now the grass was gone, chewed down to the dirt by a trio of brown and white goats. Just a few green limbs indicated the bushes still lived. The largest of the animals attacked one of the plants and detached a branch, then chewed and stared as Brooke laced her fingers through the metal fencing.

She walked around the enclosure. The doors in the back and front of the building were shut, bound by thick chains. Brooke paused and looked up and down the tree-lined street. Despite that it was the middle of the day, she saw no one. Was the school already shut down for summer break? She stared again at the desolation and chains and grazing goats. Clearly, the school was closed permanently. So where did the children go for their lessons? And where were the teachers?

Brooke walked back toward the trailer. On the way, she saw the Colorado City Marshal's Office. She mounted the steps and opened the door.

"Can I help you?" A tall young man with light brown hair that fringed over his ears and seemed too long for someone wearing the uniform of a deputy sheriff stared at her with blue eyes underlined by dark circles.

Brooke had seen him before, but she wasn't sure where. Then she remembered the face in the trees and the yellow tape, and the man approaching the woman investigator.

"My name is Brooke Neal." She pasted on a cheerful expression. "I've replaced Evelyn Garner over at the CPS office."

He did not reply.

"Child Protective Services?" Brooke said.

"I know what it means."

"I'm trying to locate one of the teachers here. A Mr. Wayland. Bob Wayland."

"He doesn't work here anymore," the deputy said too quickly.

"Oh. Well, do you know where he lives? Perhaps I can catch him at home." She reached into her back pocket and removed a small wallet. "Here is my CPS credential. I also have my driver's license if you want to check that. I understand you have to be careful about sharing private information." She smiled and held out the cards.

The deputy did not reach for the documents. He picked at his fingernails. "Wayland left town six months ago. Before I got here. I don't know where he went."

Brooke had performed hundreds of interviews over the years, mostly with people determined to keep secrets. She could tell when someone was lying.

"Is there anyone else I can speak with?" she asked, still smiling. "Is your boss around?"

"Marshal Buttars?"

"Yes, is the marshal here?

"Of course not! His wife was killed. The family's preparing for the funeral."

"Killed? You mean . . . that was the body? She was murdered?"

"Yes. I mean, no. I . . . don't know."

Brooke stood her ground, her smile fading.

"If there's nothing else you need, I'm very busy." Travis Forbush turned his back on her, sat down, and began sorting through a pile of papers on his desk.

43

Dr. Chase Allred hung up his office phone. He'd known all along the answer would be something genetic. There were simply too many similar cases in Colorado City. The cause of the birth defects stemmed from an extremely rare enzyme deficiency. In the 1930s, just two families, the Jessops and the Barlows, settled the area. Someone in that group carried the recessive gene. Because of the community's reliance on multiple wives, the group allowed first cousins to marry. Over the years, a refusal to wed anyone outside the community had added to the creation of an ever-shrinking gene pool. The illness, or rather the syndrome called Fumarse Deficiency, spread wildly through the population. In its horrible wake, the disease left children with severe mental retardation, epilepsy, and terrible disfigurement.

He slammed his hand on the desk. He'd grown up here with the Fundamentalists just twenty-two miles away. He, like the vast majority of the people in Hurricane, had been raised as a mainstream Mormon. The church he grew up in had long ago disavowed polygamy with the 1890

Manifesto: a requirement for Utah to be granted statehood. The decree supposedly ended polygamy, but just declaring multiple wifery dead did not stop the practice.

He had been told his whole life to let them be. As fellow Mormons, they were still family. And was it really so wrong that they practiced polygamy? "Who are they hurting?" his father had often remarked. "Let it go, son," the old man said, when, upon returning from medical school, Chase had condemned the practice as cruel, and, ultimately, destructive.

Chase ran his fingers through white-blond hair, one of the signs that marked him as a descendant of the pioneers who settled Hurricane Valley. He stood and stared out the window of the clinic at the massive tan rock wall in the distance. The road clung to the mountainside, twisting and turning and rising over the summit, leading to the town that Chase now equated with the spiraling levels of Dante's hell. How had he ignored the horrors in Colorado City for so long?

He had to do something. Chase slumped into his desk chair and leafed through his old-fashioned Rolodex that he kept planning to electronically update, but which he never managed to get to. There were few phone connections in the town. But he knew one, and he was pretty sure the person on the other end might listen to him.

"I really planned on heading over to the café," Trak said, when Chase appeared an hour later with a couple of pizzas.

"I need to bounce something off you, um, privately," the doctor said.

The boy entered the kitchen following the smell of hot dough, melted cheese, and pepperoni.

"You want pizza, don't you, Adan?" Chase said.

"Sure," he answered, wiping his eyes.

"Have a good nap?" Trak asked.

The boy yawned and nodded his head.

"Building a block wall in the heat is not for the faint of heart." Trak stepped up to the sink, turned on the faucet, and washed his hands.

"Geez! Andy, did you make sure to stick to the fluids all day?" Chase plopped the pizza boxes on the kitchen table.

"Yes, sir." The boy yawned again.

After they filled their plates with hot slices, the boy went out to eat on the porch. Holly padded after him.

When the screen door snapped shut, Chase placed both elbows on the kitchen table. "There's something I have to do and I don't think it's gonna be very popular."

"Sounds like your M.O. I don't remember you ever caring much about what other people thought."

Chase paused. "It might be ugly."

Trak eyed his friend. "You need a wingman? Like old times?"

"I think it might be wise."

44

The next morning, Trak, Chase, and the boy entered a meetinghouse near the Colorado City temple. A sturdy woman with bright blue eyes and gray-streaked auburn hair waved a hand in greeting.

"Beth, thank you so much for making this happen," the doctor said.

"I hope you can help. I have tried, but there is only so much . . . a woman can do here." She spread her hands wide, then mounted several steps to a stage where a podium had been set up.

"Beth Flake?" Trak stared at the woman. "She went to high school with us?"

Chase nodded. "She attended medical school at the University of Arizona and became a registered nurse. She's delivered a lot of babies."

"How did she end up back here?"

"Her family joined the community after she went to college. I don't know what made her return, but she's a rarity here in that she's seen the outside world. She was the only person I thought might understand the problem. She sees the damage this condition is causing first hand."

Most of the people in the audience stared suspiciously at Dr. Chase Allred when he stepped to the podium. While he resembled many of them physically, he was still an outsider. That he arrived with a strange, dark boy in tow added to their distrust. However, they had been summoned to listen to the man speak. As always, they did as they were told.

While Trak and Adan leaned against the back wall of the square, unadorned room, Chase explained the cause of the horrendous birth defects that were now afflicting the community.

"These children are missing portions of their brains." Chase spoke in a loud, clear voice. "As I'm sure you can see, often they cannot sit or stand. They may suffer from epileptic seizures and encephalitis. Many of them will never speak. The level of intellectual disability is severe, with IQs of around twenty-five."

The people listened in silence.

"Twenty years ago, there were only about thirteen cases of Fumarase Deficiency known worldwide. Now that you know what this disease looks like, I ask you to think. How many cases are there in Colorado City today? How many children have died at birth or shortly thereafter because of the horrible effects of this syndrome?"

Chase perused the audience and while no one spoke, he could tell that some people—mostly women—were paying attention.

"If two parents have this gene, their chances of producing a sick child are one in four. The child may die very young, or they may live into early adulthood, where they might reproduce. This child's chances of passing on the disease are now one in two.

"Here is what you must do to stop this scourge. You must not allow marriage between people who have this recessive gene. Or if two carriers do marry, they must not bear children."

Angry cries burst from the crowd. Still Chase shouted over them. "If there is a pregnancy, they should test for the gene and consider abortion. Families that produce children with the deficiency should stop having children."

The outcry from the audience was loud and swift. Some people jumped up from their seats and yelled. Others shook their heads, stabbing fingers into the air.

Chase raised his arms. "Wait, please," he implored. "Your children's welfare—"

A stooped, elderly man leaning on a pinewood cane stepped to the front of the room and stared at Chase. The commotion subsided. "We will do none of these things," he said in a calm even voice. "These children are a punishment from God. We are not yet as perfect as He demands us to be. He sends us these defective ones to remind us to heed His word and the word of our Prophet every moment of every day. Only then can we earn our way to the Celestial Kingdom."

"But can you not see the pain and suffering these children endure?" the doctor pleaded. "You're the adults; it's your responsibility to stop this . . . madness." Chase regretted the last word instantly.

The room erupted.

45

Adan slipped out the door. These people were crazy and the noise inside the meetinghouse was overwhelming. He settled in on the concrete steps. Then he saw her—the girl in the blue dress. She clutched a bundle in her arms. He watched her leap gracefully over a log, the long garment seemingly not a hindrance. On a track team they would surely have made her a hurdler.

Adan saw her take a few more long strides, and then, without thinking, he bolted after her. He watched the girl jump into a dry creek bed, cross the sand, move up the far bank, and disappear into a stand of trees with bright green foliage.

Adan quickened his pace, not wanting to lose her in the unfamiliar terrain. He kept his eyes on the spot where she entered the trees, grateful for the years of cross-country training in the sixteen-thousand-acre wilderness of Phoenix's South Mountain Park. The practice sessions had helped him hone his keen sense of balance and the ability to quickly survey his surroundings. He leapt into the sandy riverbed then scrambled up the other side, careful not to get tangled in a web of blackened tree roots sticking out of the bank.

Adan broke into the trees. The area was much deeper and darker than he'd anticipated. He slowed his pace, looking one way then the other. He wasn't sure where the girl had gone. He stood still, scanned the area, and noticed a faint—almost imperceptible—track leading north. Adan followed the trail, watching intently for any sign of the girl and any obstructions that might cause him to stumble.

The trail widened and became easier to negotiate. He increased his speed and judged that he'd gone about a half mile when the path took a sharp uphill turn. He stuck to the trail, but soon started breathing heavily. Clearly, he was seriously out of shape. Of course, there was also the difference in altitude. And his recent bout with heat sickness was affecting him. The thought of his blackout on the road made Adan pull up. He bent over and placed both hands on his knees, taking in deep gulps of air. The stupidity of the chase hit him. Not only was he in completely unfamiliar territory, he also had no water. And he had left without telling Trak.

"What do you want?"

Adan turned around, but saw no one.

"Why are you chasing me?"

Adan looked up. The girl sat on a rocky ledge about fifteen feet above him, her legs dangling over the side.

"I . . . I don't know." He collapsed, settled in a soft pile of leaf litter, and stared up at her.

"I thought you were one of the local boys, until I stopped and looked."

Adan shook his head, still breathing heavily.

For a time, neither one of them spoke.

"Why are you hiding?" Adan finally asked.

Rose gazed down at the boy who didn't resemble anyone she'd ever seen before. His skin was dark, but not like the Native Americans who lived in the area. She wished she could examine him more closely, but a sudden vision of Jacob Babbitt held her back—his hot breath in her ear, his hand grabbing at her backside.

"Who are you?" she asked.

"Ad . . . Andy," he said. "I've been doing some construction work here. I've seen you a few times. Running."

Rose flashed back on the white truck that had passed her on the road. She'd noticed this boy in the passenger seat, if only for an instant. Logically, what he was saying might be true. What else would a person like him be doing in Colorado City?

"I work with a man named Trak Benally," Adan said. "Big guy. Light-skinned Navajo."

"I don't know him." Rose stood, stared at the boy for a moment, and then disappeared.

"Don't go!" Adan sat up and wrapped his long arms around his knees. He asked her again. "Why are you hiding?"

Rose reappeared. "I'm not hiding, I'm . . . getting out of here. I'm running away."

Then she vanished.

46

"That went well." Trak led Chase down the steps of the meetinghouse, where arguing could still be heard inside.

"I did what I had to do. I told them what was causing these cases. It was my duty as a doctor."

"But it doesn't look like they plan to follow your recommendations."

"No, they probably won't." Chase fished in his pocket for his keys. "I have no control over that."

"Chase!"

The doctor turned around.

Beth Flake placed her hand on his shoulder. "I'm sorry, Chase, though not surprised."

"I appreciate you arranging for me to speak with them," he said.

"I have watched these cases, these children, being born. As a midwife, the situation is heartbreaking. Though I am loathe to admit it, I am grateful when some of these infants, the worst cases, are stillborn." She frowned and shook her head.

"I understand," Chase said.

"The children's lives are awful. Many of the people here don't care for them properly when they do survive," Beth said. "There's a belief that time should be given to the healthy ones, so little is done to relieve the pain and suffering of the disabled. The thought seems to be, if they can't marry and reproduce, why bother."

Chase rubbed his eyes. "Maybe we can try to alleviate some of their suffering, Beth. I'll check into some options and see if I can help."

"Thank you. Any assistance can't come too soon. Some of the midwives are refusing to deliver babies. The birth defects are too awful, and some men, with no training, are working in the birthing clinic. It's a very difficult situation."

Chase took her hand. "I'll see what I can do."

The two men said goodbye and walked to Chase's Chevy Tahoe. They got in, pulled on their seatbelts, and then looked at one another. "Where's the boy?" they said in unison.

Ten minutes later, they both stood by the SUV. "Where would he go?" Trak asked.

"Maybe he was hungry and walked down to the Mercantile," Chase said. "When did you last see him?"

Trak thought for a moment. "He was standing next to me in the back of the room. Then things got heated and I was concentrating on you, wondering if they were going to kick your ass and we were going to have to—"

"Fight our way out?" Chase asked.

"Shit! I don't know. I'm not sure about some of these folks. I've seen strange things here lately." Trak explained about watching Frank Jessop shoot his son's dog after trying to make the poor man kill the creature himself, and then about the truck full of dead animals he and Andy had seen the day before.

"Wonder what's going on?" Chase said. "That's bizarre behavior, even for these people."

They headed to the Mercantile. The only grocery store in Colorado City was empty, save for a girl standing behind one of the registers.

"You ask," Trak said. "You look like you belong here."

"Thanks." Chase elbowed Trak and then put on a friendly smile, grabbed a candy bar, and approached the girl. He returned a short time later and the men exited the store.

"He hasn't been here."

"So what do we do?"

"I don't know, Trak. Maybe nothing. The kid's eighteen."

"At least he says he is."

"Either way, he's not a prisoner. He can come and go as he pleases, unless we can determine that he's underage.

"I have no proof either way," Trak said. "But are you comfortable just getting in the car and leaving an Hispanic kid here. A boy?"

Both Trak and Chase had heard about the "Lost Boys."

"No," Chase agreed. "Let's keep looking around. If we can't find him, we'll go over to the marshal's office."

47

Adan stared at the empty ledge. A breeze rustled the verdant leaves, allowing a view of the blue sky and the rugged red mountain above. He should work his way back down the path. But something stopped him. He had to think.

Trak and Chase had been very kind. He'd been fed, given a place to sleep, and the chance to earn some money. Reflexively, he reached for the cash. He held the bills for a moment and then pushed the wad deep into the front pocket of his jeans.

The men had not pressed him hard for information, though Trak's continued attempts at conversation might certainly expose him if he stayed in Hurricane too long. He sensed that, if they knew he was underage, they would send him back. Adan was pretty sure the doctor was required by law to turn him into the authorities. For Adan's own good, they would say. For his own protection. He had to laugh. Protection from whom?

His head ached, but he was no longer breathing hard. He hoisted himself from the ground and stood for a moment, considering the paths open to him.

Rose moved through huge red boulders into an area where the trees thinned out, leaving only tough scrubby pines, desiccated brush, and the occasional prickly pear. When she was midway up the mountain, she walked down a thin trail that narrowed into a cut. The track opened onto the sheer cliff wall and was no more than a foot wide. Rose eased her way along the slender ledge that hugged the mountain face and was soon greeted by an outburst of green and the gentle fall of silvery water droplets.

In this spot, nature had provided a weeping rock. Fractures and pore space in the surrounding Navajo sandstone, along with erosion, helped form the alcove in which Rose now found shelter. Above the opening in the rock, a series of interconnected fractures—both vertical and horizontal—allowed rainwater to trickle down to a thin layer of mudstone. This impermeable boundary sent water flowing toward the canyon wall, where, after encountering another set of vertical fractures, the fluid trickled out, dripping over the opening in the cave. Precious water pooled in some places and seeped down the steep rock wall in others. Mosses and small patches of delicate maidenhair fern clung to the sides and floor of the cave opening, while algae in some spots made footing precarious.

The sheer drop to the canyon floor was over one-hundred-and-fifty feet, ending in what, at certain times of the year, was a heavily flowing stream that rushed over immense chunks of rock that had once been part of the mountain. Now, Rose could see only a thin trail of water moving slowly in the streambed below.

Rose dropped the bundle and went to her knees,

lapping at the water in a crystal-clear pool. A sudden vision of her disapproving mother made her want to laugh out loud. To have her daughter drinking in such a way. Like an animal. Bliss Madsen would be appalled. Surely, Rose would be whipped. Her father would say, "Not the face, Mother." And she would be hauled into that dark closet again.

She paused and shuddered at the thought of the tight, dry space. The last time, in a fit of sightless panic, she'd actually tried to stand in the closet, banging her head as she pounded on the wooden walls, ripping her nails as she tried to scratch her way out.

As the water in the tiny pool stilled, Rose saw her reflection. Bits of pale hair stuck out in all directions. The once tightly coiled braids had come loose giving her a wild look. For an instant, she regretted that the strange boy had seen her so disheveled.

Rose cupped her hands and splashed her face. She wiped the water away with the light blue sleeve of her dress, then she stood and picked up the bundle. Rose moved to the rear wall of the cave, which was, for the most part, dry, though tiny wet streaks and stains on the rock hinted that during the monsoon there might be a great deal more water flowing inside the grotto. She dumped the contents of the plastic bag on the stone floor and considered what she must do.

48

Trak threw his hands up. "I don't know about you, but I can't drive off and leave the kid here."

Chase agreed. "The marshal's office it is, then."

Five minutes later, a disheveled Travis Forbush looked up from his desk.

"Good morning," Chase said.

"Morning. What can I do for you?" the deputy asked.

Chase explained about the boy and how he was missing.

Forbush was silent for a moment. "What do you want us to do about it?" he finally asked. "You said the kid's eighteen, so he's not a runaway."

"Can you at least make a report? I have a hunch he's underage," Trak said.

Forbush took down the information.

"Keep an eye out for him and call me if he shows up. Or ask him to call me." Trak reached into his back pocket and fished out a business card. "It's probably just a misunderstanding." He stepped to the desk and held out the card.

Slowly, Travis Forbush reached up, took the card, and placed the information on his desk. "If I see him, I'll tell him to call." Forbush took a deep breath. "Anything else?"

Chase shook his head. "No."

Outside the office, Trak said, "Not much for customer service. The guy acted like he couldn't care less."

Chase unlocked the SUV. "You know teenage boys are not especially valued around here."

"So I've heard."

"And yet we've ignored this all our lives." Chase stared at his friend.

"We were told to." Trak opened the passenger-side door.

"And that's a valid excuse?"

"No, Chase. It's not. Now, do me a favor. Take me down to the Community College."

The doctor raised one eyebrow. "I sense a redhead in our near future."

"You are correct, but my intentions are pure."

"At least for now."

"Yes."

Chase smiled. "You will have different intentions later, no doubt."

"None of your business."

After parking the truck, and skirting the MCC Science Building, Chase stood on the grass as Trak walked up the steps to the trailer that had a small sign in the window that read, "State of Arizona: Child Protective Services." Trak knocked, quickly removed his cowboy hat, and ran his fingers through thick, black hair.

Chase laughed.

"Stop it!" Trak hissed.

The door opened. Brooke stood in white jeans and a diaphanous multi-colored blouse that bore an artist's rendering of a hummingbird on the front. Her short red hair rippled above her collar in waves, a few strands fluttering in the breeze, which Trak found very appealing.

Chase sighed audibly. Trak turned, pleading.

"Good morning, Brooke," Chase said before his friend had a chance to speak. "I hope you feel better. And that you've been getting some sleep and staying hydrated."

"I have followed your instructions to the letter, and I do feel better. I appreciate your help." She beamed the doctor a smile. "Since you wouldn't allow me to pay, perhaps I can make you dinner sometime."

Trak straightened and gazed at a spot over Brooke's head, grasping for something to say.

"Of course, I meant both of you. I'd like to make dinner for both of you."

Chase had to bite his bottom lip to keep from laughing out loud at Trak's discomfiture.

"And, now, what brings you here this morning?" Brooke asked.

49

"It's not much to go on, I know," Trak said.

"Do you think he's underage?" Brooke tapped the pen lightly on the desk blotter.

"I do, but I have no proof. The kid is so skittish. Like he was afraid of something."

"I see that a lot. And no ID. No license. This tells me he is trying to hide. But from what?" Brooke stood. "Coffee?"

"Sure."

"Sugar?"

Trak held up two fingers then gazed down at his waist. "Black. Black is good."

"I'm fine." Chase waved a hand. "But I do have to get back to the office pretty soon."

"OK," Trak said. "Is there time for coffee?"

"Go ahead. I'll be outside." Chase smiled and left.

After Brooke placed the mug in Trak's hands—one with an inscription saying Foster Parents Rock—she sat again behind the small desk.

"Any ideas?" When she didn't immediately reply, he added, "About the boy."

"I can only guess," she said. "Maybe he's running from problems at home—drug or alcohol abuse, domestic violence, general neglect. Maybe there are gang-related issues. If you don't want to join, you routinely get the crap beat out of you. Your siblings and other family members might be targeted. Or maybe the kid was in a gang, committed a crime to show his loyalty to the group, and got caught. So maybe he's running from the cops."

Trak sipped the strong hot coffee. "When I worked for the Maricopa County Court system, I ran into a lot of those kinds of kids. Frankly, it was depressing. I saw the same children over and over. They didn't seem to get that they were ruining their lives."

"Try to look at it from their perspective." Brooke put both elbows on the desk and grasped her hands. "Dad was in a gang. Grandpa was in a gang. Your older siblings and everyone you know is in a gang. I've seen family portraits with sometimes four generations of the same family all decked out in their gang colors, the patriarch holding a new baby wearing a bandana to match everyone else.

"But why can't they get past it? They go to school. We educate them. Give them opportunities to make something of themselves. I can't help but think of the kids in Afghanistan." Trak paused, seeing their faces. "The few times I witnessed children in classrooms, it was almost as if there was magic going on. The war melted away for those kids. Only then did I see light in their eyes. The rest of the time . . ."

"Here's the thing. If you are raised by loving parents—"

"I was."

"I can see that." She paused and smiled. "Loving parents do what's right for their children, according to their experience and way of thinking. They encourage them to learn and be nice and to do unto others. They want to see their children be successful in their world. But their world looks very different from the world of a child growing up in poverty. If the gang is all you see, and joining is something considered an admirable aspiration by the people you love, why would you think being a gang member is a problem? It is the rare child that can see through this indoctrination that begins almost at birth. And a rarer child still that manages to break away."

Trak nodded and sipped his coffee.

"By refusing to be part of the gang tradition, children who try to get out can be shunned, unwelcome in a world where family is everything. Add to that the fact that they must try to shoehorn themselves into the completely alien society where we exist."

"What are their chances of success?" Trak asked.

"In my experience, less than one percent."

50

Adan was not running from a gang, or family violence, or poverty: at least not the starvation and homeless kind. Though they didn't have much, he had never gone without food in his belly or clothes on his back. He'd had a room of his own to sleep in, one with posters of his favorite athletes: Jamaican sprinter, Usain Bolt, and Arizona Cardinals wide-receiver, Larry Fitzgerald.

Now, Adan had nothing more than the clothes he wore and the cash in his pocket, which was useless here on the jagged red mountain. He'd regretted his decision more than once on his way up the incline, where exposed roots and cactus, and scree made traveling slow and dangerous. The layer of accumulated rock periodically caused him to slide and lose ground. If he had not briefly seen a flash of blue in a narrow cave opening midway up the mountain, he might have given up. Instead, Adan kept climbing.

Now he paused and placed his hands over his eyes to shield them from the sun. Above all else he needed water. He searched the rubble and the high rock face above. Then he straightened and rubbed his cheek. A mild breeze carried the sound of water, but it quickly faded. Adan scrambled to his left, maybe one hundred yards. The stream far below was a thin ribbon, winding through jagged slabs of fallen red stone. There was no decision to be made. Adan had to have water. So he started down.

Rose stood in the shade of the cave opening, a breeze wafting in, pleasantly cool, courtesy of the falling water droplets that acted like a natural evaporative cooler.

It was time.

She looked at the items on the ground. Stealing had been incredibly easy, at least in the physical sense. Many of the town's people had walked to the meetinghouse. Rose had watched them go from the cover of the trees. After waiting to make sure no one was around, she ran into a few homes, gathering up what she needed.

Still, the stealing disturbed her. Rose closed her eyes. And again, the Lord God hath commanded that men should not murder; that they should not lie; that they should not steal . . . for whoso doeth them shall perish.

Rose exhaled, and, despite this directive, reached for the long sharp scissors she had stolen. She gazed down at her reflection in the still pool and made the first cut, somehow—and quite illogically—expecting the severance to hurt. She had always been told that her hair must remain long and uncut, so when the time came, she could, like all righteous women, use her tresses to wash the feet of Jesus. She paused thinking of the Savior. Would not a warm soapy cloth be a better tool to clean the Lord's feet?

Rose made a second clip. Then a third. While she had

planned a neat, methodical pruning, the cutting came more haphazardly with each snip. She could not stop herself. She must not. Rose refused to look at her reflection. She worked only by feel.

When the shearing was done, Rose's pale blond, once waist-length tresses rested in a silky pile on the red rock floor of the cave. She ran a hand through hair that now, only a few inches long, just touched the tops of her ears. Her head felt strangely light.

Rose waited, not yet looking at her reflection. Would God's punishment be swift? She had always heard that was how He delivered his wrath. Yet no lightning sparked. Thunder did not shatter the heavens. No cloven-hoofed devil appeared to steal her eternal soul to be deposited forever in the outer darkness.

She gazed through the cave opening, past the gently falling water droplets, and the scalloped leaves of the dainty maidenhair ferns that clung mightily to the rock. The valley beyond, from a distance, did appear to be a paradise against the cloudless azure sky. But was her home really Eden?

51

Brooke tapped her pen on the metal desk. There was so little to go on. Andy's case was much like all the others she'd encountered in Colorado City—virtually no evidence on which to follow up. She looked again at the short list of information Trak had provided.

Name: Andy
Age: Says he's eighteen: no visual proof
Height: Estimate: six feet
Weight: Estimate: one-hundred-and-seventy-five pounds
Race/Ethnicity: Hispanic
Hair: Black, medium length, straight
Eyes: Dark brown
Additional identifying information: Wearing a T-shirt with a blue Jaguars Football logo
Hometown: Phoenix, Arizona

Brooke spent the next half-hour calling her contacts in Phoenix, several of whom said they'd look into a missing teen of Andy's description, when they had time, and that they'd let her know if they found any data that might help.

Later, as she studied some of the local child abuse claim files, in the hope of finding something she might have missed, Brooke sighed and pushed away from her desk. She paced the small office. So far, she'd accomplished nothing in Colorado City. Helped no one. She knew she'd only been at work a short time, but still. She'd always prided herself on her ability to ferret out information. But she couldn't even find the one man who had filed the child abuse reports. He was a teacher—a person in a profession that generally makes them easy to locate. Teachers had to be vetted and fingerprinted and certified by state agencies before they ever stepped into a classroom. Assuming that Bob Wayland had remained in education, he should be somewhere out there and easy to locate.

But all of her calls and internet searches had produced nothing. When Bob Wayland had stopped teaching in Colorado City, he had simply vanished.

Brooke stared out the window at the grassy meadow and the striated face of Canaan Mountain. Why had Wayland left in the first place? Maybe, if she found the answer to that question, she might be able to track the man down. But who to ask? So far, with the exception of Chase and Trak and her landlady Carla Kimball, she'd been unable to get anyone to say more than a handful of words.

"Why does this have to be so hard?" Brooke looked around the claustrophobic confines of the trailer. Then she left, locking the door behind her.

Thirty minutes later, Brooke moved casually through the front door of the Colorado City Mercantile. The grocery looked no different from any other small town market. Multiple aisles boasted fruits and vegetables, canned food, soaps and detergents, personal products, frozen foods, baked goods. The people who shopped there, however, did look different. The women in their single-colored, high-necked dresses of purple, pink, brown, and blue pushed shopping carts, some with tiny girls riding inside, whose dresses mirrored those of the adults. The elaborate coiled hairdos—whether brown, gray, or blinding blond—were everywhere, all with slightly different twists and rolls and braids, the only apparent individuality these females were permitted to exhibit.

Brooke, in an effort to fit in, pushed a shopping cart of her own. She weaved her way through the aisles, inspecting produce and products, every so often placing an item in the basket.

She watched two women load twelve gallons of milk and eight-dozen eggs into a cart. Brooke stopped and reached for a pack of butter, doing her best to smile and make eye contact, but the women completely avoided her gaze and moved on.

She meandered toward the baked goods counter where the smell of fresh bread filled the air, making her mouth water. Three young women, all probably in their late teens, smiled and chatted. She heard one of the women laugh. They seemed quite happy. Brooke smiled at them and pushed her cart at a leisurely pace.

One of girls eyed Brooke, then spoke behind her hand to the others. They turned and stared for an instant. Then their smiles faded, leaving their faces drawn and seemingly much older. The group dispersed with the three women going off in different directions.

Later, Brooke waited to place her few purchases on the conveyor belt at the checkout line. Unlike most grocery stores, there were no copies of the *National Enquirer* with headlines screaming about alien babies or *People* magazines filled with Hollywood's beautiful people. There was, however, a computer screen with pictures of food that rotated through a cycle. Had these photos been normal advertisements, with trademarked products and names, Brooke would probably not have noticed. But the pictures on the screen that faced directly toward the individuals in line were just an odd assortment of foods bearing no company names. She stared at the screen. Then she saw the tiny hole. It was a camera.

52

Rose wished she had a mirror.

She'd been raised with mixed messages about her appearance. On one hand, make-up and nail polish and jewelry were strictly forbidden. Making oneself pretty was morally wrong, since inner beauty—not physical attractiveness—was essential. However, the women in the community spent an inordinate amount of time fashioning their hair. This was an attempt to attract suitors. Even little girls were painstakingly coiffed.

Women and girls were also expected to make sure their clothes and bodies were impeccably clean at all times. Whenever Rose appeared the least bit disheveled or a tiny spot of dirt touched her clothing, Rose's mother crossed her arms tightly and said, "The Holy Ghost cannot dwell in an unclean place, Rose. You must maintain spiritual and physical cleanliness."

And yet, the Colorado City men and boys did not adhere to this rule. Boys hardly bathed and went around in dirty, tattered clothing. Some of them smelled bad.

Rose took a few awkward steps. The pants—a pair of

soft blue jeans she'd lifted from a line—tightly encased her legs and narrow hips. This was a new feeling. Pants were forbidden for girls. Rose also wore a white T-shirt that was a bit too big. A dark blue, hooded sweatshirt rested in a pile on the cave's stone floor. The jacket would come in handy. Cold arrived quickly when darkness came to the high desert, no matter the time of year.

Rose stared at her white Nikes, dirty from treks up and down the mountain. Her first instinct was to wet a cloth—perhaps a strip ripped from her now abandoned prairie dress—and dab at the smudges, but then she laughed. What did dirty shoes matter now that she looked like a boy? At least, she hoped she did. Though she had managed to lean over the little pool with its mirrored surface to see the results of her hair cutting, she was unable to examine the rest of her transformation.

Rose grabbed the plain, dark blue cap. She squashed the hat on her head. Like the sweatshirt, the cap was a little big, but the bill would hide her face. Then she stepped to a dry spot on the edge of cave and sat down, dangling her legs over the side. She sighed. The moment had arrived. The now what? part of the plan. This instant was as far as she ever managed to get. Steal some clothes. Cut her hair. Dress like a boy. The last gave her more ease of physical movement, and, on the chance she was discovered, the possibility that she might fool whoever found her, and manage to get away.

But to where? That was the issue. When Bonnie—

The thought of the dead girl—her beautiful face smashed in, her bare body exposed—made Rose shiver. Still, she forced herself to think. Bonnie had said she was getting out of here. But where had she planned to go? Rose stared at the valley that nestled the only home she'd ever known. She'd never been away from this place. Her entire life had been spent in an area of only a few square miles.

She knew there were other towns and cities and even countries. She'd seen the maps Mr. Wayland used in class. He had spoken passionately about the people and beauty of these other places. But her parents and the church leaders constantly portrayed the outside world as a living hell on Earth. That was why all contact with the outside had been prohibited: to protect the people from evil.

But like the contradictory messages on beauty, all contact was not prohibited. Rose had witnessed strangers in town looking for gas and snacks at the Mercantile. They spoke into phones. The Prophet himself and the men around him were seen speaking into these devices. If the people of Colorado City were forbidden to use phones, who might the Prophet be contacting in the hell of the outside world? The one other phone Rose had seen was in the medical clinic. Did the midwives know of the world beyond Colorado City?

Rose shook her head. What was true? What was not? Why was everything so confusing? Mr. Wayland had explained that in science, one needed proof to support theories, and, if indisputable observations supported a hypothesis, the idea might become a scientific law—an ostensibly proven fact.

So was her home truly like Eden, and the outside world a living hell? Without seeing beyond the boundaries of her town, how could Rose make the observations she needed to discover the truth?

Her head hurt. Still, compared to the earlier headaches, this one was mild. And the visions had finally ceased attacking her. She took a deep breath and exhaled slowly.

She had to consider the possibility that what she'd been told all her life was true. The world beyond her community was a cesspool of evil, and that if she went there, she would be consumed. So, even after everything that had happened, Rose wasn't sure she was brave enough to leave.

53

Marshal Sterling Buttars slammed the phone on his desk.

Travis Forbush jumped. Neither man had spoken but a few words since the discovery of Bonnie Buttars battered remains.

"Another day!" Buttars roared. "They're keeping her body another day! Why can't they just let it alone?"

Forbush didn't answer.

"You couldn't keep your trap shut, could you, Travis? You had to call in the coroner. If my uncle hadn't insisted I hire you—"

Forbush stared at his desk. "I need to tell you—"

"Tell me what?" Buttars slumped into his desk chair.

"Two things," Forbush said. "First, there's a new Child Protective Services woman working out of the trailer over by the college."

"And?"

"And she asked me to help her locate Bob Wayland."

"Tell me you didn't."

Forbush straightened up. "No, I didn't. I don't know where Wayland is."

Buttars nodded. "Good, Travis. That's good. And don't ask. You might not like the answer."

"You don't trust me?" Forbush straightened in his chair. "I won't tell."

Buttars glared at the deputy. "There's no need for you to know, boy."

Forbush paused. "The CPS woman asked to speak with you, so she might be coming back."

Buttars exhaled loudly. "Anything else?"

"There's a missing boy."

"Whose boy?"

"Don't know." Forbush explained about the visit from Chase Allred and Trak Benally.

"You have a report?"

Forbush handed him the paperwork.

"I don't like this." Buttars heaved his bulk out of the chair and frowned. Should he deliver the information to the Prophet? Might the leader become angry that a teenage boy from the outside was nosing around? Or would the man be more upset if he were kept out of the loop?

"Give me the papers." Buttars retrieved the folder from the deputy, walked out, and slammed the door.

Fifteen minutes later, the marshal held his cowboy hat and turned the brim nervously.

"And we know nothing else about this missing boy?" Eldon Higbee reclined in one of the thick, leather wingback chairs. He dropped the folder to his lap.

"No, sir." Buttars stared at the thick, richly detailed carpet on which he stood.

Higbee reached for a plate piled with chocolate pecan cookies. He lifted one and bit demurely into his favorite desert. He did not offer a cookie to Buttars. Higbee slowly devoured the treat, brushed a stray crumb from his perfectly pressed button-down shirt, and wiped his fingers on a cloth napkin, which he then placed on a silver tray on the side table.

"What do you propose we do, Marshal?"

"Maybe nothing. The kid's probably long gone by now."

"Or not." Higbee rose from the chair. "I do not like the idea of an outsider here. I don't have to tell you the difficulties that might arise if this young man came in contact with any of our children. Imagine the harm he might do."

Buttars nodded but said nothing.

"Get a few men together—a search party. Perhaps the boy is injured and needs our help. Then again, perhaps the poor child has succumbed to the wilderness that surrounds our Eden." Higbee gazed at the huge window that faced Canaan Mountain. "Out there it might be very difficult to find a lost boy. It wouldn't surprise me a bit if he's never heard from again." Higbee turned and looked Buttars in the eye.

"Yes, sir." The marshal met his gaze and turned to leave.

"Oh. I'm sorry about your wife."

Buttars nodded. "Thank you, sir."

"If you take care of this issue with the boy, I'll give you another one."

54

Rose glimpsed something down below the cliff face. Something—or someone perhaps—was moving, but the pace was awkward, advancing a short way, then stopping, then starting again.

Rose stepped back into the shadows of the cave to think, her first instinct to stay hidden.

After a few moments, she crawled back to the cave opening and lay flat on her belly. A low profile would make seeing her difficult. She watched the person—a flash of out-of-place color amid the red rock convinced her that this was in fact another human being—whose progress was clumsy and slow.

Were they looking for her? She observed the person again. Most of the men in her community were consummate backwoodsmen. They had grown up in the rough, high desert country and traversed the area almost as easily as the animals that lived there. The person below was struggling.

Even the girls had been taught how to survive on their own after Mr. Wayland and the other teachers left and the school had been shut down. The responsibility for education had fallen on local women. They decided what the young people needed to learn and lessons in survival became the backbone of the curriculum.

As Rose observed the person below, she recalled the day the girls had been led to a small enclosure where a roan horse was tethered.

"There will be a great holy war," Sister Sorenson explained. "All the men of the community will have to leave to fight this battle. They will take all the weapons—anything they can use in this struggle with the evil forces." The hunched, gray woman had looked skyward. "He has commanded that we women prepare ourselves. We will be left with nothing more than simple implements like this." She produced a short kitchen knife, which she held up, the blade glinting in the sun. Then she approached the animal. "We must feed ourselves and our children. We must survive and be ready to welcome the men when they return victorious from their fight against wickedness. Only then can the worthy among us ascend to the Celestial Kingdom."

The gnarled woman had approached the horse. Someone placed a short kitchen knife in Rose's hand.

"Come, and we will learn to kill and butcher the food that will sustain us when this holy time comes." Sister Sorenson nodded to three men who laced thick ropes around the horse. They forced the animal to the ground, binding the roan's legs. The animal snorted and fought, eyes wild.

None of the girls moved. Other men appeared and herded them forward. Sister Sorenson knelt down by the horse's neck.

"Bring your knives. We will start here." The old woman eyed the men who held the beast down. She reached out and grabbed the arms of the girl nearest to her. "The neck," she said. Then Sister Sorenson plunged the short kitchen knife into the creature's flesh and the animal screamed. The knife came down again and again. At first, the girls barely made cuts in the pale red animal, but as time went on the stabbing became deeper and the girls more enthusiastic.

When the animal finally lay dead—it took a long time to kill a horse with kitchen knives—they had skinned the creature, butchered it, then cooked and ate the flesh.

After the incident with the horse, Rose and the other girls had been taught how to plant and grow crops in kitchen gardens and even how to gather wild edible foods—a lesson that she now hoped would help sustain her.

She stared into the canyon. For a moment, she was unable to find the person below. Rose squinted. Yes, there was definitely someone down there, but now they had stopped moving.

55

Rose knelt by the prostrate form that lay by a flat slab of red sandstone. The white T-shirt is what stood out, what had made him visible from her perch on the cliff side. She rolled him over. The skin of his arm was hot. Too hot. She looked around and then peered up the trail. There was no sign of a water bottle, and she remembered he hadn't been wearing a hat when they'd spoken earlier. She pressed her palm against the boy's forehead. She scanned his body and saw no obvious wounds. As she reached into the plastic bag she'd carried, she made a mental note: On her next trip into town, she would steal a backpack. She grabbed a water bottle, one of several she'd lifted from an unattended porch cooler.

"Wake up," she said, patting the boy's cheek. When he didn't respond, Rose checked his pulse, which was strong, but racing far too fast. She took the water bottle and poured the contents on his head and neck. Droplets glittered on a face that was a burnished shade of brown. Long, black eye lashes curled above sharp cheekbones. Rose stared for a moment at the boy's full lips.

She leaned over and placed both hands on his shoulders. "Wake up!" she shouted, shaking him. Then Rose slapped the boy across the face.

Eyes fluttered open, a rich dark brown. His mouth moved. No sound escaped, but he reached up and grabbed Rose's hand. She pulled away and stood. Rose was a desert dweller. Even young children recognized the symptoms of heat sickness. He must be cooled off quickly.

The stream into which the weeping cave deposited its water flowed about one hundred rock-strewn yards below where Rose now stood. She must get him into the creek.

The boy stared up at her, croaking sounds escaping his throat. She grabbed a second bottle of water and poured some on his lips, but most of the fluid leaked away.

"You have to sit up." Rose attempted to lift and lean him against the red stone slab, but he was too heavy. "You have to help."

But the boy was unable to push himself up. Rose sat and leaned on the smooth sandstone. She eased the boy's head onto her thigh. Then she reached again for the water bottle. Eventually, she managed to get him to slowly drink half the water in the bottle. Still, his body was hot to the touch and he periodically fell in and out of consciousness.

She eased his head off her leg and placed the sweatshirt, which had also been in the plastic bag, on the ground for a pillow. Then Rose gathered the three plastic bottles. She poured the remainder of the water onto the boy's chest, letting the fluid soak into his clothes, which would keep him cooler than just applying the fluid directly onto his bare skin, and then started down to the stream.

She made the trek to the bottom of the canyon and back several times. On each trip she filled the plastic bottles, drank some of the sweet spring water directly from the creek, then returned to the boy. She poured the water on his body, soaking his clothes in an effort to cool him.

Finally, exhausted, she collapsed by his side, careful to keep the water bottles ready for the moment he was able to drink. Rose fell asleep with her back against the red sandstone slab that faced west, soaking up the sun's warmth.

Later—how much later she didn't know—a violent shaking startled her. The boy lay curled on his side, hugging his knees to his chest, shivering. His brown eyes were wide open. She could see him staring at her even in the rapidly disappearing twilight.

Rose reached over and touched his shoulder. His clothes were still damp. Now the night was coming, and with it, darkness and cold.

56

Brooke wrapped a white sweater around her shoulders. The air had cooled considerably. She sipped a Chardonnay that tasted of peaches, vanilla, and a slight touch of oak, and glanced at Trak. It was their first actual date. He'd offered to take her somewhere other than the Main Street Café, insisting that Hurricane had more than one restaurant, or they could drive over to St. George, but Brooke said the café would be fine. She already felt at home on the small patio by the garden with its grove of pecan trees and cascading grape vines.

They had ordered and fallen into comfortable small talk, but she could tell Trak was distracted. She set her glass on the table. "I know you're worried about the boy, about Andy."

"I found him, practically dead by the side of the road. Did I tell you I thought he was a cow that had been hit?" He shook his head. "I've got this gut feeling about him. I think he's a good kid, running from who knows what. Smart. A quick learner. But I don't think he's ready to survive out here alone."

"His T-shirt," she said. "Do you remember?"

"The blue jaguar. And football. Jaguars Football."

"You said he mentioned he was from Phoenix, so I did a little research. There are three high schools in Arizona that use the jaguar as a mascot. Only one uses the color blue. The South Mountain High School Jaguars in Phoenix."

Dark brown eyes searched her face, questioning.

"I sent your information and the boy's description to the school and there's no one named Andy missing. But there's a boy named Adan—"

"And it's him?" he asked, hope choking his words.

"I think so. But I have to go through proper channels to find out more. That's all I have for now."

"Thank you. That's at least something." Trak reached for his bottle of beer that had remained untouched. He took a long drink and smiled, almost apologetically. "Strange how you can get attached so quickly. It's gotta be hard in your line of work."

Brooke nodded. How many nights had she spent concerned about a child? Or several children for that matter? The other social workers had often admonished Brooke for taking the job home with her. "You have to leave it at the office," they said. "You cannot survive in this profession if you take every case personally. You'll burn out!" She looked across the table. "I understand. Believe me."

Trak gazed back. Her short red hair was fiery in the light of the single candle flickering between them. "I know you do. I used to wonder how the social workers dealt with all the crap the kids in the system go through. When I worked for the courts down in Phoenix, some of the things I heard made me sick. And angry."

Brooke nodded. "In the beginning, when you're

new to the job, it's sometimes hard to get out of bed in the morning. At least, it was for me. I'd been so sheltered. Great family. Nice community where everyone looked out for everyone else's kids."

"It was like that here."

"The thing is, it's not like that everywhere. And, to be honest, there were probably families that struggled with abuse issues in our pretty little towns, too. Families can be awfully good at keeping secrets. The kids are taught early on not to share family matters with anyone. That's what makes my job so hard sometimes. Children see me as the bad guy."

Trak nodded and took a drink. "Have you dealt much with locating runaway kids?"

"I guess that's our working hypothesis, right? That Andy—Adan—is a runaway." She traced her finger around the lip of her glass.

"Traveling alone, lying about his name, and the lack of any ID, certainly points to the fact that he doesn't want to be found."

"I've had my share of runaway cases," Brooke said. "Children in the child welfare system are twice as likely to run away as children in the general public. Almost all of these kids, ninety percent, are between the ages of twelve and eighteen. Black and Hispanic children run away more than white kids."

"Were you able to locate any of them?"

"I found all the ones assigned to me, though it was a battle every time. There are, of course, some children who are never located. Sometimes families are uncooperative. They just move and leave no forwarding address. Then there are the people that don't even report a child missing.

Years can go by before anyone finds out. How can we locate a runaway if we don't know they're gone? And there are the predators, the pimps who seek out these children and lure them into sexual slavery."

"I wouldn't want your job."

Brooke took a deep breath, trying to ignore the familiar stab in her gut. "Sometimes, I don't want it, either."

57

Rose picked her way down the mountain path in the darkness, ticking off the list of items she wished she had. A flashlight would certainly help. That she was traversing the worn trail—probably a deer track—and not the layer of sliding scree just east of the weeping rock made nighttime travel easier.

She clutched only the blue dress, because there was nothing else in the cave that would keep the boy warm. She'd left him shivering in his wet clothes. Putting the hooded sweatshirt on him had been a consideration, but then that, too, might have become damp and useless in regard to stemming the cold.

Rose followed the snaking trail, careful to avoid rocks and the limbs of thorny bushes that stretched out reaching for her legs.

Matches. With matches she could build a fire and warm the boy. But someone might see the flame. A sudden thought struck Rose for the first time. Was anyone looking for her? They must be. Her father, at least, would be concerned for her safety. Were there men searching for her now? She should stay hidden. But could she just let the boy sicken and maybe die all because she didn't want to go back?

Rose saw the flat slab of sandstone in the moonlight. The boy lay curled on the ground, arms wrapped around his long legs. She kneeled and placed her hand on his cheek. He did not respond.

Rose slumped to the ground. She reached over to the boy's leg. Through the wet jeans she felt a strong thigh and, for a moment, her fingers lingered. Then she yanked her hand away. She had never seen a grown man's legs. The men of the community and the teenage boys always wore long pants. Though Rose had grown up with brothers, they slept and dressed in a separate part of the house away from the girls.

Logically, this boy's thigh should look no different than Rose's. Yet, the leg was much longer and thicker than hers. Until this moment, she had never touched a boy. With the exception of Jacob Babbitt's clumsy grope of her backside, Rose had never been touched by one, either. For that matter, aside from her sister Daisy whose flailing arms gently tapped Rose when the girl was being tended, the rare occasions when her father had allowed Rose to kiss his cheek, and her mother's punishing blows, Rose had never had physical contact with anyone.

The boy continued to shiver. Rose stood up. What she was about to do was certainly a sin, but letting the boy die would be a worse offense. She started with his sneakers, which were dry to the touch. She unlaced the shoes and pulled them off his large feet. The white cotton athletic socks were dry, as well, so Rose left them on.

Next she rolled him on his back. The white T-shirt

covered the top of his jeans. Rose gingerly lifted the shirt exposing the fly. She glimpsed the hard muscles of his belly, but quickly looked away. Rose paused then let out a long breath. She reached above the zipper for the button.

The boy's eyes bolted open. He stared at Rose then tried to bat her hand away.

"Do it, Rose!" she mumbled to herself. She reached over and quickly undid the button and drew down the zipper. She tried to yank the pants off, but the boy weighed twice what she did, so she couldn't get them down.

"Help me! You have to help get these wet clothes off!" she said.

His eyes opened again. He gazed at her for what felt like a long time. Then he reached up and touched her face. A small smile edged his lips.

Together they worked the wet jeans off, then the T-shirt with the Jaguars football logo. Rose helped him put the heavy sweatshirt over his head, his arms through the sleeves. Then she reached for the light blue dress.

An hour later, the boy slept fitfully, but he had stopped shivering.

Rose, however, was unable to sleep. Her mind whirled with so many thoughts—of her parents, of Daisy, of leaving Eden, of spending the night under the bright canopy of stars. But mostly, Rose thought about the boy.

58

The next morning, Logan Madsen sat slumped forward in his chair at the head of the dining room table. His wife, to his left, sat ramrod straight, her bony back pressed against the hard wooden chair.

"We must do something, Mother." His voice was tinged with anguish.

"Do what?" She folded her hands and placed them on the table. "Tell them our daughter has run away?"

"Maybe she didn't," he said. "Maybe—"

"Of course she ran away. That is her nature. She has always been difficult. You know that."

"But—"

"But what? You have permitted . . ." Her husband pierced her with a hard look. "We . . . have permitted her to remain unmarried all this time. She is way past the age when she should be caring for a husband and doing the job she was born to do. How many children could she have produced by now? How many?"

Logan inhaled, then eyed his wife. "You agreed that someone needed to tend Daisy."

"No, you made that decision. Sister Wife Glea could certainly have taken on that . . . chore."

He winced at her use of the term.

"Yes, chore. As you well know, caring for that one is an unpleasant task." Bliss could not even name the damaged child she had produced, the one that symbolized a mark of God's displeasure. The one that brought Bliss shame every time she had to look at the flailing arms, the drooling mouth hanging open, unable to say so much as a single word. The one, who like an infant, you could smell from down the hall.

"What if Rose is hurt somewhere and needs help?" Logan pleaded.

"So, you want to gather together a group of men and admit that your daughter has run away. I can hear the talk now." Bliss spit the words. "Logan Madsen cannot control his own family. The women of his own family. If that becomes known, do you think the Prophet will see fit to grant you a third wife?"

Three wives were required for a man to ascend to the Celestial Kingdom, and for his family to be exalted into the third heaven along with him. Logan Madsen understood perfectly well his position as a man with only two wives. He rose and stared at his wife for a long moment. Then, without a word, walked out of the house.

"How long has she been missing?" A tired-looking Sterling Buttars asked twenty minutes later.

"A few days." Madsen clasped his hands in his lap.

"Exactly how many?" Buttars asked.

"I have not seen her for three days. She left the morning that we—" Madsen paused and took deep breath.

"That you what?"

"Had to kill the bird. Daisy's bird. You understand." Logan Madsen's eyes glistened with unshed tears as the marshal let his gaze fall on the empty pink cushion in the corner that he hadn't had the heart to throw out. "But Rose grabbed the bird and it flew out the window, and Daisy screamed. Rose was punished that night, and I've not seen her since."

The marshal dropped his head. After a moment, he stared at Madsen. "Daisy? I don't recall . . ."

"One of my daughters."

"Oh, yes. That one. How old is Rose?" Buttars continued asking questions and filled out the information on a form in black pen.

When he was finished, Madsen asked, "What will you do now?"

"We'll look for her." The marshal rose and ushered the grieving father to the door. "We'll call if we have any news."

After Logan Madsen left, Buttars turned to Travis Forbush, who sat at his desk eating a chocolate donut. "We need to put together a search party. Men we can absolutely trust. You know the men I mean, don't you, Travis?"

The young deputy looked confused.

Buttars grabbed a pen and scrawled six names and addresses on a note pad. "Find them and get them here."

"They'll be looking for the girl?" Forbush asked.

Buttars adjusted his belt. "Not exactly."

59

Rose surveyed the sun. It was early morning, so the air was still cool. But the heat would come soon and they could not stay in the open another day. She grabbed the water bottles. The awkwardness of having to carry the containers in the plastic bag, which was now threatening to rip at the handles, annoyed her. She needed a sturdy backpack and so reminded herself again to add one to her list.

A short time later, Rose placed the three bottles—now filled with cold spring water—on the ground. The boy still slept peacefully, and she regretted having to wake him. But she had no choice. They must make the climb to the cave before it got too hot.

"Wake up," Rose called from a few feet away.

The boy did not stir.

Rose stepped closer and kneeled down. She shook his shoulder. "We have to go," she said. "It's a long way."

Nothing.

For a moment, Rose panicked, but then she saw the steady rise and fall of his chest. She leaned over, tilted his face toward her, and placed her wrist on his forehead. He was no longer feverish. The shivering had ceased.

The boy bolted up. His eyes were wide, but then he smiled and relaxed. "What happened to your hair?" he asked in a raspy voice. Then he started to cough.

"Here, have some water." Rose helped him drink. He downed almost half the bottle before she made him stop. "Easy, not too much at a time." She sat back on her heels.

"You know, I thought you were a boy. Last night when you were—" He looked down where the blue dress was wrapped tightly around the lower half of his body. Then he saw his jeans and white T-shirt spread out on the red sandstone slab. "—trying to take off my pants."

Rose felt her cheeks redden. "I had no choice," she said. "You were wet and freezing."

"Why was I wet?"

Rose stood. "I found you passed out on the trail. I went down to the spring and filled water bottles, and poured them on you to cool you off. But then it got cold and you were shivering horribly, so I had to take off your wet clothes." The words rushed out faster than she intended.

The boy smiled. "Well then, thank you."

"And now we have to move. We must—"

"What's you name?"

Rose paused, unsure of what to share with a stranger. She was taught to never trust outsiders. The people who lived in the hell beyond her world were often used by the devil to corrupt the good and righteous people of her community. She looked again at the dark brown eyes. Is this boy an emissary that might drag her into the outer darkness?

Rose huffed and turned away. She didn't know what she believed anymore. What she did know was that when the visions had faded and the illness stopped, a new clarity had come to her. She felt different. Were the vitamins to blame? Had she been living in a hazy world her entire life until now? She turned back to the boy who was now sitting up, arms wrapped around his long legs, still encased in the folds of her blue cotton dress.

"My name is Rose. And what is your name?"

The boy's smile faded just a bit. "I'm An—" But then he paused and the smile returned. "I'm Adan."

60

Two hours after Deputy Forbush left the office, six men stood facing Marshal Sterling Buttars. Travis, arms folded across his chest, listened from his desk chair.

"We have two missing kids," Buttars said. "I want to be very clear about how things will be handled."

"We'll find them, Sterling. I've still got Blue. He'll make tracking easier," Bill Kimball said.

The marshal looked at the heavy-set man with the gray beard and almost white-blue eyes. That he got to keep his dog angered Buttars. Working animals had been spared the Prophet's edict. A brief flash of Mouse's brown eyes stabbed at his heart.

"Do we have any clothing we can use for a scent?" Kimball asked.

"Don't get ahead of me, Bill. I have to explain what's gonna happen here. We are, first and foremost, searching for a boy—an outsider." Buttars described the little bit of information he had on the Hispanic teen, and several of the searchers narrowed their eyes. "We have been asked, no, ordered by the Prophet himself to locate this boy."

"Why should we care about finding a kid who doesn't even live here?" Forbush asked, leaning his elbows on the desk.

Buttars stared at the deputy. "Well, that's not really important, is it Travis? The Prophet has demanded we take care of this. That is all we need to know."

The other men nodded their heads, their faces hard, determined.

"But since you asked, this boy could be here to make trouble. To lead our young people astray. He is, as I've already said, an outsider. Or he might be here from the government to spy on us, as the Beast is always looking for a way to infiltrate and destroy our Eden."

Forbush sat up. "Yes, of course. So what will we do when we find the boy?"

Buttars scratched his chin then turned back to the other men. "We will not find him, gentlemen. We will search. We will tell the people who made the report that we did all we could in the rugged and dangerous land that surrounds us. But we will not find this boy. No one will."

The room was absolutely still.

"Do you understand, gentlemen?"

Grim nods all around.

"That's why I picked you."

"Who is the other missing child?" Bill Kimball asked.

"Buttars grabbed a report from his desk. "Rose Madsen. I think you know her father, Logan."

All six men said they did.

"She's sixteen. Blonde. Blue eyed. Last seen wearing a blue dress and Nikes.

"So, can we get a sample of clothing? For the dog?" Kimball asked again.

"I'm sure we can."

"Why did she run away?" Forbush said.

"Her father didn't say she ran away. He said she was missing." The marshal glared at his deputy. "I realize you haven't been here all that long, Travis, but you have to know that no father wants to say his daughter ran away."

Kimball cracked his knuckles. "I'd backhand any of mine that ran away. Then lock 'em in the shed until I married 'em off. Then it would be her husband's problem."

Several of the men chuckled.

"What if the two kids are together?" Forbush said.

All laughter ceased abruptly.

"What if they are?" Buttars stared at the deputy.

"I mean, if we're not meant to, um, find the boy, what happens if she's with him?" Forbush squinted at the marshal and scratched his head.

Buttars dropped his chin to his chest. Young witnesses could be difficult. And, of course, who would marry a girl who had run away with a stranger? Probably no one. What use would she serve then?

61

"It's time to go," Rose said a bit too gruffly. Why was she agitated with the boy who smiled up at her?

"Where are we going?" Adan asked.

Rose pointed to the sheer cliff and the opening that split the rock face like a smile.

Adan followed her finger and gazed at the red mountain that jutted into the blue sky like an impenetrable fortress. "Up there? Are you part mountain goat, or can you fly?"

Rose squinted. He was making fun of her. "Of course not. There's a back way. Over past all the fallen rocks." She kneeled and gathered the two water bottles that were now empty. "I'll go fill them. You need to get dressed." She nodded toward his jeans draped over the rock.

She turned away and heard Adan hoist himself off the ground. She felt compelled to stare, but instead forced herself to concentrate on the glittering stream that tumbled over smooth river rock that flung bright flashes of light into the morning air. Rose descended the steep incline, fighting the urge to turn and watch him get dressed.

Later, when they were halfway up the trail that led
to the weeping rock, Rose saw that Adan was breathing
heavily, so she motioned for them to sit in the shade of
several scraggily gray-green pines. She handed him one of
the plastic bottles. A cool morning breeze purled through
the shrubs rustling their short pungent branches.

After he drank, Adan said, "Why did you cut your
hair?"

Rose didn't answer. She took a long draw on a water
bottle and eyed him suspiciously. Distrust of strangers had
been ground into her since infancy. Although she could
detect no malice in the boy, she had often been warned that
the devil might work his wickedness by using sweetness
and guile. Also, she had always been taught that Lucifer
had been the most beautiful angel in heaven. And that as
the maker of celestial music so captivating, God himself
favored him above all the other angels. Until the fall.

She stared at Adan from beneath white-blonde lashes
that nearly kissed her cheeks. He was, quite easily, the most
handsome boy she'd ever seen. So different from the males
that peopled her world. So exotic with his dark eyes and
lustrous burnished skin. Briefly, Rose studied his hand—
long, delicate fingers rested casually against his thick
thigh—fingers that had never milked cows or cut firewood.
Not gnarled or rough or cracked from the heavy work of
farm life. How could a boy his age have hands like that?

She leapt to her feet. The devil did not work hard! He
used tricks and cunning to deceive the innocent. She had
a sudden urge to run. Run away and leave the boy here to
fend for himself. There was no food to feed him in the cave,
so what was the point of taking him there? She needed to
care for herself.

Adan watched Rose for a moment before he reached his bronzed arm out to her. "Gonna help me up?"

"No."

Rose crossed her arms over her chest.

Adan raised his eyebrows, then shook his head. "OK." He turned around onto his knees and pushed himself off the ground. He managed to get to his feet, but then wobbled. Rose quickly found herself at his side, holding him up, no memory of making the decision to assist.

Adan creased his brow. "I'm still a little dizzy, I guess."

Just as quick, Rose released her hold and stepped back. This was the moment. She could easily leave him now in his still-weakened state. He wouldn't be able to catch her, and he wouldn't be able to find the path to the cave.

She stared at the rocky ground at her feet for a few moments, her decision made. Rose raised her head and met his eyes. "I'll go slowly. Keep drinking your water."

62

Broken slabs of red rock that had sheared off the mountain radiated heat of their own, making the sandstone almost too hot to touch. But as they wended their way to the opening in the weeping rock, a cooling breeze kissed them. Adan stopped abruptly and sniffed at the wet air, so out of place.

"Come on," Rose said. "We are almost there."

After edging their way along the thin trail, a towering rock on one side, and a sheer drop to the canyon floor on the other, they rounded a sharp bend. Adan stopped and stared at the veil of crystalline water droplets that fell from the top of the cave's mouth. Tears of water grew fat, then fell, some dripping into a hollow on the rock floor and forming a small pool in the stone basin. He looked at Rose.

"Go ahead," she said.

Adan got on his knees and leaned into the shockingly cold water, sucking the fluid in. He felt the liquid, so cold on his lips, course down his throat and drain into his stomach where an ache of pleasure filled him. Somewhere in his primal brain, he knew that water was the most important— the most priceless—substance on the planet. More valuable than gold or platinum or oil. Even more precious than food. How had he been stupid enough to get caught in the desert twice—to have to be rescued twice!—just because he hadn't taken the need for water seriously? Hadn't his teachers and coaches, even his mother, always emphasized the need to stay hydrated when out in the sun? What had he been thinking?

He splashed water on his face, then sat back on his heels and gazed out over the canyon and into the valley beyond. He saw a thin ribbon of pavement splitting the golden grasslands, which he assumed was the road leading from Colorado City to Hurricane. Was Trak looking for him? Adan was assaulted by a sudden surge of guilt. The man had been nothing but kind and concerned. He pushed the thought away; he couldn't worry about that now.

He sat cross-legged on the cool stone floor, resisting the urge to plunge his feet into the pool. He caught Rose staring and watched her turn quickly away, busying herself with several plastic bags in the back of the cave. Clearly, she was uncomfortable being with him. Yet, she had not left him to die down in the rocks.

Even with her almost white hair shorn, strands of varying lengths sticking out haphazardly, she was pretty. Adan was used to the girls in his school, faces often coated with elaborate and multi-colored makeup. When asked, most of his friends admitted they preferred the girls who presented themselves less like music video sirens, which the boys often found intimidating. This girl wore no makeup. No adornments. The females in her town seemed to only wear the strange single-colored ankle-length dresses. The jeans and T-shirt she now wore were obviously too big. He guessed she'd stolen the items. But why? What was she doing here in this cave, tucked up alone, living like a wild creature?

Rose crumpled the plastic bag and pushed the container into her front pants pocket. She walked to the edge of the cave, a little too quickly, which caused Adan to draw in his breath. Then she sat down in a dry spot and dangled her legs over the side.

She did not look at Adan as she spoke. "There is no food here. I have eaten all I had. I will have to go get some more."

"You're going steal it?"

Rose whipped her head around and faced him, light blue eyes radiant against alabaster skin. "I have no choice!" Stealing was a sin. But did God want her to starve? Did He want them both to die? "I will go to town and find what I can. There also may be some plants that I can collect. I will see."

Adan stood. "I'll go with you."

Rose's laugh startled him and he frowned.

"You barely made it here. You are probably still ill, and it will be quicker and easier if I go alone."

Adan stared at her. "What if they catch you?"

Rose met those brown eyes, then turned and focused on the valley below. "They have not found me yet. And today is Sunday. The people will be in church much of the day. Most houses will be empty. But I must go quickly."

"Are you sure you don't want me to go with you?"

"You will stay here." Rose surprised herself. She had never in her life told a man or boy what to do. She left her perch on the lip of the cave, kneeled by the pool, and filled two plastic bottles, then slipped back through the veil of water droplets and was gone.

63

Brooke snapped her cellphone shut, rubbed her eyes, and headed for the coffee pot, before taking what had become her customary seat on the wooden steps outside the trailer. Another bright, blue day in Colorado City and still no local people willing to speak with her.

She held the hot beverage in both hands, the chipped mug green with CPS emblazoned in red around the sides. She was grateful she had Adan's case to work on. Without this one missing boy, she'd have nothing to do. None of the follow-up inquiries on any of the Colorado City cases had garnered so much as a single response. And the search for the man who'd made the reports, the teacher, Bob Wayland, had gone nowhere. How could the man just disappear? Teachers were fingerprinted and had background checks, and so were some of the easiest people in the country to find. Had he just walked away from Colorado City and decided to never teach again? Her friend at the Phoenix PD said he'd make a few calls, but still, the search for Wayland shouldn't be this hard. This one man was the key to all the abuse cases filed in the town; without him she had nothing.

Brooke watched a hawk circle lazily above the spot where the girl's body had been found, her head bludgeoned in, a murder still under investigation. Married at thirteen, dead at sixteen. Clearly, another abused child.

Her phone chirped. The ringtone a cheerful *tiu–tiu–tiu-tiu*: a cardinal. Football was still a few months away, but in the time she'd been in Phoenix, Brooke had become a fan of the local NFL franchise, despite the team's sometimes dismal record. Her dad had teased her that rooting for the Cardinals was akin to being a Chicago Cubs fan, only without the panache.

"Hello." She listened, her eyes drifting up to the still-looping hawk. "Great! Let me get something to write on." Brooke rose and went into the trailer.

After numerous calls, she examined her notes, grateful she had so many contacts. Even though today was Sunday, she'd been able to gather some information. There were individuals always on call who could access records, especially if a child might be in imminent danger. While the Family Educational Rights and Privacy Act—known as FERPA—protected the privacy of student educational records, in some cases student information on minors could be divulged without a subpoena to specific parties if that child was missing or thought to be in danger. Brooke had used this clause in the FERPA law to glean information on missing children numerous times over the years. And now, she used it again.

Specific facts, referred to as non-confidential directory information, included verification of the child's name, school enrollment, and current address, all available without the parent or guardian's consent and without prior court approval. If the child is not located at the address listed, it was also possible to talk to a school counselor to see if the child discussed the possibility of moving. Phone numbers of any emergency contacts listed in the missing child's records could also be divulged without a judge's prior permission.

Now Brooke learned that a boy named Adan Reyes had, in fact, officially been reported missing. She requested his original file, and, since she'd briefly seen the boy Trak was searching for, added what she knew. Her years at CPS had taught her that even the tiniest scrap of evidence might help locate a missing, exploited, or abused child.

Outside again, seated on the steps, she heard the hawk cry as the bird swirled in the currents, wings extended, floating. Brooke's heart beat rapidly. She wanted to help find this boy. She needed to find him. She squeezed her eyes shut. Not too long ago, she swore she would quit. That she was done with the rotting homes and the disgusting smells: feces, vomit, decay. She would not be a witness to another big-eyed infant starving in a land filled to the brim with food. She would never again have to look into the faces of adults who performed unspeakable acts on children, even babies, or have to listen to their rationale for their horrifying actions, convinced that what they were doing was out of love. Brooke shuddered. She'd vowed not take one more case. Because even though some ended happily for the children, others tore at her heart, leaving permanent open sores. Wounds that scabbed over for a while, only to break open again when memories of the children and what had happened to them pried the edges apart.

She forced down the despair that hovered on the periphery of her world, the anguish that nestled in her belly poking with barbed claws. Brooke open her eyes and exhaled, having been unaware that she was holding her breath.

She should talk to Trak. Tell him what she knew.

For an instant, the creature released its claws.

64

Rose traveled down the rocky path, swift, surefooted, no longer questioning which way to go. She had made the trip enough times over the last few days that the route was cemented in her brain. However, she was unsure of exactly where to go once she reached the edge of town.

The easiest place to locate specific items she needed was her own home. Rose was fairly certain that the house was empty, save for Daisy. Her sister rarely went to the temple. Would someone have stayed behind to care for the girl? In the past, Daisy was left alone for short periods of time, and either Rose or Sister Wife Glea checked on the child during the day's religious observances.

She reached the edge of the dry wash that backed up to the town. Not even a trickle of water remained in Short Creek's sandy bottom. Crouching, she peered from the brush. To her left she could see the boulder where Bonnie Buttars had laid splayed in the dry grass, her religious garments torn off, her backside exposed, reddish-gray ooze seeping from her ruined skull. The memory was shrouded in a shiny haze, a curtain that Rose had seen through as long as she could remember.

Now, that veil had lifted. Rose could not explain exactly what was different about the way she now viewed her world, but something had changed. Mr. Wayland would have expected Rose to analyze the situation. So she did. I stopped taking my vitamins. I got sick to my stomach. I had strange dreams and visions. When these things passed, I began to see—to think—more clearly.

Had the vitamins affected her thinking? Rose had been told that the pills kept her healthy. Church doctrine insisted that her body was a precious gift from God. That she must remain strong for the Lord. What was in the tablets that she had taken all of her life? Had they kept her healthy? Or had the pills done something else?

She focused on the spot where she had pulled Bonnie's dress down, covering her, keeping her modest, even in death. She took a deep breath and looked away. Scanning the area, she saw no one, and she stood and ran— long smooth strides, arms pumping at her sides, no dress to hinder her movement.

"Hey!"

Rose stopped so quickly she almost fell over. She did not turn and face the voice that called to her.

"You're late for temple, boy!"

Rose lifted her head slightly. She started to speak, but the sight of the hawk circling above made her pause.

"You git now," the man said. "They'll be a whippin' when they see you come in so late, but I expect you know that."

Rose nodded almost imperceptibly and bolted. She ran down the worn dirt path faster than she ever imagined she could move. She traveled around a bend, through a thicket of young cottonwoods. The long trailing branches caressed her face. Her foot hit a rock that jutted from the ground, but she did not fall. She righted herself and kept going. Was the man following her? She did not turn around to look.

When she was within a fifty yards of her back door, she slid behind the barn and collapsed against the wooden slats of the wall. The air was filled with the smell of hay and horses, cows and manure, sour milk and dry pine from the firewood stacked against the building. She sucked in deep breaths and wiped the sweat from her face with the edge of the T-shirt. She dared a glance around. Saw no man or any other human. The hawk still circled high in the air above.

The exhilaration of running was overwhelming. Certainly, this feeling must be a sin! Perhaps that was why her mother always told her to slow down, to walk. "Be a lady, Rose. Keep sweet." Rose searched her brain for any church teaching that said one must not run. But she could think of none. And the boys in the community were allowed to dash anywhere they wanted. What of that?

The more Rose considered her life with this new-found clarity, the more confusing her existence became. But she had no time for contemplation now.

Focus. Rose went over the list of things she needed, then tried to remember exactly where each of the items was kept inside the house.

65

Careful to mount the back stairs one at a time, avoiding the one with the soft spot in the middle that groaned when stepped on, Rose slowly pushed open the kitchen door so that only the screen remained between her and the inside. The house was always unlocked, so it was possible no one, save for Daisy, was home.

She stood still and listened. Nothing. She waited a full minute, then eased the screen door open and slipped inside. She was desperately hungry and wanted to eat, but she needed to retrieve the other items first. Silently, she went over the list one more time, then she moved through the house, but not before grabbing the slice of fresh bread sitting on the cutting board almost like a gift. She jammed the thick wedge into her mouth, crumbs dusting her T-shirt.

She found a backpack in the room where the boys had been housed, before they had all married or gone visiting. Rose could smell them—stale sweat, old shoes, something akin to overly ripe peaches. She missed her brothers. Why, once they left, did they never come back? In whose home were they now guests? Had they married? Certainly, mischievous. Bret—always playing practical jokes and laughing uproariously whenever Rose had been caught in one of his games—hadn't settled down. Had he ever been sentenced to the dark, airless closet? He had certainly been whipped often enough.

Before Rose left the room, she searched the closet for a pair of jeans that fit her better. Then she ransacked the drawers and located some athletic socks and another smaller T-shirt. This one, dark blue, which, unlike the white shirt she now wore, would make her less easy to spot. Rose pulled the navy T-shirt over the one she had on.

She paused and gazed at her dusty reflection in the small mirror over the bureau. The Rose she knew was gone. She could pass as a boy, but for how long? She shook her head. Hurry.

Methodically, Rose went from room to room, grabbing what she needed and stowing the items in the backpack. Then she approached the stairway that led up to Daisy's room. She listened. Slowly, she edged her way up the wooden stairwell, again careful to avoid the steps that might creak.

Outside Daisy's door, she paused. Could she walk by without being seen? For a fleeting moment Rose considered that Daisy might be distracted by her little bird, but then the memory assaulted her—her parents trying to make the child break the struggling creature's tiny neck, snap the twig-like vertebrae in her bent, warped hands.

Rose wanted to run, but two steps would get her past the threshold. She walked.

"Wa, wa, wa!" Daisy cried out, flailing her fists on the tray before her.

Rose stopped on the other side of the doorway, out of sight. But Daisy had seen her. She should run, but the damaged girl's cries broke her heart.

"Wa, wa, wa!"

Rose stepped back and smiled at her sister, who was slumped over in her chair, drool streaming from her malformed mouth. The girl stopped calling, and tilted her head almost imperceptibly. She pierced Rose with one dark eye. There was a spark there. Of this, Rose was sure.

Rose smiled at her sister, removed the cap, and ruffled her fingers through her shorn white hair.

"Wa, wa, wa!" Daisy pounded her fists on the tray harder and rocked her frail, broken body back and forth in the metal chair.

Rose dropped the backpack to the floor, crossed they room, and hugged her sister, tears purling down her cheeks.

66

Brooke closed the trailer door. Mid-afternoon in Colorado City was clear, comfortably warm, and breezy. A sweet smell of dry pine tinged the air. While she waited for more information to come in on Adan's past, she decided to become more familiar with the area. Perhaps, if the townspeople saw her more, she would become less of a stranger. She would walk around, nod her head, and smile, wave and try to became part of the community, and hopefully be seen as something other than an outsider and a threat.

Brooke wended her way through town, turning down tree-shaded streets and some with nothing but weed-covered, empty lots. Two-story houses stood solid, well-built, with bushy flowers in window boxes and luxurious kitchen gardens. Others wore skeletons of unfinished construction—concrete pads sprouting rebar, walls supporting roofs with no doors or windows. She passed rusting hulks of ancient cars and trucks, horses swatting their tails at flies in tiny mesh-covered enclosures, and black-and-white cows in the shade of dilapidated farm equipment. The smell of smoke issued from piles of burning garbage she could not see.

Where was everyone? Brooke had not encountered a single human being on her walk through town.

A short time later, near Township Avenue and Memorial Street, Brooke stood before a white, wrought iron archway. The sign read Isaac W. Carling Memorial Park. The jagged face of Canaan Mountain, striated sandstone evidence of the ancient sandy desert that once covered the area, rose behind the cemetery.

Brooke entered the park that was flat and dusty, and here and there dotted with juniper and pinyon and small Christmas tree-like pines. And then she remembered it was Sunday. No wonder she'd seen no people in town. They were probably at church services.

She wandered in the quiet among the graves, many neglected. A brown marble marker indicated that David R. Bateman rested here with his wife, Arlene, and their children: April, Randal, Coral. More untended graves were surrounded by leggy weeds, stones, and dirt paths lining the rows. Brooke read the names and dates of the deceased. So many children. Young people everywhere, dominating the cemetery real estate. Red mounds rose in spots, with no markers or any indication of who might lie beneath. Brooke found this curious.

She continued walking up and down the rows, and, without thinking, began to count the dead children— anyone under twenty. She had been to the funerals—a heartbreak no one should have to endure. And yet, she always forced herself go, even if the child was not one of her cases.

The creature slowly sunk one barbed claw into her gut.

Brooke stopped near the edge of the cemetery and closed her eyes, took several deep breaths. When she opened them, she noticed the earth had been disturbed outside the white fence that enclosed the park, a section of earth devoid of vegetation. Who had been digging there?

Curious, Brooke left the confines of the cemetery and walked to the back fence. She kneeled and pressed her palm to the ground. Fresh digging, soil darker than the rest, appeared at one end of the plot. She turned back to the cemetery with its headstones and markers. Was something, someone, buried here? If so, why was there no indication of who it might be? Why, if indeed these were graves, did the dead rest outside the white fence of the cemetery?

To the east she saw an enormous cottonwood, massive green branches spreading before the red rock of the mountain. That young girl had been killed nearby. A chill shivered down her spine.

Two white butterflies flitted across the broken earth. Then Brooke was knocked to the ground.

67

She pin-wheeled—all flying arms and legs—into the turned red earth. The bulging backpack landed with a thud. Rose rolled onto her hands and knees. A woman, on her back, sat up, twisting her neck from side to side. Rose scrambled for the pack, grabbed the straps and jumped to her feet. She eyed the woman for an instant, and then ran as fast as she could.

"No, wait!" Brooke cried.

Rose did not wait. She slid her arms through the straps and pumped her arms and legs as fast as she could, her mind racing along with her body. Why hadn't she looked where she was going? Who was the woman? Clearly no one from the community. Her clothing said as much.

Rose rounded the turn by the cottonwood, swiping her hand across the top of her head. The cap was gone. She slowed her pace. The hat would help her hide, but she would not go back to retrieve it.

She paused, turned three hundred and sixty degrees, and scanned the area. She saw no one, so she crossed the dry bottom of Short Creek and ran toward the narrow opening in the trees.

Brooke got up flexing her arm. Her elbow was bruised, but other than that she was unhurt. While her assailant appeared to be a boy, after looking at the child's face, she was sure a girl had knocked her to the ground. She reached down and retrieved a navy blue ball cap.

Obviously, the collision was an accident, so why had the child run off? A bigger question was posed by the way the girl was dressed—jeans and a dark T-shirt. Perhaps she was from a farm outside the community, but then what was she doing here? Brooke had seen outsiders at the Mercantile, purchasing snacks and filling up gas tanks at the station across the street, but she doubted any of these travelers stayed in town. There were no hotels or rooms for rent that she knew of in Colorado City. The locals did not encourage mixing with outsiders, but there seemed to be nothing they could do to thwart drivers from pulling off SR389.

Brooke brushed red dirt from her pants. Her tumble had left several impressions in the turned soil where her knees, elbows, and back had impacted the ground. She had a sudden urge to dig, to see what the loose dirt covered.

A cloud blocked the afternoon sun, throwing a shadow across the cemetery and the small plot of disturbed earth. Did she really want to see what lay beneath the surface? Images, like a Power Point on steroids, raged in her head, the horrors racing one past the other, children who had suffered at the hands of those who should have loved and protected them.

Brooke turned away and walked along the white iron fence that enclosed the cemetery, the spearheads pointed, sharp. She slapped the cap along the rungs. The girl who ran into her was frightened. Brooke had seen the look often enough. A protective wave surged through her that she was powerless to control.

A short time later, Brooke stood in front of the marshal's office. Perhaps the girl was a runaway from the community. Which meant that the child needed help. In Phoenix, she would contact her friend at the police department. So, Brooke mounted the steps and went into the office.

She read his nametag. "Officer Forbush." She smiled at the thin young man with the dark hair and angular jaw.

"Deputy Marshal," he corrected. "What do you need?"

Brooke paused. He stared at her blankly, remaining seated behind the desk. She kept the smile pasted on. "I was wondering if you have any reports of a missing girl."

Forbush squinted. "Why do you ask?"

Why were these people so obstinate? Couldn't they see she was trying to help? She exhaled. "Well, I was knocked down, accidentally, by a girl who seemed to be dressed as a boy and—"

"Where?"

"Out behind the cemetery and—"

"What were you doing there?" He came out from behind the desk.

"Um, I was just walking and—"

"Where did she go?" He towered over her.

Then it came to her: the face in the trees, the blue dress. Could it be the same girl?

"Tell me!" The deputy demanded.

68

Rose tossed the backpack to the floor of the cave, then collapsed to her knees and sank her face into the crystalline pool. Adan jumped, the dreams ripped away so quickly not a thread remained for him to hold on to.

Rose came up for air, coughed, then drank some more. When she was done, she rolled over on her back and stared at the moss-covered edge of the rock ceiling where the droplets clung and fell, sparkling jewels in the late afternoon light.

Neither of them spoke.

Finally, Rose sat up. "Are you hungry?"

Adan laughed. She turned and stared at the boy.

"I'm starving. I'd pretty much eat anything. I was thinking about foraging out there." He nodded toward the cave mouth.

"Well, it's good you didn't. Do you know anything about poisonous plants?" she said a bit haughtily.

"Um ..."

"I didn't think so. Mr. Wayland ..."

"Who's he?"

"My old teacher. He taught us about plants. Since you know nothing about them, you must never, ever eat a wild plant, no matter how hungry you are." She retrieved the pack and sat cross-legged with her back against the cave wall.

Adan leaned on his elbow and stretched his legs. "What should I eat then?"

Rose narrowed her eyes. Was he teasing her? "Bugs."

"Bugs?"

"Yes, insects of all kinds are just protein, not much different from chicken." She recited Bob Wayland's lesson verbatim. "Insects are sanitary and cannot make you sick, unlike certain plants that can kill you in any number of horrible ways. So, even if a plant has berries that look fat and juicy and quite eatable, never, ever eat them unless you're sure of what they are."

"OK." Adan tilted his head, still smiling. "And what is your favorite bug? I mean, what is the best tasting bug you've ever eaten."

Rose just stared.

"I'd like to know what I should look for, just in case you ever abandon me." He grinned.

Rose turned away. The boy was annoying.

"Well?"

"I've never eaten a bug."

"Ah, then how do you know they taste like chicken?" Adan burst out laughing, something he hadn't done in a very long time.

"Mr. Wayland never lied. He promised us that he would only tell the truth. We could ask him anything and if he didn't know the answer, he found out. He is . . . was . . . different from all the other teachers."

"Was?"

"He's gone now. He doesn't teach here anymore." Rose felt a sudden urge to cry.

"Why not?" Adan sat up.

"I don't really know." Rose dumped the contents of the backpack on the floor. "One day the school was closed. We were told that all the children would be home schooled. Some of the teachers stayed in town, but Mr. Wayland—" She let the statement float between them, then sorted through the pile of items she stole.

"You miss him, don't you?" Adan said, a hint of compassion in his voice.

Rose lifted a package of peanut butter crackers, the cellophane crinkling in her hand. "I do. He was the only adult who ever talked to me. No, the only one who ever listened. He said I could be a science teacher."

"So be one," Adan said with a shrug.

She tossed the crackers at him. "You don't understand."

69

Sweet mesquite smoke wafted over the backyard. Trak stuck a long-handled fork in the last of the chicken breasts and removed it from the barrel smoker. The pork tenderloin was already resting in the kitchen, waiting to be sliced.

"Let me help," Brooke said.

Trak watched as she moved back and forth beneath the massive pecan limb to which the worn wooden swing was tethered. She held a sweating bottle of beer to her forehead. "You look far too comfortable to move. Just give me a few minutes."

She smiled and took a swig.

A short time later, they sat at a planked picnic table that had been painted multiple times in various colors over its long life. Currently, it was a moss green. A round, white linen tablecloth that sported fine filigree edging covered the middle of the rectangular table.

Brooke ran her hand along the delicate design. "This is beautiful. Are you sure we should be using it on our . . . picnic."

"Of course. My mother would be delighted. She made it." Trak placed several rounds of pink-centered pork on her plate. He followed with slices of smoked chicken and a medley of grilled red, green, and yellow peppers topped with cloves of roasted garlic. Then he spooned dark wild rice and and a mixed-green salad with cucumbers, red and yellow cherry tomatoes, and thin slices of avocado. "Here's some dressing." He lifted a small white pitcher dotted with tiny roses. "Balsamic vinaigrette."

Brooke stared.

"What? Surprised a country boy can cook a meal that's not hotdogs?"

"Well," Brooke spread her hands as if to showcase the whole spread.

Trak handed her a basket covered with a linen napkin. Underneath were thick slices of homemade bread and a ramekin of whipped butter.

She raised her eyebrows. "You bake the bread, too?"

"No." He poured two glasses of wine from a bottle of chilled Chardonnay. "That's from the mayor."

"Of course, I should have known. Carla does like to feed me."

Trak laughed. Brooke did look better than she had when she'd arrived in Hurricane. "Go ahead and eat."

Crickets were out in full force sounding like thousands of tiny stringed instruments, on what was a clear, warm evening. Stars above the high desert glittered, the thick gauzy swath along the Milky Way splitting the night sky.

After Brooke had tasted all the offerings on her plate, she looked at Trak. "This is delicious," she said. "Really."

He twirled his glass of wine and gave her a wide smile. "What can I say? I'm multi-talented."

"Did your mom teach you to cook?"

He laughed. "No. Like any good Mormon mother, she believed men did not belong in the kitchen."

"So then who . . . ?"

"I dated a chef when I lived in Phoenix."

"How nice for you. She cooked your meals."

"Gosh, no. She cooked for other people every day. When she came home, the last thing she wanted to do was turn on the stove, or have to think about food. Though she happily opened a bottle of wine, sat at the kitchen table, and told me what to do."

Oh. Private chef lessons."

"Exactly."

When the table had been cleared and the dishes put away, Trak and Brooke sat together on the wooden swing. On the plate resting between them, a single pecan brownie remained.

"You want the last one?" Trak felt a surge of nervousness in his stomach.

"No, though they were wonderful." She smiled up at him.

Brooke's red hair practically glowed in the darkness. Pale skin. Blue eyes. The freckles that bridged her nose. He leaned over to kiss her.

"Trak!"

70

They'd eaten peanut butter crackers, several apples, half a loaf of fresh-baked wheat bread, and a thick slab of white cheese. Rose and Adan washed the food down with bottled water from the pool, which at night, shone liked the polished glass of a dark mirror.

Adan did not feel comfortable dangling his legs over the side of the cliff. Still, he sat next to Rose, cross-legged, a foot back from the ledge, while she tapped her heels lightly on the still warm rock face, looking out into the valley that was her home. Lights twinkled in the distance—in the houses of the residents of Colorado City—and now and then, a miniscule beam threaded down the ribbon of SR389—a vehicle on its way to what lay beyond Rose's world

She turned to Adan. His profile was regal in some vague way. She had read of kings and queens, but in the picture books the monarchs were always pale skinned, light haired, and blue eyed, like her. Dark-skinned people were never mentioned in the equation that included royalty. There had been some mention of these people in the scriptures, but always as a lower type human, often slaves. Did the word of God somehow place her above Adan? Certainly, he was far more beautiful than any boy she had ever seen. How could someone like him be a lesser person than she was?

"What are you?" she blurted out.

Adan cocked his head. "What do you mean?"

Rose waved her hand up and down. "I have not seen a person that looks like you before."

"I still don't understand."

Rose pursed her lips. Was he teasing her again? "Your ... face, your color."

Adan raised his eyebrows. "Did your Mr. Wayland not teach you about people that lived in other parts of the world?" he asked. "Those from Africa and Asia and South America."

Rose turned away and looked back out over the valley. "He told us about some other places, but I don't ever remember seeing any pictures of the people who lived in them."

Adan scratched the back of his neck. "I'm what you call Hispanic. That means my ancestors come from a country where the main language spoken is Spanish."

"You speak another language?" Rose's eyes were wide.

"Yes, I'm fluent in Spanish."

"Spanish." Rose rolled the word in her mouth. "Say something."

"Eres muy hermosa," Adan said suddenly shy.

"What does that mean?" Rose asked.

"Um ... it is a beautiful night," he lied.

"Oh. And does everyone who speaks Spanish look like you?" A flash of heat struck Rose. A bright red swath spread across both cheeks.

"Well, people in Spain, the country where Spanish comes from, tend to be lighter skinned than I am. "These people from Spain traveled all over the world in great ships. When they landed, they mixed with the local people who lived in those places."

Rose pursed her lips.

"Like the Native Americans," he said. "The Indians."

"But you don't really look like the Indians here." Rose waved her hand before her face.

"I think the Indians where my people lived look different from the ones up here."

"And what is this place called. Where you come from?"

"America."

Rose frowned. He'd insulted her.

"Really, I'm American. I was born in Phoenix, about six hours south of here."

Rose squinted her eyes.

"But my mother is from Mexico." He smiled. "A place where there are a lot of tan-skinned people who look like me." Then the smile faded and Adan turned away from the girl with the white blonde hair.

71

Trak still stared at Brooke, at her eyes, her lips, but she had turned away.

"Chase." He did not need to look. It was the doctor who had walked into the yard.

"Oh, gosh. Man! I'm sorry."

"That's OK." Brooke smiled.

"No, it's not. Go away." Trak leveled a poisonous gaze at his friend.

Chase dug both hands deep in his pockets.

Trak hung his head. "OK, go get three beers."

Brooke giggled. Trak pushed the ground with his feet and sent the swing creaking backward. At the same time, he put his arm along the back of the seat. The rusted chain that secured the swing to the tree limb groaned as Trak and Brooke went back and forth. He squeezed her shoulder, which felt small and delicate. Brooke's hand held the brownie plate on the seat between them. Compared to his, her hand seemed tiny, fragile.

"Here you go," Chase said cheerfully when he returned. He held three dark bottles, the caps already removed.

Half an hour later, Trak sprawled on his back in the cool grass, while Brooke and Chase chatted on the swing. Not a single one of the annoying looks he tossed in the doctor's direction could get the man to leave.

"How's the job going?" Chase asked.

"It's very frustrating. No one will speak to me." Brooke sipped her beer.

"Not at all surprising."

Trak directed another stink eye at his oldest friend, which the doctor summarily ignored.

"What's the matter up there? What are they so afraid of?"

"They are Fundamentalist Mormons," Chase answered. "Quite frowned on. It's much different than being a regular Mormon."

"Or a Jack Mormon." Trak tipped his beer bottle in Chase's direction.

"Yes, I am of the Jack variety, to the disdain of many of my more observant relatives. And don't be so quick to point the bottle at me, my friend. You're holding a beer, too."

"You're a Mormon?" Brooke asked.

"No. And you know I'm not, Chase, so cut the crap." Trak sat up.

"But your mother was."

"This is true. But my father was a Navajo traditionalist. So I had a choice."

"And you checked the none-of-the-above box?" Chase said.

"How did I become the center of the conversation? Brooke asked you about Colorado City."

"True. Here's the thing, Brooke." The doctor turned his pale eyes toward her. "The ancestors of the people there used to be regular mainstream Mormons. It's just that mainstream in the old days meant polygamy. Which made some sense in the context of those times. Farms needed lots of people to keep them going, so children were seen as a huge asset. But childbirth was difficult and dangerous. If you don't believe me, go out and read the headstones in some of those pioneer cemeteries.

"Many non-Mormon men lived through the passing of multiple wives. At the turn of the twentieth century, the average life expectancy in the US was forty-eight, not because some people didn't live to be one hundred, but because so many women died in childbirth, and so many children died before the age of two. So having multiple wives having multiple babies assured that, at any given point, there would be women around to tend to the children. Some of whom might actually live into adulthood and help out on the farm."

"But in 1890, the church issued the Mormon Manifesto, making plural marriages illegal from that point on," Trak said, staring up at the sky.

Chase shrugged. "The Federal Government threatened to confiscate church property if the people didn't renounce the practice. Mormons would also lose their civil rights."

"OK, all of that makes sense," Brooke said, "but then why are these people still practicing polygamy today and why are they so afraid of outsiders? And, since polygamy is illegal, why are they allowed to continue living this lifestyle? And what about the public school? I walked by there and it's closed up? Why hasn't the state done anything about all this?"

Neither Trak nor Chase offered an answer.

72

The sun was barely above the eastern horizon when the door opened at the marshal's office. The smell of strong coffee lured the men inside. Travis Forbush handed paper cups around and filled them from a stained glass pot. Only one of the men on the search party abstained, waving the cup away.

"We're doing God's work, William," said Bill Kimball. His dog, Blue, fidgeted at his feet. "Don't think he'll mind if we wake ourselves up a bit."

William Flake just shook his head. Even though the inhabitants of Colorado City had the Prophet's permission to drink coffee and alcohol, some still abstained.

Buttars came through the door holding a plastic bag. Dark pouches underscored his eyes. The marshal dropped the container on his desk, grabbed a bottle of water from the refrigerator, and took several long draughts. Then he addressed the team.

"Sunday worship held us up, but today we'll find those kids."

"I thought you didn't want us to find the boy." Flake's face was expressionless.

Buttars sighed. "We will locate him, William, but he will not be coming back with us."

There was a long silence while Flake digested this information. He looked at the others who had clearly gotten the message during Buttars' earlier talk. Finally, William sniffed loudly and nodded.

Buttars reached for the bag on his desk and pulled out a worn athletic shoe. "This belongs to the girl." He handed the stained item out to Kimball and watched as the dog, a mottled bluetick coonhound, dance on the leash. Kimball refused to take the shoe.

"Wish ya hadn't touched it. Give me the bag, Marshal. No need muddyin' up the scent."

Buttars complied, placing the shoe back in the bag then handing it to Kimball.

"Where are we starting?" the tracker asked.

"You tell me. No one remembers seeing Rose Madsen leave, and there have been no sightings since she disappeared."

Travis Forbush looked down at his desk, and said nothing of his encounter with the CPS caseworker.

"This is your area, Bill. Where do you think we should start?" Buttars asked.

The tracker pinched his nose, then placed his hand on the hound's head. "Don't think she would have taken to the road. That's a twenty some mile hike into Hurricane."

"She ever been away from here?" William interrupted. "She even have any idea which way to go?"

Buttars shook his head. "Her father said she's never been out of town."

"OK. Then the mountain is the obvious place to start. Let's go down along the creek. It's dry now. Maybe there are some tracks. If she went that way, Blue'll sniff her out."

"Let's keep this quiet," Buttars said. "No need to let folks know what we're doin', all right?"

Nods all around.

"And Bill, keep Blue quiet if you can, at least until we get outta hearing range."

"Will do."

As the men filed out the door, Travis Forbush rose from his desk, walked across the office, and grabbed a rifle that hung with several others on hooks along the wall. He squashed a cap on his head and followed the group.

"Where you think you're goin'?" Buttars asked the deputy.

"With . . . with you," Forbush stuttered.

"You're not part of the team, boy. You stay here."

"But I have a lot of experience tracking—"

"What, squirrels? No, we got plenty of experience on the team already." Buttars adjusted his cowboy hat. Could the deputy pull the trigger with a human being in his sights? He doubted it.

"But I can help." Forbush looked like he might cry.

"Stay here, boy." Buttars turned and walked out the door.

73

Brooke felt guilty collecting her paycheck, derisory as it was. There was still practically nothing for her to do. The only thing she accomplished Monday morning was locating and talking to the caseworker in charge of Adan Reyes. The woman was forwarding a photograph to confirm that Andy was indeed Adan.

The young woman—fresh out of college and only a few months on the job—had seemed a bit dazed during the conversation. No doubt the caseload was smothering her. Social workers at CPS were tasked with accounting for a staggering number of children. Average caseloads in Arizona ran two-thirds above state and national standards. And still, bright-eyed, young people eager to help others arrived regularly, insisting that they could handle the daunting amount of work and the horrors that came with the job.

Brooke dragged her index finger down the list of information she'd written on a yellow legal pad: Adan Reyes would be eighteen in seven months. He'd been born in Phoenix and attended South Mountain High School. She smiled, pleased that she had managed to link the Jaguars mascot with the school. Her job often left her feeling like she was part detective.

She continued reviewing the information. Adan was an excellent student. He held a 3.94 grade point average. He would be a senior when school started in the fall and was a captain and starter on the football team, a basketball player, and a member of the cross-country team, where he was currently the school's top runner.

Brooke looked up. She had dealt with hundreds of children in her six years at CPS, all ages and races, single kids and sibling groups. But none of those children were anything like Adan. Here was what appeared to a bright, fabulously well-adjusted kid. He'd even been in the school's aerospace magnet, and was working on earning his pilot's license.

What makes a child like that run away?

Brooke had asked the young caseworker why the boy was in the Foster Care system, but that information was elusive. The woman repeatedly checked her notes and kept apologizing because she couldn't answer the question. And no, off the top of her head, she just couldn't remember why it was that Adan Reyes had become a ward of the state. She promised to find out and send the reason along when she could.

While others might be surprised that the woman could not recall all the details concerning a child under her protective care, Brooke sympathized with her plight. Sometimes, Brooke was jolted awake in the middle of the night after the dream that regularly visited in the dark. Damaged children, miserable faces assaulting her, all pleading with Brooke to say their names. She always started out well, smiling and reciting each child's appellation, eliciting bright, cheerful smiles. But as Brooke proceeded down the endless line of children, her memory failed her. She would stumble on one child's name and then forget them all, becoming yet another adult who had hurt and disappointed them, who had let them down. The nameless children slewed away from her in a never-ending queue, their wails and tears tormenting, pinpricks in her heart.

Brooke rubbed her eyes. Was there anything in her notes that would give her an idea of where the boy might be running to? What was he doing way up here on the Arizona Strip, in this rugged stretch of land so far from Phoenix? The caseworker told her that Adan was an only child. No known father. No known relatives save for his mother, Maria Reyes. And no, the woman had been unable to contact the mother. The listed number was no longer in service.

For a moment, she was angry with the young caseworker. Why couldn't she do her job properly? The missing information was important to the case. Then Brooke paused, the scratching in her stomach a signal of imminent pain. She sighed. Who was she to criticize someone for not doing their job?

74

Both Adan and Rose slept well into the morning.

Adan lay huddled in the blue hooded sweatshirt, his head on a wadded-up red flannel shirt that had once belonged to one of Rose's brothers. Rose, who reclined on the other side of the cave, had wrapped herself in a knitted blue and pink baby blanket that she found—long unused—in a drawer in Becky's room.

Rose looked at the wrap's delicate pattern of tiny flowers. Because of several stillbirths, there had been no infants in the Madsen home in almost four years, which had been a much-discussed point of contention between her parents. Logan Madsen would not be assigned that coveted third wife, if the babies stopped coming. The family hopes had been pinned on Sister Wife Glea, who, they prayed, might produce a living child for the family sometime soon.

Rose sat up, pressing her back against the now cold stone. She shivered and pulled the blanket around her shoulders. The mid-morning sun gilded the rock mouth, illuminating the never-ending rain of water droplets that seeped from the moss-covered ceiling. A clump of purple and white columbines had opened in a patch of rich moist soil near the pool.

Rose glanced at Adan and saw that he was staring back. He graced her with a beatific smile then sat up, stretched, and yawned.

Rose turned her head away quickly.

"Something wrong?" Adan asked.

"Shhh!" She held up her hand.

"What?"

"Quiet," she said in a low voice. "Listen." A few moments ticked by. "A dog."

"Why is that a—"

She cut him off. "You hear how the dog is barking? It's a hound." Rose stared at Adan. "They're searching."

"For what?" But Adan knew the answer.

Rose got up, dropped the blanket, and backed into the furthest recesses of the cave, her hand covering her mouth. "I won't go back. I can't go back."

Adan approached her. "I'll help you." He placed his hands on her shoulders, dark eyes worried.

His touch produced a shiver that raced through Rose's body, going all the way to her toes. The hound brayed again, the sound echoing up the canyon and the rock face of the mountain. She pulled away from him.

"What can you do?" Panic rose in her.

He spread his hands wide. "I don't know. But I've been hiding for a while now, so at least I have some practice."

Rose started to pace. She had found the cave easily. The searchers probably knew the place, as well. They also knew she needed to be near a source of water. And they had the hound. Was the dog Blue? A friendly animal, renowned for his ability to find missing livestock, and who, just a few months earlier, had located a three year old who had toddled off alone into the woods. There had been much celebration when the child was discovered unharmed, though the caretaker—a teenage girl like Rose—was severely punished, and forced to suffer a long, gruesome stint cleaning the birthing clinic.

"We have to leave," Rose said. "Gather up anything that shows we've been here."

A short time later, the backpack had been stuffed and zipped. The dog barked in the distance. Rose tried to remember that day when the child went missing. The story had been told repeatedly about how Blue had managed to find the little girl.

"An article of clothing," she said.

Adan cocked his head.

"They've given the dog something of mine to smell, so he can track me."

"So, even if we leave here, he can still find us?"

Rose thought for a moment then she bent down and untied her shoes. She walked to the pool and removed her socks. Then Rose stepped into the water, the cold seeping up her legs.

74

An hour later, Travis Forbush cautiously moved in behind the search party.

"Marshal Buttars!" he called out, lest he spook anyone who might be trigger-happy.

"That you, Deputy?" Buttars called out. "What the hell? I told you—"

"I thought you'd want to know right away." Forbush appeared from behind a massive red boulder. "They're bringing Bonnie back."

Buttars, set to ream the young man for ignoring his orders, dropped his fleshy arms to his sides.

"I headed after you as soon as I got the call," Forbush lied. He paused, waiting for some kind of backlash. But none came.

Buttars was quiet for a time. "I'm goin' down. You keep looking," he told the searchers. The marshal turned and passed Forbush. "Come on, Deputy."

"Wait . . . why don't I stay with the search party? They're losing your help. Really, I don't mind."

Buttars noticed for the first time that Forbush was

carrying a rifle. "You needed that to come and give me a message?" He raised his eyebrows.

"I . . . well . . ."

Buttars stared at the deputy for a moment. But all he could think about was poor Bonnie—her beautiful white skin and those long legs—the body she bared for him without the least hint of shame. He bit his lower lip, then looked at his deputy. "You don't belong here, boy! You're coming with me." Then he trudged down the trail and disappeared around a bend into a small copse of junipers.

Forbush paused for a moment, then dropped the rifle to his side and followed.

The searchers moved across a thick fall of scree. The footing was loose and difficult, but the dog seemed intent on continuing up the mountain. Bill Kimball stopped, then held up his arm, signaling to the other members of the party that they should gather.

Kimball shielded his eyes as he looked up the sheer rock face that confronted the group. The dog danced excitedly. "Easy, Blue. Hold on." He turned to the men. "There's a weeping wall up in that cave. Fresh water, cover. You can see a long way from up there. If I was hiding, I might well do it in a place like that."

Several of the other men nodded in agreement.

"But there's an easier way up there," Kimball said. "Over to the right, past all this loose rock is a trail, if my memory serves. It's a small one. Easy to miss if you're not lookin' for it. But it should take us right up to that cave, which is where Blue wants us to go. Don't ya, boy?" The dog strained at the leash.

The men formed a long queue, following Kimball and his dog. Seasoned trackers, they observed the area around them as they climbed, looking for any evidence that either of the teens had passed this way. They did not speak. Instead, they listened intently to the sounds around them, checking for any hint of voices on the wind.

When the trail thinned and wound around toward the front of the cave, Kimball paused, allowing the other men to catch up. He peered over the side of the cliff at the sheer rock face that plummeted down into a rushing stream. Then the dog and the men carefully edged their way along the narrow trail.

They entered the stunning cavern with the mass of columbine magically poking out of the rock floor. Bi-colored flowers—purple and white—reflected in the still pool. The dog barked, pulling at the lead. Kimball allowed the animal to roam about the stone room. At one point, he kneeled, swiping his finger across the floor. He touched his tongue.

"Whadayagot, Bill?" one of the trackers asked.

Kimball stood. "Just a bit a peanut butter, I think."

"Got 'em," Forbush said, finger on the trigger of the rifle.

"Not yet. Come on, Blue. Where'd they go?" Kimball extended the dog's lead. Blue sniffed the entire cave floor, then he stopped by the pool. The dog turned his head from side to side then pulled at the leash, leading the party toward the side of the cave opposite the trail on which the team had entered.

26

Rose's plan did not work. The idea had come to her when she recalled the conversation between her father and her brother, Joseph. The two had argued about whether a hound could track someone through a stream. Her father had insisted that walking through water makes the animal lose the trail. Her brother, meanwhile, countered that a well-trained animal could indeed stay on the scent for one simple reason. Humans shed millions of skin cells into the air. Shirtsleeves and pant legs work like giant saltshakers. The faster a person runs the more cells waft out. These cells are attacked by bacteria that give off an odor. This is the smell dogs follow. The scent is in the air, not on the ground. So crossing a river only slows the person down and the dog stays on course. Rose remembered wondering where Joseph had come by this scientific explanation. He had always been inquisitive. Something the two of them shared. At the time, she thought that perhaps Mr. Wayland had explained the process to her now long-gone brother.

Unfortunately for Rose, she couldn't believe her brother knew something her father did not. So, in the short time she'd concocted the plan, she assumed her father must have been right. By washing her feet in the pool and ditching her shoes, might she throw the animal off?

Adan had protested, saying the trail was too rough to go off barefooted, but Rose was stubborn. And then, when she had proposed leaving by the west side of the entrance, Adan had looked down over the cliff and backed away. The ledge was barely a hands width wide and led off into a blind turn.

"Then stay," she said, hoisting the pack onto her back.

They both heard the dog coming from down the trail. Rose had stepped out on the precipice, her face kissing the red rock, hands searching for something to grasp. And Adan, despite his better instincts, had followed her.

The ledge threaded around the rock face. They made slow progress on the harrowing crawl, inching their way along the thin sandstone lip. Rose lost her footing once, the pack appearing to drag her backwards. But she righted herself. Adan was suddenly nauseous, visions of her body splayed on the rocks below, vivid, bloody. Still he followed. At one point, Adan glanced toward the cave mouth. He desperately wanted to convince her to return, but the opening seemed horribly far away. And then, when he turned back, Rose had disappeared.

First Rose, then Adan entered a thin crevice, walls high and narrow that soon widened into an inverted V. The footing was difficult, especially with Rose shoeless, but then the floor flattened out. A wedge of blue appeared far above—sunlight slanting in a triangular beam. The cave snaked along smooth, twisting rock faces, a testament to the floodwaters that sometimes surged through what was a massive stone tube. Eventually, the cave emptied into an enormous room.

Rose and Adan stopped and stared at the turquoise pool that filled the grotto. Small green aquatic plants reached up to the beam of sunlight that sparkled on the surface. A spring caressed one wall, cascading over rocks, draining into the pool. Perhaps, this was the source of the water that seeped down and fed the weeping rock.

"Your feet are bleeding, Adan said. "Sit down. Let me take a look."

Rose dropped the backpack, sat, and placed both feet into the cold water, the sensation numbing and somehow pleasant. After a few minutes, suddenly exhausted, she lay down, placed her head on the backpack, and lifted her feet from the pool.

Adan reached over and gently took Rose's leg in his hands. He placed her foot in his lap. Feeling his touch, she resisted the urge to jump. He checked her toes. Rose closed her eyes.

He ran one finger down her arch. "You have a cut here," he said. "Not too bad. Only a little bleeding." He checked the other foot. "Two toes look bruised." He dried both feet with the bottom of his T-shirt.

Rose didn't want to move. Ever again. She was happy being right here with Adan holding her damaged feet. The waterfall burbled beside them. A black-chinned hummingbird darted above the water, stopped—tiny wings flitting almost imperceptibly—then darted away.

Then she heard the blow and saw Adan's face slam down onto the cavern floor.

77

Bill Kimball, rifle in one hand, loomed over Adan, his boot crushing the boy's hand. Rose jumped, scuttling away like a crab. But there was nowhere to go. "You touchin' that girl, boy? We don't do that here." Kimball kicked Adan in the ribs, causing him to coil into a tight ball.

"No, Mr. Kimball! Please stop!" Rose pleaded.

Kimball pointed the weapon at Adan. "And you, runnin' away, worryin' your daddy." He stared at Rose. "What were ya thinkin', girl?"

Rose did not reply. She stared at Adan.

"Now git up! Both of you!" Kimball glared at Rose, then the boy.

Adan tasted blood. His head buzzed. He tried to push himself off the smooth stone floor of the cavern, but was too dizzy.

Tears streamed down Rose's face. She got to her bare feet slowly. "Please," she reached out to Kimball. He eyed her for a moment. Adan shot his arm out and grabbed the man by the leg, jerking him off balance. Kimball dropped the rifle and fell into the turquoise pool.

"Go! Please, Adan!" Rose screamed.

"No!"

Kimball thrashed and then poked his head above the water. He got his footing and spit. Then he narrowed his eyes and climbed toward the boy, but the rocks in the bottom of the pool were coated with algae and he slipped, flailing in the water.

"Run away! They'll hurt you! They won't do anything to me!" she lied.

Adan ran through his options. If he stayed, could he do anything to help her? Kimball gasped and coughed up some water. What could he do? Not much alone. He needed help. He had to get away. Adan gazed at Rose. He didn't want to leave her.

Rose grabbed the backpack. "Take this and go." She threw the supplies at him.

Adan stared. His feet wouldn't move. "I can't leave you here." He turned and they both faced a dripping Bill Kimball who was climbing out of the pool.

"We won't go with you," Adan said, sounding braver than he felt. He'd hit and been hit in football games. Some of the boys who tried to take him down were bigger than this man, whose face was haggard, his mouth punctuated by several missing teeth. Adan stood in front of Rose.

"Put your shoes on, Rose," he said, not taking his eyes off the man.

Kimball wiped his face and shook the water off his sleeves. Silver droplets glistened in his beard. He surprised them both with a crooked smile. "I got eleven sons, boy, and there ain't one of 'em that can take me. So go head and try." He cracked his knuckles.

Adan—almost a head taller than the man—lunged.

He didn't see the knife. Kimball slashed at the boy, slicing a gash in Adan's upper arm. Blood ran freely, dripping from his fingers, spotting the stone floor.

Rose gasped. Adan wrapped both arms around Kimball's torso and shoved the man into a stone wall. The knife went up again and came down, this time aimed at the boy's spine. But it was Rose, in an effort to protect Adan, who got the edge of the blade, a strike to her chest just below the shoulder blade. She fell back, and, for a moment, both Kimball and Adan stood still. In shock.

"See what ya done, boy!" Kimball hissed. He pushed Adan away and went to Rose.

"Don't you touch her!" Adan yelled. Tears formed in his eyes.

Kimball snorted. He kneeled and peeled back the torn fabric of the two T-shirts she wore, one blue and one white. Rose's pupils were dilated, her breathing rapid.

Adan's mind raced. The rifle that had fallen by the turquoise pool beckoned him. He took two quick steps, picked the weapon up by the barrel, ran at Kimball, and swung it as hard as he could. The stock connected with the side of the man's head producing a loud crack.

Adan stood over Kimball's prostrate form. The dog barked from somewhere outside the cave. Rose's eyelids fluttered and she stared up him, her hand clutching the bloody wound. "Go, Adan, please." Her voice was barely audible. Adan turned and gaped at Rose, watching as a dark stain bloomed on her shirt.

"I can't—"

"You have to. Go before they get you."

78

Adan's chest heaved. He stopped for the first time since leaving the cave, where he'd left Bill Kimball bound securely with the dog leash. Once the hound had entered the cave, Adan had ordered the animal to sit, and it compliantly reclined by its master. It made no menacing moves or any attempt to abandon the fallen man.

Adan had no idea how long he'd been running. Although he was out of shape, he had forced himself into cross-country competition mode. The vision of Rose bleeding on the cavern floor was more than enough motivation for him to disregard the burning in his legs and lungs.

Now, he peered from the cover of the trees—the same spot into which he had seen Rose disappear when he had decided to follow her.

Would these people harm him? They had no reason. Certainly, the search party with the hound had been looking for Rose. They probably didn't even know he existed. Had Trak or Chase made any inquiries about his absence? Probably not. Why would they—strangers, really—care what happened to him?

To Adan, there was no choice. Rose was hurt, maybe dying. What did it matter if he was caught and taken back? He couldn't live with himself if he didn't do everything in his power to help her.

Adan burst from the trees, deftly maneuvering among the rocks and scattered roots on the trail, then crossing the sandy bottom of Short Creek in four long strides. He passed a massive cottonwood and a red boulder the size of an SUV. Further down the small trail he saw the ornate white fencing that enclosed a cemetery. Suddenly, the ground relaxed beneath his feet. He sank into a turned plot of earth, but quickly passed the spot without giving the disturbed ground another thought.

He needed to find people now—not avoid them. So he turned along the cemetery fence, his eyes on the roof of the Mercantile in the distance.

Half an hour later, Deputy Travis Forbush jumped from his chair. A boy stood in the doorway. Dried blood covered his shirt and jeans. The kid breathed in great gulps of air and bent forward, placing both hands on his knees.

"You hurt?" Forbush pushed a rolling desk chair toward the boy. "Sit down."

The deputy went to the small refrigerator, retrieved a cold bottle of water, and gave it to the boy. Then he checked for injuries.

Adan placed the container to his lips and took several long pulls. The fluid went down the wrong way and he started to cough.

"Easy. I'm Deputy Forbush. Tell me what happened?"

Adan pulled away as Forbush examined the wound on his upper arm. "I'm fine."

"You're not. You need medical care. No one's going to

hurt you." Forbush jerked his head to the door and waited a few moments before turning back to the boy.

Adan creased his brow. What was the man looking for? "You don't need to worry about me. But you have to get some people up the mountain to help." Adan coughed again.

"Who needs assistance?" The deputy stood up and reached for the phone on his desk. "Her name is Rose."

"Rose Madsen. You know where she is?"

Adan described the grotto and the cave's location above the weeping rock.

"And what are her injuries?" The deputy punched a number on the keypad.

"She was stabbed in the chest." Adan bent forward. He gripped his thighs. His head sagged.

Forbush glared and spoke into the phone. "We need a medical unit. We have to go up the mountain! Now!" He slammed the receiver back into the cradle. "You stabbed her!" He stepped toward Adan.

"No! It was that man with the dog—Kimball. We were fighting and he tried to stab me. Rose got in the way." Adan watched the deputy come toward him, but he was too tired to run or wipe the tears from his eyes.

79

The sun was midway down the sky when Rose Madsen was borne on a stretcher toward a white van parked in the field where the helicopter had landed earlier in the week. Word had gotten around town quickly that the runaway girl had been located, so a crowd had gathered. Logan Madsen hurried to his daughter's side, but his wife stayed back in the crowd, stiff, erect, hands clasped in front of her.

Brooke was drawn to the scene by the townspeople who drifted past her office window. By herself on the edge of the crowd, she watched a woman run toward the men who carried the stretcher. While dressed in the usual Colorado City female garb, the woman also sported a white medical-style jacket over her yellow prairie dress. She indicated that the men should stop where they were. They complied, and, after a short time—during which the woman examined the girl—she inserted a needle into the child's arm. Then the woman held up a clear pouch that was attached to a coil of tubing. The men were instructed to move toward the vehicle.

As they hurried by, Brooke caught a glimpse of the

child's face, the third time she had seen her. The first time—that flash of blue—was when the girl was off alone in the trees shortly after Bonnie's body had been discovered. The second time was at the cemetery when she and the girl had collided. And now Rose Madsen—everyone was whispering her name—was unconscious on a stretcher carried by six men.

The group arrived at the van. Someone opened the rear doors. Rose was placed inside and the medical woman, still holding the saline bag, climbed up beside her. There was no room in the vehicle for Logan Madsen, so when the vehicle pulled away, he was left in the dry field with the stretcher-bearers, hands at his sides, a look of desolation on his face.

Brooke stood frozen as the van drove away from the assembled crowd. She expected to see the driver take the road that led to SR389. Hurricane was the nearest town, and surely had better medical facilities than were available here in Colorado City. But the van stayed on Central Street.

The crowd dissipated. Brooke walked back toward the trailer. Why she felt a connection to this girl, she could not say. Still, a child had been harmed. Stabbed was the rumor. Had it been a family member? What was the girl running from?

Later, Brooke sat at her desk, but she couldn't concentrate on anything save the girl on the stretcher. While she could have placed a call, she decided to make the inquiry in person. Since she felt a sudden unexplained urgency, she decided to drive.

Brooke parked the beat-up Nissan Centra on the street, then mounted the steps and pushed at the door. The entrance to the Marshal's office was locked. She knocked.

No one answered. She stood on her tiptoes and peered into the office through one of the two small windows in the door. The main room was dark.

Then Brooke heard something. Pounding, and a voice, but the sounds were coming from the back. She went down the steps, around the side of the office, and faced two small windows. Blinds had been drawn preventing her from seeing inside. Brooke continued around the building.

"Hello," she called at another set of windows. These had black security bars inserted into the brick and were made of thick Plexiglas. Brooke stuck her small hand through the grillwork and knocked on the window.

A face appeared out of the darkness. The apparition stared.

Brooke jumped then composed herself. "Adan?" she asked on a hunch.

The boy inside squinted and turned his head, as if he were unsure of what she said.

"Adan!" Brooke said the name in a louder voice.

For a moment the boy looked defeated. Then he lifted his head and stared at Brooke. "Get me out of here."

80

Chase and Trak leaped from the doctor's truck, slamming the doors behind them. Both carried dark bags. Elizabeth Flake stood at the entrance to the Colorado City Clinic and Birthing Center in a blood-spattered green surgical gown, the hem of her canary-colored prairie dress peeking above her shoes.

"As I told you on the phone, she's lost a lot of blood," the midwife said as they hurried down the hall. "I've tried to stitch the wound, but it's not working." She pushed open the doors to the birthing clinic's main room. Bright lights illuminated what appeared to be a clean, though somewhat dated medical facility.

"Put the bag there on the counter, Trak," Chase ordered. "Then leave. There's nothing you can do in here right now."

Trak glanced at the pale child on the stainless steel gurney, her skin translucent, devoid of all color. "Are you sure, Chase? I was a medic."

"Go!" Then the doctor softened his voice as he scrubbed up in a white porcelain sink. "I know you were a medic, my friend. "I'll call if I need you. Wait outside."

Trak nodded and backed out the door. His phone rang.

Ten minutes later, Brooke appeared. She stared at the double doors to the birthing clinc, and then turned to Trak. "How's the girl? Rose. Her name is Rose."

"She's lost a lot of blood."

"I'm surprised to see you here."

"Beth Flake is a midwife who Chase and I went to high school with. She sometimes calls him when there are difficult cases."

"Aren't there any doctors here?" Brooke asked.

"Not on a regular basis. And in this case," Trak nodded toward the door, "Chase was the one who could get here the fastest."

They went outside and sat on the concrete steps. Neither spoke. Two canyon maples over thirty feet high flanked the walkway leading to the clinic entrance. Their bright green leaves rustled in the soft breeze. High clouds streaked the sky.

"I want to find out what happened to Rose," Brooke finally said. She told Trak about her previous interactions with the girl. "She was running away from something. It takes a lot for a child to decide to leave home, to consider that the unknown is better than what they're dealing with."

Trak's eyes met Brooke's. "The poison they know is preferable to the one they don't know."

"Exactly. It's amazing what children can put up with." She stared at him for a moment and resisted a sudden urge to touch his bronzed face. Instead, she reached into her back pocket and drew out a piece of folded paper. "It's only black and white. They didn't spring for a color printer." She handed the sheet to Trak.

"That's him!" he said.

"His name is Adan Reyes."

Brooke explained what she knew about the boy. "And now, he's locked up in the marshal's jail."

"Why?" Trak creased his brow.

"I don't know. Maybe he stabbed the girl."

"I don't believe that for a minute."

"Considering his past, I don't think he'd harm the girl either, but remember, the boy was in foster care, and those kids come with baggage."

"You didn't say how he wound up as a ward of the state," Trak said.

"That's because I don't know. His caseworker is still trying to locate that piece of information."

"You're kidding."

"I'm not. She's young and new to the job, and, frankly, seems overwhelmed."

A silvery-blue Steller's jay alighted in one of the trees and squawked above them. Brooke watched the bird for a moment. "So, what are we going to do?"

"I have to wait here until I know Chase doesn't need anything," Trak answered. "Then we are going to find the marshal."

81

Forty-five minutes later, a white Chevy Tahoe pulled to the curb and stopped. Logan Madsen and his wife Bliss got out and walked between the towering maples toward the entrance of the medical clinic. Trak and Brooke rose from the steps and watched the couple approach.

"Her parents?" Brooke said quietly.

"Probably." Trak nodded at the couple. The man returned the greeting, while the woman—long mud-brown dress touching the tops of her shoes, chin in the air—ignored them.

As they mounted the steps, Chase pushed open the doors. Blood dotted his green surgical gown. A matching cotton cap covered his hair. "Mr. and Mrs. Madsen? I'm Doctor Allred."

"How is Rose?" Logan Madsen asked.

"She is out of imminent danger. The wound to her chest was deep. I have cleaned it and stitched her up, but she needs to see a specialist. She's lost a lot of blood, but Beth Flake and I have stabilized her. We've called for an ambulance to take Rose to St. George for further treatment."

"Absolutely not!"

Chase stared at Bliss Madsen. "But she has to go. The stitching I've done is a temporary solution. There is also the possibility of infection."

"You will not take my daughter away from here. She will not go . . . out there."

Logan Madsen placed his hand on his wife's arm. She pulled away. "Is there not something that can be done for Rose here?"

"No," Chase said. "She needs better equipped facilities, and she must be seen by a vascular specialist."

Bliss Madsen folded her arms across her chest. "We will not let you take her."

Chase pinched the bridge of his nose. "Mrs. Madsen, your daughter is still not out of the woods. She could die. Do you understand?"

"Then that is God's will. Perhaps that will be the child's punishment for running away."

Logan Madsen's jaw dropped. "Surely, you don't mean that." His wife shot him a poisonous glance.

Brooke, who had observed the exchange, squinted her eyes and stepped forward, but Trak put his hands on her shoulders and squeezed. She got the message and did not intercede.

Chase removed the surgical cap exposing a rumpled shock of white hair, and ran a hand over his head. "The ambulance is already on the way. We will take your daughter to the hospital in St. George. Feel free to follow us."

"You can't take her without our permission, and we will not allow it!" Bliss Madsen barked.

Chase stared at Logan Madsen. Their eyes met.

"Take her, Doctor," Rose's father finally said. "Save my daughter. Make her well again."

"No!" Bliss shrieked. "Do you want her to be in that world among the devils? It's better for her to die here among the righteous than to be tainted by outsiders."

Logan Madsen stared at the ground, then raised his eyes, and leveled them at his wife. "The most important thing is that Rose live." He turned to the doctor. "We will follow you."

"I will not go."

"Then I will go myself. I will not have Rose wake up in a strange place alone."

"But—"

"And you will say nothing more, woman!"

Bliss Madsen looked as if she'd been slapped.

"Now get in the truck, Mother. I'll drive you home." He turned to Chase. "I'll be back in a few minutes, Dr. Allred. Please don't leave without me."

82

"Holy shit! These people are crazier than I thought," Brooke blurted out after Rose's parents had departed.

"I'm going to go clean up." Chase turned to leave.

"How long will it be before the ambulance gets here?" Trak asked.

"St. George is about forty miles away. They left about ten minutes ago. Do the math."

"We need to make a quick trip over to the Marshal's office."

"You want the keys? the doctor said wearily. "They're inside. I'll get them."

"We'll take mine." Brooke pulled the keys from her jeans.

Trak glanced at the battered Nissan.

"Good luck getting in that, big guy," Chase said. "Be back in half an hour, or we'll leave without you."

Travis Forbush looked up from his desk. "Can I help you?"

"We'd like to see the young man you have back there in your cell," Brooke said.

Forbush leaned back in his chair and clasped his hands. "Can't do that."

"Why not?" Trak asked. "He's the boy we reported missing, isn't he?"

"I don't know who he is. He has no identification."

"Here, I have a picture." Brooke produced a folded piece of printer paper from her back pocket. "It says here he's Adan Reyes, an underage child missing from a group foster care facility in Phoenix."

"All I know is that the boy is wanted in a crime. He stabbed a girl." Forbush stood and walked to the front of his desk.

"What proof do you have that he stabbed her?" Trak said.

"Not your business."

"The boy is my business, though. I'm his caseworker," Brooke lied. "I have a right to speak with him, and I demand you let me do that right now."

Forbush stared at the bird-like woman with the red-hair. He picked at the skin on his thumb and glanced at the round, black and white clock on the wall. "OK. You've got five minutes."

The deputy led them through a short hallway past two offices with cheap, dark wood paneling. He unlocked a door at the end of the passage, inside of which was a small cell closed off with floor-to-ceiling bars. Adan Reyes lay face up on a thin, striped mattress that covered a flat surface jutting out from one wall.

"Adan," Brooke said.

For a moment, the boy didn't speak. Then he sighed and got up. "Yes."

"We're here to help," she said.

Adan laughed. Tears seeped into the corners of his eyes. "What does that mean?"

"I'm a caseworker for—"

He didn't let her finish. "Child Protective Services? I don't know which is worse, you people, or these crazies here." He waved his arm.

"Careful, boy," Forbush said.

"They won't even tell me what I'm doing in here. Don't I have the right to a lawyer if there gonna lock me up? Don't they have to tell me why they're holding me?"

"They claim you stabbed a girl," Trak said.

"Rose! I didn't stab Rose. The guy with the dog did. The same one that stabbed me." Adan turned his arm toward them.

"Has he had any medical care?" Brooke asked upon seeing the still bloody gash.

Forbush didn't answer.

"I demand you release this boy to me." Brooke's face was redder than her hair.

The deputy checked his watch. "Time for you to go."

"We'll be back," Trak said to Adan.

Forbush hurried them back down the passage and to the front door. He looked again at the clock on the wall. Trak stared at the deputy.

"Go," Forbush said. "You need to leave now."

83

Deputy Travis Forbush didn't have a lot of time. The fact that the caseworker and Trak Benally had appeared unannounced muddied things up. He looked at his watch again. He needed to attend the viewing.

He picked up a backpack he'd found in the office closet. Everything was there. He zipped the bag closed, looped the container over his shoulder, and switched off the lights. He walked down the now dark hallway and unlocked the cell-room door.

Adan stood. "Why did you turn off the lights?"

Forbush stared from the other side of the bars. "I'm going to a funeral viewing."

"OK." Adan felt an upsetting twitch in his stomach.

Forbush reached into his pocket and unlocked the cell door. Then he shoved the gate open and stepped inside.

Adan backed away, but there was nowhere for him to go. He was pressed up against a brick wall. Slowly, Forbush removed the backpack from his shoulder and let the bag drop to the floor. "What are you—"

"Shhh," the deputy placed one finger to his lips. Then

he walked out, pushed the cell gate shut, and disappeared down the hall.

Adan sat in the dark for what seemed like a long time. Then he heard a door close, making a surprisingly loud noise. He jumped. Had the deputy left the building? He rose and paced the small room, staring at the entrance to the cell. Had he imagined it? He stepped up to the steel bars and placed his hand on the cold metal. Slowly, he pushed the cage door open.

Adan backed away. Why had the deputy left the door unlocked? He gazed at the floor outside the cell. And why was a backpack sitting there? Adan cautiously stepped through the doorway, expecting the deputy to tackle him at any moment. He reached for the bag, which he dragged inside the cell. He unzipped the backpack and found the container filled with power bars and plastic bottles of water.

Adan stuffed one of the granola bars in his mouth and swallowed the food half chewed. Did the deputy want him to run? If not, then why leave the cell door open and a bag of provisions? The bigger question was why was the deputy helping him? He'd seen enough police shows on TV to know that this behavior was not normal. What would the deputy gain by allowing Adan to get away?

He tried to think rationally, but the last few days and the blow on the head had left him mentally and physically exhausted. He reached in the backpack for another nut bar and found a piece of paper folded into a square. He smoothed out the page and saw a simple map leading to SR389. An arrow indicated the direction to Hurricane.

Adan crumpled the map in his hand. This made no sense. Then he thought of the tiny CPS worker. If he stayed and convinced the police that he did not stab Rose, they would let him out. But then the CPS worker would be there waiting to gather him up and send him back to Phoenix.

His head was splitting. He looked at the open cell door. Adan stood, grasping the backpack, and walked out. He moved down the hall silently and gripped the handle of the next door. He turned the knob and that door opened as well.

All the lights in the narrow hallway were off, but there was enough ambient light coming in the windows to illuminate the passageway. Once in the main office, Adan paused, expecting someone to grab him. But no one did. He quickly stepped across the room and slowly eased open the front door. He glanced up and down the street, but saw no one, neither a person, nor a moving vehicle of any kind. He slipped out the door, thought briefly about the map, and oriented himself. Then, sticking to the shadows, he headed south on Central Street.

He did not see the dark car that pulled out behind him.

84

Marshal Sterling Buttars stood with his two wives, welcoming mourners to a small room off the main temple. As was customary when a death occurred, everyone in town who was able attended the viewing.

The funeral director had done what he could to repair the child's bashed-in skull, but Buttars, after seeing the corpse of his third wife—pasty and resembling plastic, a dent in her once pretty forehead—ordered the coffin closed. He had gone against precedent, lowering the ceremonial white veil—a cultural tradition steeped in mystery—over Bonnie's face himself.

In a daze, he accepted condolences and vaguely heard his wives doing the same.

"A lovely girl . . ."

"Such a sad thing . . ."

"Thank you for your kind words . . ."

Buttars shook the hands of men and women he couldn't name. There was a time when he recognized just about everyone in town. But his brain didn't seem to be reacting as it should.

He glanced at his wives and saw one whispering to the other behind her hand. He'd had little to do with them in the bedroom since his marriage to Bonnie. He had been sure that the women would be delighted that the Prophet had assigned him a new wife. With three spouses, the entire family was ensured a spot in the Celestial Kingdom. How had everything gone so terribly wrong?

Whenever Buttars had been down before, little Mouse had always been there, wagging her cute curly tail, eager to cheer him up. He often thought he saw the little dog scampering around the corners in the office or out in the field near the house where he used to toss a tiny red ball that she would joyfully ran after, short legs flying. Then she'd find the toy and bring it right back for him to throw again.

"I'm sorry for your loss, Sterling."

The Prophet stood before him in a perfectly pressed silk suit. Although Buttars was unaware of the origin of the outfit, Eldon Higbee wore an Italian-made William Fioravanti custom ensemble that cost more than Buttars made in six months.

The marshal forced his shoulders back. "Thank you, sir. I appreciate you coming."

"I'd like to chat, if you have a moment. I realize this is not the ideal time or place, but it is rather important." Higbee graced him with a greasy smile.

"Of course." Buttars followed the Prophet to the undertaker's office.

"Go ahead and close those," Higbee said, nodding at the double doors.

Buttars complied.

"Now, I need to know where we stand with regard to

the missing boy. I don't like surprises, as you know." The smile again.

"Didn't Deputy Forbush contact you?"

"No." Higbee sat in an overstuffed, wingback chair and looked up at Buttars.

"I have been very busy with my wife's—"

Higbee held up his hand. "While I commiserate with your loss, Marshal, that does not exonerate you from your duties."

"Of . . . of course not, sir." His mind raced. For a moment he couldn't remember where the boy was. "In the cell. The boy is in our custody."

Higbee jumped from the chair. "That's not what I asked you to do!"

"I know. He turned himself in. The girl, Rose Madsen, was injured and needed assistance, and he came to tell us where she was."

"Bliss's daughter?" Higbee composed himself. "Yes, I heard there'd been an incident. But again, Marshal, I had no word on this from you. So, the question here is, are you capable of handling your job? Right now, it doesn't appear so."

"But—" Butters glanced toward the door.

Higbee spread his hands wide. "You are now again seeking that ever important third wife, Marshal. This is something you must earn. So please, take care of the boy."

"There is a plan in place."

"Good. I look forward to the closure of this problem shortly."

"Yes sir."

"You may go, Sterling. And again, my condolences."

"Thank you, sir."

"Oh, wait. Where is the Madsen girl?" Higbee asked.

"She has been taken to St. George for further medical care. I spoke with the ambulance driver when they came to pick her up."

Higbee creased his brow. "And again, no one tells me anything."

"I . . . I'm sorry . . ."

Higbee waved one hand in the air. "Just go!"

85

Rose opened her eyes and blinked. A window with vertical blinds framed the night. She was groggy. She felt sick to her stomach and tried to get up to find a bathroom.

"Wait, child. You need to stay in bed," a lilting female voice said.

Rose felt someone ease her forward. She threw up into a stainless steel bowl cradled in dark brown hands. When there was nothing left in her stomach, a cup of cool water appeared at her lips.

"Just a little now," the musical voice said.

A hand rubbed gentle circles on Rose's back, then she was eased against soft cool pillows.

A while later, Rose awoke again.

"Are you feeling better, sweetheart?"

The question came from a dark-skinned woman with high arched brows and almond-shaped eyes that sparkled when she smiled, the warmest smile Rose had ever seen.

"Are you still feeling sick to your stomach?"

"No. Who are—" Rose was interrupted by strange beeps and whirring sounds.

"Those are just some machine noises. We are monitoring you, since you had surgery."

"I don't remember." Rose reached to the left side of her chest.

"The surgeon gave you some medicine that made you sleep. That's why you were feeling a little sick in your belly." The woman, who was wearing a flowery jacket over blue scrubs, patted her own stomach.

"What's your name?" Rose asked.

"My, how rude of me not to tell you sooner. I am Nurse Tanice Breeze. You can call me Tanice, if you'd like."

"I've never heard a name like that before."

"I am from Jamaica. Do you know where that is?"

Rose shook her head.

"It is a beautiful island in the Caribbean Sea. The ocean there is the prettiest in the world. More shades of blue and turquoise than you can count."

"Do all the people in Jamaica talk like you?"

"Many do, yes." Tanice smiled as she checked the various devices to which Rose was attached. "Now, are you hungry?"

"No, I don't think so."

"When you're ready, I'll get you something to eat."

Tanice pointed at a small button attached to the metal bars on the side of the bed. "When you are hungry, or if you need anything, just press this button and I'll be here straightaway." She patted Rose's arm.

After the nurse left, Rose stared at the ceiling. She was fairly certain that she was no longer in Colorado City. One thing she was sure of was that she'd never seen anyone like Tanice Breeze at home. So where was she, and how did she get here?

Rose's whole body ached, especially the area around her upper chest and left shoulder that was covered with a thick layer of bandages. A clear bag of fluid hung above the side of the bed. A long tube snaked down from the bag and ended at a needle that had been inserted into her arm on the inside of her elbow.

Rose understood surgery. A doctor had cut into her. Tanice was her nurse. Was this, then, the outside world? That these people were devils conspiring to corrupt her was a difficult idea to comprehend. Perhaps the doctor had even saved her life. Why would a devil do such a thing? And Tanice, seemingly all gentle sweetness, was kinder than any of her family members had ever been—save her father.

She briefly considered the idea of escaping this place, where wickedness and sin probably lurked around every corner. But a wave of exhaustion overcame her and she couldn't even make her arms and legs move.

Rose fell asleep and dreamed of Adan and the cave, where the purple and white columbines and maidenhair ferns grew beneath the weeping rock.

86

Adan looked behind him. He sensed someone watching, but saw no one on the dark street. He loped in the shadows, staying off the road, following the map with directions that pointed toward Hurricane.

The two-story house ahead, like the others he passed, showed dark windows. Where was everyone? Surely, at night, people were in their homes, lights on, eating or reading or doing whatever it was families did in this strange little town. Although Adan was unsure of the time, he imagined that somewhere his mother was hovering at a table, watching other people eat. He had often tried to convince her to sit down and enjoy the meal with him, especially since there were only the two of them. His father had gone off in search of a better-paying job when Adan was in elementary school. At first he sent money to them every week, but then the envelopes stopped coming. They had never heard from his papa again.

Adan guessed his father was dead. But there was a possibility that he had taken up with another woman, and that somewhere, he had brothers and sisters. But when he remembered the way his parents used to look at one another, he doubted his father would have abandoned them intentionally.

The man had worked so hard to provide for Adan and his mother. As a small boy, his father had once taken him into the fields where Adan had played among the grapevines. It had all seemed a grand adventure to the child sitting in the shade of the bright green leaves strung up on either side of the rows, thick clusters of purple fruit hanging down that his father gently plucked and placed in heavy cardboard boxes. Every once in a while, Adan was given a handful of the fat globes. Sweet juice squished in his mouth and ran down his small chin. The workers were allowed a break for lunch, and the men and women would sit in the shadow of several sprawling oak trees. Adan's father carried his lunch in a plastic bag—a meal he shared with the boy sitting cross-legged on the ground.

Adan's foot hit something, a root perhaps, and he pitched forward, but he straightened and stayed on his feet. If the map was correct, the next right turn should lead him to SR389.

He glanced behind him, out of habit now, and saw a car moving slowly in his direction. Another house loomed ahead, this one with a single light shining on the top floor. He darted to the side of the home, a large structure with a wrap-around porch and a garden. He flattened himself against the wooden siding among a row of tall sunflowers, their brown disc centers and golden petals like giant eyes, watching.

The car paused, then continued creeping down the street. Adan searched the area and darted behind the house. He almost tripped over a dog bowl and a chain with one end tethered to a tree and the other to nothing—the only remains of the animal that had once lived there. Adan envisioned the handicapped man forced to shoot his golden dog. The blood. Still, he was glad there was no creature here now to give him away.

He bolted through two more backyards and into an open area. There was a sign pointing the way to SR389. He ran faster. Bright headlights splashed the road. Adan took the turn, backpack bouncing, holding him down. If he dropped the provisions, he could run more freely, but without water, he might die. He knew that now.

A vehicle—big—a semi perhaps, roared past up ahead on what was surely the road to Hurricane. The car behind him sped up.

It wasn't his imagination. He was being followed.

Frantic, he hunted for cover. A thicket of bushy foliage appeared to his right. He took a chance and bolted inside.

The car pulled to a stop close to where Adan had entered the scrub. He held his breath and watched as a person exited the vehicle. The man removed a jacket, stepped in front of the car, and scanned the area. On his hip, illuminated by the headlights, was a holstered handgun.

87

Trak, Brooke, and Chase sat at one of the outside tables at the café. Holly lay curled at Trak's feet. Chase pushed back his chair and gazed at the night sky, the food on his plate untouched.

"You all right?" Trak asked.

"I'm exhausted. That girl—"

"Rose," Brooke said. "Her name is Rose."

"Yes, Rose." The doctor let out a long breath. "Another fifteen, twenty minutes, I think we might have lost her."

"But she's fine now, right?" Trak asked.

"The surgeon over in St. George said she's doing great."

The question is, who stabbed the child?" Brooke, with a newfound appetite, dug into a thick patty melt with glossy grilled onions, glued together with Swiss cheese.

"Last I heard, they're still blaming the boy," Chase said.

Trak placed both hands on the table. "I realize I only knew the kid for a short time, but damn, I just don't believe he's that vicious."

Brooke put the thick sandwich back on her plate, finished chewing, and swallowed. "How'd they catch him?"

Trak looked at her for a moment and grinned. Then he reached over and wiped a dab of catsup off her chin. Brooke blushed a color that nearly matched the condiment.

"You two want to be alone?" Chase said with a tired smile.

Trak raised an eyebrow. "Would it matter if we did?"

"Touché. But as you know, my friend, considering your history with red—"

"That's enough, Chase."

Brooke stared at Trak.

"It's nothing. Really. Let's talk about something else. You asked how they caught him. I don't know."

"Neither do I," Chase said.

"OK." She eyed them both." So what happens now? I mean with Adan and Rose? There will certainly be a criminal investigation of some kind. After all, the girl was assaulted."

"I guess the marshal's office will do an investigation." Trak sipped his beer.

"The marshal?" She burst out laughing. "I get the feeling that's like giving one bullet to Barney Fife."

Trak smiled. "I wouldn't have taken you for a Mayberry fan. Aren't you a little young?"

"It was my dad's favorite show. I'm pretty sure I've seen every episode. Anyway, his deputy refused to answer any questions I asked. I've never had such a hard time dealing with law enforcement. They're supposed to help, especially when kids are concerned."

"The problem is that the marshal and almost all of the folks over there are completely into the Fundamentalist thing," Chase said.

"What does that mean?" Brooke held her hands out, palms up.

"That they'll do whatever Eldon Higbee tells them to," Trak said.

Brooke reached for her glass of wine and took a drink. "I've seen him on TV. He's creepy."

"To them, Higbee is practically God," Chase said.

"There has to be someone else who can look into criminal activity there." Brooke put the wine glass on the table and leaned on her forearms.

"The Mohave County Attorney's office has a special investigator, a Victim's Advocate." Chase stabbed at a salad topped with red and yellow cherry tomatoes and sliced avocado.

"Scott Parker?" Trak said.

"That's him. His job is to see that victims are treated fairly and that they receive support, crisis intervention, and referrals to local programs and services. He's got an office over on Central Street."

"Maybe we should go talk to him," Trak suggested.

"He might be helpful with regard to Rose," Brooke said. "The child's not only dealing with being stabbed, she ran away. Why? What was happening in her home that made her take that drastic step?"

"You want to talk to her?" Trak asked.

"Of course, I do."

"Chase, do you think Parker can also help Andy?"

"Adan." Brooke patted his arm.

"Sorry. Adan." His forearm tingled where she touched

him. Why couldn't Chase take a hint? He turned to his friend and was greeted with a grin. He sighed.

"As far as we know, Adan is not a victim," Chase said. "So I'm not sure Parker can do him any good. But since the people in Colorado City don't have a good track record with teenage boys, it's probably worth a shot."

Brooke tilted her head. "What do you mean?"

"Haven't you ever heard of the Lost Boys?" Chase asked.

"No."

"When boys get to a certain age in Colorado City, usually around twelve, decisions are made concerning their qualifications to become important members of the church," Chase explained. "Not all boys make the cut. When they become teenagers and it's obvious that they're not suitable Fundamentalist material, they become expendable."

"And there's another problem," Trak said. "If you're a teenage girl, who are you going to be attracted to? Not the sixty-year-old guy you're given to in marriage. Those teenage boys are a liability to the Fundamentalists. They distract the girls."

"And . . . they are driven out." Chase spread his hands. "Sent away. Many end up in the streets. They're mostly uneducated and unfamiliar with the outside world."

"How the hell do they get away with this?" Brooke demanded, as if the two men at the table had the answers.

Chase frowned. "It's complicated."

88

Adan covered his mouth with his hand and tried to stifle his instinct to cry out.

The man—he was tall and well muscled with a head of light-colored hair—went back to the driver's side door, reached inside, and shut off the headlights and motor. He glanced up and down the street, then walked deliberately toward the outcrop of bushy foliage where Adan was hiding.

Adan moved farther back and into a grove of trees, half-dead junipers, victims of the long-term draught. He tripped over a large limb, a casualty of a fire or perhaps a lightning strike, and fell on his hands and knees, but kept his head up, looking and listening for his pursuer. Rooting among the rocks and plant litter, he reached around for something with which to defend himself. He grabbed onto a short, thick branch.

"Adan," a voice called. "Come on. I'm not gonna hurt you. I'm with—"

Adan bolted, running blindly, holding the branch like the baton in a relay race, expecting a bullet in the back. He dropped the backpack. The trees gave way to an open area and a trench that paralleled SR389. He leaped into what was an irrigation ditch and lay flat. He gulped in air, the sound of his gasps deafening in his ears. As he would in a cross-country race, Adan forced himself to control his breathing: slow and steady.

He heard steps coming toward him at an even clip, the man making no effort to conceal his approach. Adan moved into a crouched position. The steps stopped above him. He would have just one shot.

"Adan?"

A head appeared over the edge of the channel and—like a batter hitting a pitch high in the zone—Adan swung. But there was no sweet-spot sound when the tree limb connected with flesh and bone. Blood erupted from the man's nose and mouth. For a moment he gazed at the boy and appeared confused. Then he tumbled on top of Adan and they sprawled into the dry ditch.

Adan pushed the man away, blood covering his hands and shirt. He froze. Had he killed the man? Did he care? All he knew was that he didn't want to die. He waited, holding the tree limb firmly in his right hand. If the man moved, he'd hit him again.

A short time passed. The man breathed, but only faintly. Adan kicked the man over with his legs, rolling him onto his back. He did not move or open his eyes. Adan leaned over and placed the stick where he could reach it quickly. Then he unlatched the man's weapon. He grasped the grip of the Glock 40 and slipped the gun from the holster. Then Adan took one more look at the man's broken face and ran.

With the weapon pointing down, Adan retraced his steps. He glanced back periodically to see if he was being followed, but saw nothing. He cut into the trees, searching for the backpack, but there was less light penetrating inside the wooded area, so he didn't find it. He slowed his pace.

A great rumbling sounded. Scattered light pierced the darkness in the grove, illuminating the backpack ten yards ahead. Then the light and sound disappeared as another semi-truck passed by on SR389.

Adan scrambled to the provisions. He unzipped the backpack and placed the Glock 44 inside. He grabbed a bottle of water and drank, forcing himself to take slow, measured gulps. He considered the extra weight and dropped the plastic container to the ground. But then remembered how important those empty bottles had been to him and Rose in the cave.

Rose. Where was she? Did she live or had she died? He forced the thought away. He didn't know how long he'd be out here. He did not want to ever again suffer from dehydration or heat sickness. He picked up the empty bottle and dropped it into the pack, then put his arms through the shoulder straps.

Hurricane was a little over twenty miles away. They were still looking for him, so he could not stay on the road. Adan closed his eyes and tried to think of the lay of the land between the two towns, much like he would consider the course prior to a cross-country race. There were vast areas of flat open land, rocky cliffs, rolling hills, fields spotted with conical evergreens, patches of ancient rusted farm equipment, and—near Hurricane—steep switchbacks leading down into the valley.

Adan opened his eyes. Moonlight played along the road. He moved off into the brush, away from the beams cast by passing cars and trucks. His pace was even. He told himself that this was just another race.

89

The next morning, Brooke was ushered into Scott Parker's office, which, as it turned out, was only a short walk from the CPS trailer. The white-haired man in his mid-fifties met Brooke at the door and offered her a cup of coffee.

"Thank you for seeing me on such short notice," she said.

"No problem at all." Parker pointed Brooke to a padded chair and then sat behind his desk. "I need all the help I can get up here. I didn't know we were getting a new CPS worker. In fact, I was going to call your office to see if you had any possible abuse reports on Bonnie Buttars."

"The girl who was killed. Was she murdered?"

"She was."

"Any idea who did it?" Brooke asked.

Parker scratched the back of his neck. "I can't share that with you."

"On-going investigation, yes?"

"Correct."

Brooke blew on the scorching hot coffee. "I don't recall Bonnie's name in any of the reports. But I'll check the files again."

"I'd appreciate it," Parker said.

"How'd you end up here?"

"I used to be a police officer, but I got shot and stuck with permanent desk duty. When I learned about what was going on here, I wanted to help."

"I had no idea what this place was all about before I got here." Brooke shook her head.

Parker spread his hands. "I have three daughters."

"Ah, I understand."

"When you have a guy like Eldon Higbee handing out girls, some as young as thirteen, like they're some kind of carnival prize, well, if you'll excuse me, it really pisses me off."

"As I'm sure you know, as a CPS worker, I'm here to provide services to children and their families. To make sure that children are raised in positive, safe, and loving environments. In my experience, most parents want to take good care of their children. It's just that sometimes, they don't know how. Maybe it's because they're too young themselves, or maybe there's a history of abuse that's been passed down, or maybe there's substance abuse issues or problems associated with poverty. But this?" She waved her hand in the air. "I have never dealt with anything like it."

"You'll get no argument from me. I agree completely," Parker said. "I'm a Special Criminal Investigator. I gather evidence for prosecution. Which is tough, since almost no one here will talk to me. I get called devil a lot."

"I have the same problem. I have fifty-seven open cases of possible abuse, and I haven't been able to gather information on any of them."

"Let me guess. Bob Wayland made those reports."

"He did. But I can't find him," Brooke said.

"They fired him when they closed down the school. And he complained loudly. And then he just disappeared. I haven't been able to locate him, either."

"It's very strange." Brooke sipped her coffee.

"Eldon Higbee told his followers to pull their kids out of the public schools so they wouldn't have to associate with apostates. That's anybody who doesn't subscribe to Mormon Fundamentalists beliefs. Tax dollars were still going into the school district, but the money was being funneled to Higbee. I heard he went and purchased an airplane with some of it. So, the government put the district into receivership."

"I saw the main school all fenced up. Goats eating the shrubs. Have you heard about the situation with Rose Madsen?"

"The girl who was stabbed? That's all I know," he said. "But again, it's almost impossible to get anyone to talk about what happens here."

"She's at the hospital in St. George," Rose said. "I spoke with the doctor who first worked on her."

"What's the doctor's name?"

"Chase Allred."

He nodded. "I've met him."

"Anyway, Chase said she's doing well. So, do you want to take a drive over to St. George? You can talk to her about the assault, and I'd like to know the reasons she ran away."

"I didn't know she ran away," Parker said, pulling open a drawer and grabbing his keys. "Let's go. I'll drive."

90

"You must release her to us!" Bliss Madsen said.

Nurse Tanice Breeze stood her ground. "You cannot just walk in here and take this child. Only the doctor can release her."

Rose, still attached to multiple tubes and wires, stared wide-eyed at her parents. That her mother was even in this place—beyond the confines of Eden, mixing with apostates—was astonishing. Bliss Madsen glared at the Jamaican nurse, who turned away to adjust a needle in the crook of Rose's arm.

"Do not touch her again!" Bliss stepped toward the nurse.

"Wait!" Logan Madsen moved between them. "We will have the proper paperwork in just a moment. Sit down, Mother. There, in that chair." He pointed to a seat by the window. "We will wait for the lawyer."

The women eyed one another.

Two men entered the room. One was Rose's surgeon. The other announced that his name was Jeb Farnsworth, an attorney for the Madsen's.

"This is not in the best interest of the child," the doctor said.

"Her parents have a legal right to take her home, if she's out of danger." The attorney adjusted a thick pair of glasses. "You yourself said Rose was doing extremely well. So, her parents will now be taking her back to the clinic nearer to their own home."

"But it's better if we watch over her for a few more days. There is always the possibility of infection."

"Please, Doctor. Don't insult my intelligence. Seventy-five thousand patients die every year from infections they acquire in the hospital. Rose will be safe in the much smaller setting the Colorado City clinic can provide. Fewer patients, fewer chances of a nasty bug infecting her wound." The attorney turned to Tanice Breeze. "An ambulance is waiting to take Rose home." His forced grin barely sufficed for a smile. "So prepare her for the ride."

Jeb Farnsworth turned and left the room. The surgeon followed. Rose could hear them arguing as they departed down the hallway.

"Mother." Rose reached out.

Bliss Madsen stood, but did not move toward her daughter. Then she lifted her chin and exited the room. Rose's arms fell to the bed. She turned to her father. Tears pooled in the corner of his eyes. He stepped over and embraced his daughter as best he could through the hoses and wires that tethered her to the bed. "You want to come home, Rose, don't you?"

She felt his warm breath on her ear. Her chest still throbbed and an almost constant headache—despite the painkiller that moved through a tube and into her arm—kept her on edge. Did she want to go home? Her father leaned back and their eyes met. He loved her. Daisy loved her. And there was little Iris. But there was nothing, and no one else in that town that she couldn't live without seeing again. Yet Rose could not get those words out.

"Let me prepare her," Tanice Breeze said in her gentle, singsong voice. "Give us a few minutes."

Logan Madsen released his daughter and nodded. "Thank you," he said addressing the nurse.

After he left, Tanice Breeze took Rose's hand in hers and sat on the bed beside her. "Do you want to go back there?"

"No," Rose said. "I mean . . . I don't know." Tears streamed down her cheeks.

"You don't want to hurt your father, am I right?"

Rose nodded.

"Listen to me. You are not the first child from Colorado City that I have taken care of. There are people that can help you. People who know what you've been through."

At that moment, Jeb Farnsworth appeared in the doorway. "It's time to go, Rose."

91

Trak put the breakfast dishes into the sink and grabbed a sponge. But before he reached for the soap, he stopped, startled by what he saw through the kitchen window. The boy lay sprawled on the wooden swing, one leg dangling down, one arm across his face. A backpack yawned open on the grass next to a bottle of water that had tipped over on its side.

Holly, who'd been sleeping on a multi-colored rag rug by the door, lifted her head and looked up at Trak.

"Quiet, girl. Stay!" Trak opened the door, walked down the steps, and into the yard.

The sun slanted through the trees. A breeze pushed the swing, chains creaking, and caused Adan to open his eyes.

Trak Benally sat in a green metal rocker watching the boy. "Hungry?" Trak tried not to stare at the bloodstained T-shirt.

Adan sat up and scratched at a ragged cut that ran up his forearm, evidence of the precarious trek he'd made from Colorado City the night before. He yawned and nodded.

Fifteen minutes later, Trak deposited a plate filled with scrambled eggs, crisp bacon strips, and thick slices of buttered toast in front of the boy. The aroma almost made the Adan faint.

"Thank you." He dug into the food.

Trak sat at the opposite end of the table, sipping a mug of sweet black coffee. Neither of them spoke.

Following a shower, Adan changed into one of Trak's T-shirts, which was too big, and an equally large pair of workout shorts. "I think I need to get some clothes," he said, pushing open the door to the front porch.

Trak, who was sitting in a metal rocker, looked over the top of the *USA Today*. "I don't have any jobs scheduled for today. I can take you over to Target in St. George."

"Just a minute." Adan went back into the house. A few minutes later he returned holding some bills in his hand. "I wasn't sure I still had this after last night."

"Do you want to talk about it?" Trak asked.

Adan plopped down in a chair beside him.

"Did the marshal let you go?"

Adan looked over the green lawn that spread beneath an ancient pecan tree. The mottled dog stuck her head underneath his hand. He scratched Holly behind the ears and told Trak what had happened.

"Is the man dead?"

"I don't know. He was breathing when I left."

"And you ran all the way from Colorado City?"

"Sometimes I had to walk. I had to stay off the road, just in case I was still being followed. And the land was rough in spots—uneven, rocky, lots of vegetation, and sometimes none at all. I stopped and fell asleep a few times, but the thought of running in the heat of the day kept waking me up. I didn't want to end up face down on the road again. Took me about twelve hours. A time that certainly wouldn't win me any medals."

"Still, impressive," Trak said. "We really should make a report. This is all pretty bizarre. And Andy, I still don't understand why the deputy let you out." He didn't let on that he knew the boy's real name. There was time for that later.

"I think he wanted me to run so the other guy could kill me. They'd say I was trying the escape." Adan stared at Trak.

"It doesn't make any sense. Why let you go if they think you stabbed Rose?"

"Shit! I would never hurt her!" Adan slumped in the chair. "How is she?"

"She's recovering from surgery in a hospital in St. George."

"The same place as the Target store?"

"The same," Trak said.

"Let's go there."

92

Beth Flake fussed over Rose, plumping pillows, gathering extra blankets, and adjusting tubes. The room down the hall from the birthing center was small but immaculately clean with a window looking out onto Canaan Mountain. Rose stared at the massive stack of stone and tried to pinpoint the location of the weeping rock and the beautiful crystal pool. Where was Adan?

Nurse Flake clasped her hands and settled them on her belly. "Is there anything I can get you, dear?"

Rose looked at the woman with the neatly pressed white coat buttoned over a purple dress. A few stray strands of gray hair hung by her right ear.

"How about some water? I bet you're thirsty. I'll get you some." The nurse smiled and left Rose alone.

Rose quickly fell asleep and was buffeted by a strange combination of dreams. She and Adan were running from a pack of dogs. Then Daisy, in her wheelchair, was trying to tell Rose something. But when the girl opened her mouth, the tiny blue parakeet flew out. Nurse Tanice Breeze held her hand as they walked along a sandy beach, white foamy water caressing her feet. The Jamaican woman pointed to the ocean and she and Rose tried to name all the colors of blue in the Caribbean Sea. Mr. Wayland appeared. He was giving a lesson on the water cycle: rain, evaporation, and transpiration. The science teacher opened his eyes wide and went to the window. "Everyone come here," he said to the students. "What do you smell?"

"Rain," Rose answered.

"Yes!" he said. "We call that scent petrichor. The name comes from—"

Rose's eyes bolted open. She was, for a reason she could not explain, fearful. She glanced around the room. The Prophet was sitting in a chair by the window, elbows resting on the upholstered arms, fingers tented. He graced her with an oily smile.

Eldon Higbee examined the child in the bed. Her light blond hair appeared as if it had been pruned by a blind man. Her once waist-length tresses stuck out in short uneven tufts that gave the impression of a ragged halo. Her face was angelic, pale and blue-eyed, wisps of red across her cheekbones. Higbee felt something stir in him that had been still for many months.

"We are glad to have you back, Rose," he said, drawing out the single syllable of her name.

She shuttered. "Where is Nurse Beth?"

"I sent her away so that you and I can . . . talk." He stood and moved to the edge of the bed. "Why did you run away, Rose? Whatever made you leave our Eden?"

Rose had never spoken to the Prophet. How could she explain?

He continued smiling at her, a greasy smear exposing several of his yellowed front teeth. He reached out and ran a finger down Rose's cheek. She jerked away.

"I do need to check her wound, sir." Beth Flake stood in the doorway. "So— "

"Get out, woman! Didn't I tell you to leave? I said I'll let you know when you can return."

"Yes, but— "

He turned to the nurse. "Who are you to make me ask twice?"

Beth Flake observed Higbee for an instant. "Of course. I am sorry. I was just concerned that she might be in pain." The nurse stood her ground.

"Are you suffering discomfort, child?" He looked at the bandage that covered her chest and shoulder.

All Rose could do was nod.

"Then I will visit you later." He patted Rose's hand and walked to the doorway. Elizabeth Flake studied her shoes. "Be very careful," he said. "Make sure our Rose gets well soon."

93

Not many people attended Bonnie's Buttars gravesite service. The viewing had been a show of community support—one had to be seen sharing sympathy with the bereaved—but since Bonnie was a known renegade as far as her behavior was concerned, most did not feel the need to be on hand when the girl was lowered into the ground.

Sterling Buttars wept openly, to the shock of the few mourners, and to the total disgust of his two wives. They all listened as the girl's uncle—a member of the Melchizedek Priesthood, and so a holder of the keys of all the spiritual blessings of the church—asked God to protect Bonnie's grave from the elements or any other disturbances, calling the plot a hallowed resting place until the resurrection.

Following the brief service, a meal was served at the marshal's home: ham, rolls, funeral potatoes—a cheesy, au gratin dish—salad, Jell-O, cakes, cookies, and Kool-Aid.

Travis Forbush, stuffed from the meal, walked a few paces behind Sterling Buttars. Once they reached the office and the marshal had unlocked the door, the deputy walked to his desk and waited. This was when the question would come.

Buttars slumped heavily into his chair, eyes red from crying. He reached to a box of tissue, grabbed a handful, and blew his nose loudly. Finally, he took a deep breath and stared at Forbush.

"Did you take care of the problem with the boy?" he said.

"Yes. You won't be seeing him again."

All the deputy could do was hope that the kid was smart enough never to come back. Why would he? The plan had failed rather miserably. But Buttars didn't need to know that. And since the man was obviously severely unsettled by Bonnie's tragic death, perhaps he would let the thing with the boy go.

The door opened. "Sorry about your wife," Scott Parker said to Buttars.

The marshal mumbled his thanks and then said, "What do you want, Parker?"

"I have something I want you to take a look at."

The special investigator opened a black folder and produced a glossy eight-by-ten color photograph of a piece of torn fabric. The brown material formed a neat triangle on one end. The opposite side was ragged with what appeared to be a small hole sown into the cloth. A button, the same color, was positioned next to the material.

"It's a piece of cloth and a button. Is that what you want me to say?" Buttars raised his eyebrows.

"I'm trying to find who killed your wife. I thought you might care to know that these items were located at the scene. In fact, the victim was holding the fabric in her hand. The button was found in the brush beside the body."

"Do you have any other evidence to share?" Buttars asked.

"Not at the moment. But perhaps you've seen something, or spoken to someone in town who might know something about this evidence. I would be happy to take their names and interview them," Parker said. "You know I had to ask."

Buttars snorted. "Go away. We'll handle this."

"Will you, Marshal? Do you even care? Or will Higbee just assign you a new wife and say no harm done?"

Buttars got up from his chair, face red, fists clenched. "Of course, I care! Get out. You're not welcome in this town. We'll find out what happened and handle it ourselves."

Parker faced Forbush. "How about you, Deputy? Got anything to say?"

The two men stared at one another. Forbush turned away and fumbled with some papers on his desk.

"How surprising. Go ahead and keep the picture, Marshal. Maybe it'll jog your memory." Parker turned to leave. "Oh, one more thing. I will need to interview the young lady who was stabbed—Rose Madsen. Can you tell me where she is, since she is no longer at the hospital in St. George?"

"Got a warrant?" Buttars said.

"You know I don't need one to interview a victim."

Buttars stared at the man. "I'm sure she's too ill to speak with you now. We'll let you know when she improves."

"I trust I'll be seeing you again soon." Parker turned and walked out the door.

94

Eldon Higbee was giddy. A seventy-fifth wife was exactly what he needed. After all, the seventy-four women he was already married to were all rather boring, clones in the same outfits with the same hairstyles. Admittedly, the prairie-dress idea had been his. He had designed the outfit specifically with his own tastes in mind. He detested women with curves, so the pattern purposely flattened the chest area. The pleats, just above the waist, fell over the hips, another technique designed to downplay the female body's tendency to curve with age. Hence his desire to marry ever-younger girls. Unfortunately, even the youngest of his wives rounded out disgustingly once they gave birth, but there was nothing he could do about that problem.

Higbee slipped off his hand-made Italian loafers, poured himself a brandy, and slumped into one of the leather wingback chairs to watch Canaan Mountain change. He loved the nightly play of light across the massive rocky parapet that protected his Eden. As the sun set, the sentinel was bathed in a rainbow of colors.

He sipped the brandy and thought again of Rose

Madsen. Why had she so stimulated him? Her short chopped hair had certainly been different. Perhaps that was it. He had for so long been inundated with women whose tresses had been swept up, coiled, and braided. An edict made before he was born. His father, from whom he inherited the mantel of leadership, had explained. In 1953, Arizona law-enforcement raided the area and took four hundred Mormon Fundamentalists—including over two hundred children—into custody, because of the group's practice of polygamy. The raid backfired, however, when public opinion sided with the polygamists.

After that, the women's clothing in the community changed. At first, it was decreed that women could no longer wear pants. Their dresses or skirts had to cover a certain amount of leg. And their entire chest had to be covered up to the neck; plus, all women had to wear long sleeves.

Female sartorial alterations were made about every five years, until only one dress style was permitted, and in only a few plain, pastel colors bearing no stripes or patterns of any kind. Flowered fabric was expressly forbidden. Why this particular edict was in force, Higbee couldn't say. Women's hairstyles, too, had become more restricted: long, loose hair was provocative to men, overtly sexual, so hair had to be combed up and worn on the top of the head.

The rules made all women look alike. And that, as Higbee knew, was the point. God had personally told him that the people were to breed a perfect race. Everyone should be blond, blue-eyed, strong, and straight. Only then could the holy war begin and the people be promised residence in the Celestial Kingdom.

Higbee sighed. He thought again of young Rose

Madsen. Of course he hadn't seen the child in real clothing. She was wearing a hospital gown and covered with blankets. But he sensed she was flat all over. He felt himself get hard.

Suddenly the thought occurred to him that the child was Bliss's daughter. The irony. In fact, he saw the young Bliss in the daughter.

He and Bliss had grown up together. She had been attracted to him way back when he was a pimply youth to whom no one else had paid much attention. He had encouraged her, stealing a few clandestine kisses before being caught and punished. After that, he found himself much more attracted to her younger sisters. Until they got older and he no longer found their female forms appealing, either.

At one point, his father—infuriated when he found his son naked with a young boy—had mercilessly whipped Eldon, calling him a sodomite. But Higbee wasn't a homosexual. He just like smooth-skinned, flat, hairless children. Gender was unimportant. Why was that so hard to understand?

Was that it? Rose Madsen with her short halo of hair was an androgynous child? What an intriguing thought.

He must marry her very soon.

95

Adan dropped the bags on the small bed in the guesthouse. He was proud that he made the purchases himself, using money he earned while working with Trak. He showered and changed into new black jeans and a black slim-fit Nike T-shirt with an Arizona Cardinals logo across the chest. He pulled on clean socks and laced up a pair of black and white Nike running shoes.

The knife slice that Bill Kimball had inflicted, which snaked from the top of his wrist to his elbow, along with the cut he sustained during his run to Hurricane, looked much better after he'd showered and Trak had cleaned the wounds. However, his ribs still ached from the spot where the man had kicked him, and the twenty-two mile trek had taken a toll on his hips, lower back, and legs. Still, considering what he'd been through, he felt surprising good.

Then he pictured Rose and frowned. How could the hospital have let them take her back there? Would he ever see her again?

He picked up the backpack and placed the bag on the

bed. Then he emptied his new clothes into a pile: socks and underwear, two T-shirts, and a pair of compression shorts, since he thought he might like to keep running.

"Hey." Trak stood in the doorway. "There's someone here to meet you. Formally, this time." He stepped aside and the petite red-haired woman entered, the one he'd seen briefly outside the jail window and now recognized as the woman Trak had been so taken by. She wore an emerald-green T-shirt and white cotton shorts. Silver hummingbirds with scarlet eyes dangled from her ears.

"Hi, Adan. I'm Brooke," she said smiling. She stepped over and extended her hand. Trak pulled over a wooden chair and motioned for Brooke to sit down.

Adan remained standing, unsure, and suddenly nervous. So much had happened, and he'd forgotten she'd called him by his name outside the jail window. He glanced at the screen door, his only avenue of escape, but Trak would easily get to him before he got anywhere near the exit. Trak folded his arms across his thick chest and leaned against the counter, his body framed by a myriad tools—hammers, screwdrivers, tape measures, pliers, handsaws, and wrenches—hanging from the pegboard.

Trak sensed the boy's discomfort. "Brooke is here to help."

"Help how?" Adan said.

Brooke looked up at him. "Why don't you have a seat so we can talk?"

Though he did not wish to be rude, Adan remained standing.

"Listen, Adan."

The boy jumped. "I'm not going back." His hands trembled. "What are you, CPS?"

Brooke nodded her head. "I am, but I'm here to help."

Adan let out a high laugh that surprised them all, even himself.

"Help! Do you have any idea what it's like in a group home? No one gives a shit about the kids. It's nothing like being in a family. There's just a revolving door of people who are probably paid minimum wage keeping track of us like prison guards. They even lock up the food like we're all thieves. There's no privacy. The boys beat the crap out of each other when no one is looking. You have no friends. Everyone is in it for themselves. You have to be mean—cruel—or they'll think you're weak. And then . . ." He spread his hands wide. "Two boys in my 'home' ended up in the hospital, but we didn't know who attacked them. Do you know what it's like trying to sleep in a place like that, wondering if someone might stick a pillow over your face for a pair of sneakers, or for no reason at all?"

"But Adan, children placed in foster care are removed from dangers in their own homes. I know the system isn't perfect, but we're just trying to protect you."

"Protect me from what? My mother is the nicest person you'll ever meet."

Brooke paused. "You know, Adan, many abused children protect their abusers. They think the way they're being treated is normal, because that's all they've ever known."

"My mother cooked and cleaned and spoiled me my entire life. She never complained about anything, even when my father disappeared. I always had clothes, my own bedroom, and whatever I needed for school, because she got down on her hands and knees and scrubbed other people's toilets."

"Then how did you end up in foster care, Adan, if your life was so perfect?" Brooke placed her hands on her knees, her voice calm, soothing.

Adan stared. "Really? You don't know?" He scratched his neck. "My mother was deported. I was born here. She was born in Mexico and had no green card. She made me stay here. Wanted me to get my education. When they sent her back, I became an orphan."

He moved so quickly, Trak didn't have a chance to stop him. The boy reached into the backpack and leveled the Glock 40 at Brooke.

96

Chase put the phone back in his pocket. What could he do? This had all been going on for so long. His father had always insisted that the Fundamentalists had the right to live the way they wanted. But did they? What about the children?

He paced. In his dad's time things were different. While polygamy was practiced by some in the community, the majority of men had only one wife. And young girls were not generally part of the picture.

He pulled the phone out and punched in Trak's number. The call went to voicemail. "Pick up, Trak. Come on." He waited, thinking his friend would call him back, but he did not.

Chase grabbed his white coat and bag and headed for the truck. Forty-five minutes later Chase mounted the steps to the Colorado City Clinic and Birthing Center.

Beth Flake stood inside the double doors. She grabbed the doctor's hands. "Thank you, Chase. I didn't know who else to call."

"Take me to her."

Rose lay on the bed under a cotton sheet and white blanket. Her face was red from crying.

"She keeps trying to leave," the nurse said. "She pulled her saline tube out twice."

"Hi, Rose. Do you remember me?" Chase walked slowly toward the bed. "I'm Doctor Allred. But you can call me Chase."

The girl pushed herself into the pillows and turned away.

"When you first came down the mountain. I operated on you here with Nurse Beth."

"I've never seen you before," Rose said. "You're from the outside."

"I am, but Nurse Beth and I were friends when we were children." He nodded at the woman.

"We went to school together," Beth said.

Rose squinted. "Then you are an outsider, too?" Why was everything so confusing? How could Nurse Beth and Nurse Tanice be bad people? How could they be devils?

"Let me take a look at your wound, Rose."

Chase washed his hands in the sink and dried them on some paper towels. Then he pulled on some plastic gloves, stepped to the bed, and peeled back the tape and gauze that covered Rose's incision. After examining the wound, he said, "It looks good. No infection. But you need to stay here at least another day or two. Are you in pain?"

"Just a little," she said.

"That will pass."

"What are they going to do about Mr. Kimball?" Rose asked.

"Bill Kimball?" Beth Flake said.

"Yes. The man who owns Blue."

"Who's Blue?" Chase asked.

"Blue's an old hound dog." She turned back to Rose. "Why should they do anything to Bill Kimball?"

Rose stared at the nurse. "He's the one who stabbed me."

"No, sweetheart. It was that boy. That outsider."

Rose jerked up in bed and then winced and grabbed her shoulder. "Adan? Adan didn't stab me. He was trying to protect me."

"What are you doing here?" Eldon Higbee glared at the doctor from the doorway.

The wall clock ticked off three long seconds before Chase answered. "I wanted to see how Rose was doing. I operated on her when she first came down the mountain." He forced a smile.

Higbee stared at the doctor as he ran his thumb over manicured fingernails. Then he walked to the bed and placed his warm moist hand on Rose's arm. He looked toward the ceiling. "I have had a revelation. No more will male doctors be permitted to see female patients. It is forbidden. So you must leave now, Doctor. And don't ever come back."

97

"Relax, Adan." Trak flashed on the young soldier who'd had his legs blown off by an IED. He was trying to staunch the flow of blood when the kid pulled out his sidearm and raised the weapon to his own head. Before Trak could do anything, the boy put a bullet through his skull.

Brooke remained frozen in the chair.

Trak put his hands in the air, palms facing Adan. "I know you don't want to hurt her. Brooke's done nothing to harm you. You're just frustrated. I understand that. But don't make things worse. Give me the gun." He reached his hand out to the boy.

Adan backed up, clutching the grip tightly. The Glock was now pointed at Trak.

"Get out, Brooke. Get up nice and easy and leave," Trak said. "Let Adan and me take care of it."

"But," she gazed at him.

"Now, Brooke! Adan's going to let you get up and walk out the door. Aren't you?"

Adan nodded. Tears pooled in his eyes. He pointed the gun at Brooke then back at Trak. "I just want to—"

Slowly, Brooke rose from the wooden chair. Adan watched her move toward the door.

"Look at me, Adan." Trak said, staring intently at the boy.

Brooke backed away. She reached the screen door and slipped outside. She ran into the backyard and crouched behind the pecan tree's huge trunk. She reached for her phone to call the police, but the battery was dead.

"We can work this out, Adan. Just give it a chance. This one decision will affect you the rest of your life." Trak was out of things to say.

"You don't understand." More time slipped away. Adan, exhausted, sat down on the bed, still gripping the gun. His shoulders sagged. He lifted the weapon.

"No!" Trak hurled himself through the air, hitting Adan full on. The Glock fell, skidded and bumped against the tool counter. Trak rolled off the boy, scrambled across the floor, and grabbed the weapon.

Adan sat on the bed rubbing his neck. Trak, still sitting on the floor, leaned against the storage doors of the counter.

"Shit!" Trak placed his hand on his chest. "You trying to give me a heart attack?"

"No, I was trying to hand you the gun," Adan said. "And I would never hurt you or her after everything you've done for me. Even if—"

Trak stared at the boy. "Oh, I thought you were—"

"Going to shoot myself?" Adan laughed. "It's not even loaded."

Trak pulled himself to his feet with a groan. "I may have to knock you over again just on principle. Where'd you get this anyway?" He held up the Glock.

"I took it from the man chasing me. The one I left in the ditch."

"Did he drop it?"

"No, I took it from his holster after I hit him."

"That doesn't make sense. If he was trying to kill you, why was his weapon not in his hand? And why wasn't it loaded?"

Adan was silent for a moment. "I removed the clip, but I don't know why he wasn't holding the gun."

"Maybe he wasn't there to hurt you."

Adan stood up. "Shit! What if I killed him?"

98

Buttars stared at the photograph of the torn fabric and the button, then tossed the picture onto a pile of papers he hadn't bothered with in weeks. He looked over at Forbush. The kid had gone out of his way to pick up the slack at the office, and Buttars had never once thanked him.

"You did a good job. I appreciate it," the marshal said.

The deputy's head popped up. He looked surprised. "Thank you."

"No really. You got rid of that boy without any fuss." Buttars got up.

"What'll we do about Parker?" the deputy asked, hoping to change the subject.

"There's not much we can do except ignore him. Getting rid of him would cause a lot of outside complications. And there isn't a person in town who would give the guy the time of day, so there's nothing to worry about."

"But?" Forbush pursed his lips.

"But what?"

"Bonnie. How will we find out what happened to Bonnie? You want to, don't you? Someone killed her."

Buttars stared at the deputy. The boy was damned confusing. "Of course I want to find out who killed her. We'll get him, Travis. We don't need Parker, and we'll take care of it ourselves. Just like you took care of that kid."

The marshal turned and stared out the window. Dark clouds hovered over the mountains. "Is it supposed to rain, Deputy? We could certainly use some." But then he pictured the newly dug grave of his third wife—all fresh red dirt. Maybe rain wasn't such a good idea. "I've gotta go. I promise things will be better around here."

"Yes, sir." Forbush buried his head in a pile of paperwork.

Sterling Buttars had no particular destination in mind. He just wanted to be alone. It used to be, at times like this, he'd snap on little Mouse's leash and they'd go for a walk together. He sighed and lumbered down the steps and into the street.

Something about the picture Parker had given him gnawed at his stomach. The fabric and the button stirred his memory. *Think*, he admonished himself. The shade of the material—a pale, nondescript brown—was one of the few permissible colors allowed for a woman's dress: plain, pale brown cotton. The implication was so obvious that he had to assume Parker knew. The murderer was not a he. If, in fact, the fabric was in Bonnie's hand, she had ripped the piece from a woman's dress, and torn the button off with the material.

A woman? What woman would kill his Bonnie? He wracked his brain. It was true that her family had seemed happy to be rid of the girl. He ticked off her female relatives, but couldn't imagine a single one of them angry enough to bash the child's head in.

Buttars blinked a few times. The triangle. Again, so obvious. Bonnie had ripped a collar from someone's dress. The pointed V was the only part of The Prophet's demure design shaped that way. How could he not have recognized the piece when he first glimpsed the photo?

The marshal walked home, eyeing the gloomy clouds above Canaan Mountain. That a woman could be so brutal, was a completely shocking thought. Men were ruthless and cruel. Women were the givers of life, subservient, and sweet. Well, maybe not always sweet. Some were annoying.

Buttars entered his yard. The mourners had eaten and left quickly. Two of his daughters were taking down several lines of clothing that had been pinned out to dry.

The wind increased. One of the girls looked up at the clouds and encouraged her sister to hurry.

Buttars walked over and did something he'd never done in his life. He helped them take down the clothing. Both girls stared at him with wide eyes. "Thank you, Father," they said practically in unison.

He smiled. "Maybe we'll beat the storm." Buttars nodded at the fast moving clouds. He unpinned several flapping shirts and dropped them in a basket. Then he reached for a pair of jeans, the legs dancing merrily in the breeze. A dress was next.

Buttars hand froze.

99

"Right here! This is it." Adan pointed at the span of thick foliage.

Trak stopped the truck, did a U-turn, and parked off the road.

"His car pulled up behind me and I ran in there to hide.

"Do you remember what kind of car it was?"

Adan thought for a moment. "A Crown Vic."

"You know anything about cars?"

Adan stared at him.

Trak raised both eyebrows. "Got your license?"

"I do."

"Then of course, what teenage boy with a license doesn't know something about cars?" Trak said.

"Exactly."

"So, a Crown Victoria?"

"From what I could see."

Trak had a hunch. "Any markings?"

"On the car? None that I saw. It was dark, though."

"Well, the vehicle is gone, so maybe that's a good sign."

Adan jumped out of the truck and started into the undergrowth. Trak followed him through the bushes and into a stand of drought-damaged trees. Adan paused and looked at the ground, then turned three hundred and sixty degrees. He walked to his left and pointed.

"Here is where I dropped the backpack." Then he took off again.

They broke out of the trees into the open area, with the irrigation ditch winding about thirty yards away. The trench curved back toward SR389. Adan slowed and waited for Trak to catch up. Then the boy stopped and stared.

"Geez! You're killing me," Trak said, sucking in gulps of air. He leaned forward and placed both hands on his thighs. "Where do we go now?"

Adan dropped his head to his chest and closed his eyes. After a few moments, he pointed straight ahead. Then he collapsed to the ground cross-legged and put his face in his hands.

"Do you want me to look? You can just wait here."

"What if I killed him?" Adan said.

Trak had seen that look before. Young soldiers new to battle were sometimes repulsed when they were forced to take a life, even when they had been protecting their own, or that of a comrade. "Just stay here," he said.

Trak walked, preparing himself for what he might find. He'd seen plenty of dead soldiers and civilians in Afghanistan. After a while, he became numb to the carnage, something he thought might be the mind's survival mechanism. The problem was dealing with the living, the wounded who cried and screamed and begged him to stop the blood and pain and calm their fears. Those were the faces that peopled his dreams.

He took a breath and stepped to the edge of the irrigation ditch. Weeds grew up the sides and in the bottom of the trench, where water flow was an intermittent event. He looked to the right and left. He turned back to Adan. "Are you sure this is the spot?"

The boy looked up. "It was dark, but it was right around there."

"Well, I don't see anyone. Come on over. It's OK."

Adan pushed himself off the ground and trotted to the edge of the canal.

"Let's go down. You walk that way, and I'll go this way. See if we find anything."

Adan nodded and they split up.

Ten minutes later, Trak kneeled down and yelled. "Adan, come here!"

The boy quickly appeared at his side.

"See this. It's dried blood." Trak pointed at the ground.

"How do you know?"

"I was an Army medic. I've seen all kinds of blood. And, judging from the way this looks, I'm gonna guess that you did not kill this guy. Though you probably gave him one hell of a headache."

"So what do we do now?"

"Maybe we should go pay the marshal a visit."

100

"I'm so glad to see you both." Eldon Higbee looked at Logan and Bliss Madsen with an unpleasantly eager expression. "Do sit down. I have some wonderful news."

Bliss smiled. She hadn't seen the prophet without being surrounded by hundreds of others in a long time. She had longed for this moment. Bliss smoothed the skirt of her tan dress. She didn't have to look in a mirror to know her hair was perfectly coiffed: a gray-brown roll pulled back from her forehead. The rest of her never-cut hair was fashioned into a twisted mass at the back of her neck.

Logan Madsen stared at his wife. Her smile—so extraordinarily rare—was disconcerting.

"I wonder if you know why I've ask you to come?" Higbee said.

Logan and Bliss stared at one another, then back at the Prophet. Neither spoke.

"Come. Sit down," Higbee opened his hand and indicated a leather sofa.

Rose's parents settled on the edge of the massive couch, while Higbee took a spot in one of the matching leather chairs facing it. Bliss clutched her hands tightly in her lap.

"As you know, God insists that we be fruitful and multiply," Higbee said.

Bliss could barely control her excitement. Finally, she would be married to a man with three wives. And she would always be the first, the most important woman in a household where there would now be a guarantee of reaching the Celestial Kingdom. Of course, the Prophet had to give the ultimate approval for the Madsen's to enter that coveted realm. But hadn't Bliss spent her life adhering to the requirements to cross that holy threshold? She had received the ordinances of salvation: baptism, confirmation, the temple endowment, and the marriage sealing. She'd kept the commandments and repented her sins. She had even refrained from ever hugging or kissing her children, since the only two people who were permitted to make a child feel valued were the head of the household—her husband—and the Prophet himself. Though early on in motherhood, she had to fight the urge to cuddle her children, and she sometimes looked longingly at Logan when he had fawned over them and become their favorite. She had resisted for the family's sake. And now, her lifetime of righteousness would finally bear fruit.

Who would the new wife be? Then again, did the choice really matter? It was the number that was important. The vital number three.

"I have decided to marry again," Bliss heard the Prophet say.

"What?"

Logan Madsen jumped, startled by his wife's unsolicited comment.

Higbee kept the smile pasted on. "Yes. And I will marry your daughter, Rose."

Bliss Madsen's mouth fell open. "Rose? Why do you want to marry that child?"

Eldon Higbee raised his eyebrows and fought down the urge to strike the woman. How dare she even deign to question him.

"No!" Logan Madsen stood. "You can't have Rose."

Bliss, too shocked to speak, reached up and grabbed her husband's arm. He shook her off.

Higbee leaned back in the chair. After a few moments of silence, during which he inspected the cuffs of his suit coat, he slowly got to his feet. "I brought you here to give you both this wonderful news in person. Of course, you know I do not require your permission. And I am quite surprised by your reaction. I am sure when you have a moment to think about this blessing, you will be as delighted as I am." He waited.

"No," Logan Madsen said again. "No. The child is injured. She only just came back from the hospital."

"Because I made the arrangements to get her back." Higbee's voice was menacing.

Logan stared at the floor. Then he put his shoulders back and fixed Higbee in the eyes. "You can't have my daughter." He turned to his wife. "Let's go."

Bliss Madsen stood, still unable to speak, or even look at either man. Her husband strode out of the room and she followed without question.

Higbee made no move to stop them. After all, it didn't matter what they thought. He stared out the window. He would have the girl . . . and soon.

101

Travis Forbush choked on his coffee when Trak Benally appeared in the doorway with the kid.

"Deputy."

Forbush evaluated the man. Benally was big, probably strong. While he had no record—the deputy had checked—he had been a soldier, and could, no doubt, take care of himself in a fight. He was not part of the community, which, at this point, was a plus. The deputy glanced at the clock on the wall. The marshal was due back any moment.

"You two need to leave," Forbush said, rising from his desk.

"We will, as soon as you explain some things." Trak smiled.

"I've got nothing to say to you. Now leave."

"Why did you let Adan go?" Trak nodded toward the boy.

"What difference does it make? Just get him out of here." Forbush looked at the clock again.

"Expecting someone? If you are, maybe we'll just wait

and speak to . . . who is it . . . the marshal? We have another question, too, about the man who was following Adan."

Forbush swiped a hand through his short brown hair. Then, almost imperceptibly, he stood taller.

"Mr. Benally, it's very important that you and the boy leave here immediately."

Trak noted a change in the deputy's voice. "Have the charges against him been dropped?"

"There were never any charges filed." The deputy looked at the clock again.

Trak examined Travis Forbush. He'd been right. "I understand. Quick, Adan, let's go."

"Thank you," the deputy said.

Forbush sat behind his desk. If the marshal saw the kid, everything would be over. That his partner had failed in his attempt to corral the boy was problematic. And now, the man was out a week with a concussion. Forbush ran a hand through his hair again and turned his attention back to the paperwork on his desk. He had to look busy and unbothered when the marshall returned.

Twenty minutes later, the door opened. The deputy casually looked up when the marshal entered holding a plastic garbage bag as if it held a big pile of dog shit. Travis looked up at Buttars. "You all right?"

Buttars put one hand in his pocket then quickly pulled it back out again. He opened his mouth to speak, but said nothing.

"Want some coffee?" Forbush squinted at his boss.

"No! Shit! I don't know what I want." Buttars slapped the bag onto his desk, collapsed into his chair, and put his face in his hands.

"Can I help?"

No answer.

"Do you want me to look in the bag?"

Buttars pushed the bag toward the deputy.

Forbush approached and dumped the contents on the desk. A brown dress and a crumpled photograph fell out. He looked at the picture of the mostly ragged piece of fabric that had a neat triangle at one end and what appeared to be a button of the same color, both of which matched the hue of the garment before him. The deputy recognized the triangle as the corner of a collar. He rotated the dress and held the picture next to a spot where material had been torn away. A button was missing, too.

Forbush looked at Sterling Buttars. "Where did you find the dress?"

"My house." Tears ran down the marshal's face. "What are we going to do?"

102

For the second time that day, Chase sped down Central Street toward the Colorado City medical clinic. He stopped in front of the building, turned off the ignition, and jumped out. Trak and Adan stood on the walkway waiting.

"What did Beth say?" Trak asked as the doctor passed him, heading for the steps.

"Only that the child was in some kind of danger, and that she didn't know what to do."

"I don't suppose you've got anything for protection," Trak said.

"I'm here as a doctor. Not a hunter. Besides, I've got you."

"Great."

Chase paused and nodded toward Adan. "He should probably wait out here."

"But I want to see her."

Trak held up a hand. "We don't have time to argue. Wait by the truck."

Before Adan had a chance to respond, both men leaped up the stairs and entered the double doors.

Chase led the way down the hall. "If anybody comes in, look big and menacing."

"At least I've got the big part down."

Beth Flake met them and ushered Trak and Chase toward Rose's room. "He's coming for her."

"Who?" Trak asked.

"The Pro . . . Higbee." Beth stopped outside the girl's room. "He's going to marry her. And he's not going to wait."

"But she's still injured." Chase reached for the door handle.

"She's asleep and doesn't know." Tears welled in Beth's eyes. "He ordered me to bathe her and dress her and do her hair. He said he was sending his people over to help."

"When?" The doctor asked.

"I don't know. He just said soon."

Trak looked at Chase. "So what's the plan?"

"I'm thinking," Chase said. A minute passed. "She's having a medical emergency. Hemorrhaging. Infection. I don't care. Beth, you had to call an ambulance to take her back to St. George."

"But she's not. She's doing very well."

Chase looked at Beth. "You're going to have to lie. Now let's bundle her up and get her in the truck without anyone seeing. Hurry!"

103

A knock sounded at the Madsen residence. Bliss answered the door and faced Oran Coombs. She blinked. What was the Prophet's assistant doing on their doorstep?

"I need to come in." He did not wait for her to respond, just pushed the screen open. "I will speak with your husband immediately."

"But . . . why?"

"I will speak with your husband, not you. Now, where is he?"

She pointed. "In the dining room." Out of years of habit, Bliss straightened her skirt and swept her hand over her hair in case any strands had strayed. Then she followed the large, well-muscled man down the hall.

Logan Madsen sat at the head of the long wooden table, his head in his hands. He had not heard the knock on the door and appeared puzzled when Coombs approached and sat in the chair next him.

"I have a message from the Prophet," Coombs said in a low voice. "He has considered your response to the news of his pending marriage to your daughter Rose."

"No, he can't. The child is still hurt and—"

"She is his to do with as he pleases, as I'm sure you know." Coombs glared at Logan. "You have been declared an apostate."

"No! Please don't do this." Bliss reached out and grabbed Coombs by the shoulder.

He stared at the woman for a moment. "Remove your hand."

Bliss released her hold and stepped back, her hand over her heart.

Coombs turned back to Logan Madsen, who remained seated at the table. "You will gather only what you can carry in a single suitcase. You may take one hundred dollars and not a penny more."

"Why are you doing this?" Logan stood. "Have you no daughters of your own?"

"They are not mine. They belong to the Prophet."

Logan looked down and entwined his fingers. Then he glared at Coombs. "Tell the Prophet he may not have my daughter Rose, or any of my children. He has taken enough of them already."

"You are effectively banished by the end of today," Coombs said in a voice devoid of emotion. "You no longer have children. Or wives. They will all be reassigned to men, who, unlike you, realize that the Prophet speaks with the voice of God."

Logan stared at the man. His comment seemed sarcastic. But that couldn't be.

"You will be escorted from town in two hours. So be ready."

"But what about—?" Bliss began, but the man cut her off.

"As I said, you and your children will be reassigned." Coombs rose and walked back down the hall and out the door.

104

Chase pushed Rose's wheelchair down the hallway to the front double doors. It wasn't until the entryway was shoved open by Trak that the barrier before them became obvious. A dozen women in pastel-shaded, ankle-length dresses filled the steps and cement walk that led to the doctor's truck. He paused with Rose's wheelchair straddling the threshold.

The women appeared surprised, speaking nervously behind their hands to one another. No one made an attempt to move.

"We need to get this young lady to a hospital immediately," Chase finally said. "Please give us room."

The women remained still. Then a sallow, paunchy matron with a thick, gray braid twirled around the top of her head silently moved to the front of the crowd. The other women parted to let Belle Higbee pass. She squinted through rimless glasses at the two men and the child in the wheelchair. Rose blinked several times and shrunk down into her blankets.

"Where are you going?" Belle's voice sounded almost uninterested in the answer.

"The child needs more medical care than can be provided here," Chase said.

Belle looked again at Rose. "She does not look sick to me."

Beth Flake had pressed herself out of sight inside the clinic's doors when she'd seen the wall of women. Now she took a deep breath and stepped outside. She held her hands tightly in front of her. "The girl . . . needs to go."

Belle appraised the nurse with small, cold eyes. She walked up the steps and moved to the side of the wheelchair. "Are you sick, child?"

When Rose did not answer, Belle placed a clammy wrist on the girl's forehead. She sniffed and looked at Chase. "She has no fever." Belle turned back to Rose. "Are you bleeding?"

"I . . . I—"

"I didn't think so." Belle motioned to the other women. "Come. We have a job to do."

The Prophet's wives shuffled their athletic shoes toward the doorway.

"You may leave the girl with us." Belle addressed Chase and Trak. "As for you, Elizabeth, you will assist us in preparing the child. The Prophet asked specifically for you to be available, just in case the girl needs any medical care. Though it certainly appears that she is just fine. Aren't you?" Belle stared at Rose without a hint of compassion.

"N . . . no! I think I need to go." Rose peeked up at the sour-looking woman who smelled incongruously of lavender. She ducked down, expecting to be slapped, but Belle just graced her with a sickly, brown-toothed grin.

"You are just nervous. It is a big day for you." Belle turned to the crowd of Eldon Higbee's wives. "Evelyn, come push the chair. And the rest of you, we are wasting time. The girl must be perfect."

A few minutes later, as the last of the gathered Higbee wives disappeared inside, Chase and Trak sat in the truck in stunned silence.

"We can't leave her here." Trak stared at the clinic's double doors that were being closed by a despondent-looking Beth Flake. "Jesus!"

"Shit!" Chase balled up his fists and hit them on the steering wheel. He turned to his friend. "What were we supposed to do? Knock over a bunch of women?"

Itching to do something, Trak rubbed his hands on his jeans until it made his palms burn. "We've ignored what's been happening here our entire lives."

"Because our families are Mormon, we let them be." Chase turned his pale eyes toward the clinic. "Your parents and mine always said just let it go. It's their way. They're hurting no one."

"But they are," Trak said. "She's just a kid, and Brooke is right. Higbee is a creep. How can they make her marry him? And what about Bonnie Buttars? Head bashed in for . . . for what?"

Chase pinched the bridge of his nose. "How many more girls are in the same boat as Rose? And, with all the inbreeding, how many children are permanently damaged, their lives miserable? I think if my parents were alive today, they would be appalled by what's happened here. Somewhere along the line things got seriously out of whack."

"OK, Chase. You're right. But what are we going to do about it now? How are we gonna convince anyone here that their entire way of life is absurd?" Trak paused. It was the first time he had ever said the words out loud.

The doctor shook his head. "I don't know. Maybe one kid at a time?"

Trak reached for the door. "Let's start with Rose. I'll get her. I won't knock anyone down. I won't hit any women. I'll just find her and get her out of there."

Then the back door of the truck opened. Both men had forgotten about the boy. He'd heard everything.

105

While the Prophet's women prepared Rose for her marriage to Eldon Higbee, the two wives of Marshal Buttars found themselves facing strangers at their front door. One was Special Criminal Investigator Scott Parker. The other, a twenty-year veteran of the Mohave County Sheriff's Office, Detective Barb Turner. While she was armed and carrying two sets of handcuffs, she didn't need to use them.

Silent and stone-faced, Sterling Buttars' wives were led to the waiting car.

In his office, Buttars sweated profusely. He should have been there when the arresting officers came. But he couldn't bring himself to face the two women with whom he'd shared a bed, the mothers of his children. He still wanted to believe they were incapable of such an act. A vision of Bonnie's caved in skull assaulted him. Buttars suddenly found breathing difficult. A foul odor emanated from his pores, the smell of fear. He glanced at the clock, waiting. Will they come for me next?

For an instant, he considered just leaving, getting into his car, driving down Central Street then over to SR389.

Either direction. It didn't matter. But the thought was fleeting. Buttars had spent little time in the outside world. He didn't belong there. But did he belong in prison? He placed his meaty hands over his face and sobbed.

The door to the office opened. Travis Forbush stood, hands in his pockets, staring at the marshal. "I think it might be OK." The deputy retrieved a box of tissues from the counter and placed them in front of Buttars.

The marshal looked up. "How can it be OK?" He reached for a Kleenex and blew his nose loudly.

"I took the evidence in, like we agreed," Forbush said. "I told them you had every intention of doing the right thing, of turning it in yourself, but you were overcome, too distraught by what you'd found. I said I'd volunteered to do it for you, but that you promised to cooperate."

"Why couldn't we just get rid of it?" The marshal stared through bleary, red-rimmed eyes"

"As I said before, that Parker guy, he would have been all over this place. Who knows what else he might have found, who else might have been implicated."

Buttars nodded, fat tears glistening on ruddy cheeks.

"This way, you're good. And while I'm sorry about your wives, I know how you felt about Bonnie." Forbush did his best to look sympathetic. "I'm sure, under the circumstances, the Prophet will give you some more wives."

The marshal nodded slowly, then leaned forward in his chair and let his hands fall heavily to the desk. He tried to wrap his mind around the fact that his wives had murdered his beloved Bonnie in a fit of jealous rage. Or had they planned the whole thing? A swift tide of nausea swept through him. "I think I'm gonna to be sick." He rose and headed for the bathroom.

As Buttars quickly passed, he reached out with one thick hand and grasped the deputy's shoulder. "Thank you for being such a good friend."

Forbush watched the marshal lumber to the bathroom and close the door. Instantly, the sound of retching filled the office. The deputy turned and walked outside. He stood on the cement steps watching the slate-colored cloud that hovered over Canaan Mountain.

Then he smiled.

106

Rose still ached from the wound in her chest. As the women fussed over her, there was much discussion about whether the bandage should be removed. Would the blemish be unacceptable? Would the bride be considered imperfect?

Beth Flake stood in the corner of the room, a conference area with a long table and chairs that had been pushed back to the wall so all of the women could fit inside.

"Remove the bandage," Belle Higbee ordered a young wife, who was just fourteen.

The girl fumbled with the tape. Rose winced.

Beth took a deep breath. "Please leave the bandage alone," she said in a voice that belied her nervousness. "You have not washed your hands. You'll infect the wound."

Belle turned and glared.

Standing taller, Beth forced herself to speak. "Do you want the Prophet to blame you for making the child ill? He clearly favors her. If the wound becomes septic, I would certainly have to tell him why." The nurse's hands shook, so she crossed her arms tightly over her chest.

Belle narrowed her bead-like eyes. "Leave the bandage be," she said, her gaze still focused on Beth.

Two other women approached Rose and helped her to stand. Another held some thin white articles of clothing that resembled a tight T-shirt and a pair of knee-length leggings. The pink hospital gown was untied and tossed onto the table.

Rose clasped her hands over her small breasts, horrified to be naked in front of these women. She looked at Nurse Beth, pleading for help through tear-filled eyes. Then a slap caused Rose to stumble backward.

"Why are you crying, girl?" The Prophet's first wife sneered at Rose with a wrinkle-creased mouth that made her appear years older than she was. Then she turned suddenly, appalled to find that the nurse had actually laid a hand on her arm.

"Do not hit the child again!" Beth riveted the older woman with a determined gaze. "And the rest of you. We don't need all of you in here. You are bringing infection into the room. Three of you may stay, the rest need to leave. Now!"

No one spoke. Beth and Belle eyed one another like two bulls, each daring the other to make a move.

"Infection is dangerous, Belle," the nurse said in a low voice. "It can be fatal."

The first wife's eyes widened. To be addressed by her first name by this woman was an affront.

Beth leaned in, so that only Belle could hear her whisper. "And I promise you, the Prophet will have you to blame if Rose comes to any harm. You might never have that twentieth child, should he have any reason to think you have interfered here."

Belle reared back as if she herself had been slapped. She clutched at her neck as if something was encircling it, something choking her windpipe. "You have no right—"

"I am the medical professional here." Beth's voice shook as she turned to the other women in the room, many of whom had their mouths hanging open. "Everyone needs to leave. I will prepare the girl. Now get out!"

After the last of Eldon Higbee's wives left the room and closed the door, Beth Flake collapsed into one of the hardback chairs. For a moment, she forgot about Rose and placed her face in her hands, attempting to steady her breathing. Her mind raced. What had come over her that she behaved so badly? She had been taught to honor her elders. To always keep sweet. But then she opened her eyes. Rose, naked, sat slumped in the wheelchair, a dazed look on her face as she tried to cover herself with the hospital gown with one hand clutching her wound. The girl's close-cropped blond hair stuck out in all directions, her scarlet cheek a map of Belle's palm.

Beth jumped up, took the hospital gown from Rose. "Here, let me help you. You'll have to put these on, I'm afraid." She reached for the religious undergarments and held them up.

"But I can't . . . I don't want—" Rose didn't finish. She wiped the tears away with the back of her hand and looked up at Beth with a face so sad and hopeless, the nurse thought her heart might break.

107

A black, late model Mercedes pulled up to the front of the clinic. A man got out, glanced briefly at Chase's truck, noted the occupants inside, and made a quick determination that they were not hostile. He made it his business to know everyone in the area and recognized both the doctor and the handyman, but could not see Adan who had his head down, hiding, around the other side of the truck cab. Then he bound up the front steps. He was surprised to find twelve of the Prophet's wives standing idly in the hallway. Belle Higbee's sour expression was hard to read. But, she pretty much always looked that way.

"Where's the girl?" Oran Coombs asked.

Belle nodded her head toward the closed door.

Higbee's assistant walked down the hall, put his hand on the door latch, pushed down, and entered the room. Rose was dressed only in the white religious garments, which, of course, Coombs was not supposed to see. But the Prophet had insisted that the girl be brought to him immediately. "Cover her with something. She's coming with me now."

Beth Flake stood immobile. It was one thing to talk

back to other women, but one just could not refuse a request from a man, especially the Prophet's second in command. Still, her conscience assaulted her. She stared at Rose. The nurse grabbed the blanket that was draped over the sides of the wheelchair and wrapped the cover around the child's body and shoulders.

Coombs checked his watch, then grabbed the handle on the wheelchair and pushed it toward the door.

"No, wait!"

Coombs turned his head. Had the nurse given him an order?

"I mean . . . let me do that." Beth softened her tone. "The Prophet asked me to make sure Rose is well. So, I need to be with her."

"The Prophet did not instruct me to bring you along."

"I'm sure he meant to," Beth said as sweetly as she could.

Rose coughed and groaned, grasping at the wound.

Coombs removed his hands from the wheelchair. "Push her."

Track and Chase stood by the truck holding Adan pressed against the vehicle. They watched as Beth Flake guided the wheelchair out of the clinic's front door and down the ramp that ran alongside the stairs.

"Who's the muscle?" Trak asked.

"The Prophet's assistant, Oran Coombs, who also acts as Higbee's personal bodyguard."

The twelve wives, led by Belle Higbee, exited the building and headed for two large SUVs. Coombs opened the passenger door on the Mercedes, grabbed Rose roughly from the chair, and moved to place her on the front seat. But as soon as Rose caught a glimpse of Adan, the will to fight—the will to run—came roaring back.

"I'm not going!" She hit Coombs with her fist, a glancing blow to his eye, and tried to push him back.

"Rose!" Adan struggled to get free from Chase and Trak.

"No, Adan. We'll find another way." Trak pinned the boy against the truck.

Rose pierced the three of them with a look of desperation.

The bodyguard gripped her tightly to his body. "Touch me like that again and you will be very sorry."

"Hey!" Chase moved toward Coombs. "She's hurt. You can't handle her that way."

Coombs stared at the doctor then at the big Navajo who stood on his other flank, holding a boy he did not recognize. Rose momentarily quieted and Coombs took the opportunity to unceremoniously dump her on the front seat and slam the door.

He faced the trio. "I don't take orders from any of you."

"We can't let you take the girl." Trak's voice was ominous.

"And what are you going to do to stop me?" Coombs studied the man. In an instant, he pulled the concealed weapon he carried in the holster under his jacket and leveled the gun at Trak.

"What? You're going to shoot us?" Trak asked, incredulous.

"If I have to."

Adan struggled. "Rose!"

Trak tightened his grip on the boy. "You can't fire that

weapon here. There are women and children who might get hurt."

Coombs surveyed the area. The Prophet's wives had stopped loading themselves into the SUVs, and, like a heard of cattle, stared dumbly at the gun that was aimed at Trak's midsection. The women were, in fact, in Coombs line of fire. The bodyguard grinned and holstered the weapon.

"Load up, ladies. Let's go!" Coombs rounded the car, got in, and started the engine.

Adan squirmed in Trak's rock-hard grip. "You can't let them take her!"

Rose stared from the tinted car window, her feverish gaze meeting Adan's. She placed her palm on the cool glass. The car jerked forward. The Mercedes accelerated and pulled away.

Adan stopped fighting.

"We'll figure it out," Trak said. "Now get in the truck."

But as soon as Trak released his grip, Adan bolted and took off running behind the speeding vehicle.

"No, Adan! Come back!"

108

"Please, Bliss, don't do this!" Logan Madsen stood next to his wife, staring at the dark car in the driveway.

"You want me to ignore the Prophet?" she said. "He has ordered me to see him. You know I have no choice in the matter."

A bald man with bulging biceps held the sedan's backdoor open, waiting for Bliss to comply with Eldon Higbee's directive.

Bliss exhaled and shook her head. Logan had been a disappointment. While he was kind to her and the children, and she had loved him when they were younger, he didn't seem to understand what was required to enter the Celestial Kingdom. He would never have a third wife now. Where did that leave her? Out of reach of Paradise for all eternity?

"Goodbye, Logan." Bliss surprised herself by laying a rough palm on his cheek. She pursed her lips and quickly withdrew her hand. Then she turned, walked down the steps, and joined Sister-wife Glea in the backseat of the vehicle.

Logan watched his wives disappear. His heart felt like it was being crushed in a vise. Then a wave of cold sweat engulfed him. He burst through the kitchen doors and up the stairs. He didn't have much time.

An hour later, Brooke jumped when she heard frantic knocking. She had grown accustomed to being ignored by the locals and was momentarily stunned. She put down the coffee cup and opened the trailer door.

"I'm sorry, I don't know your name. But I need your help."

Brooke recognized the man. "Mr. Madsen? You are Rose's father?"

"Yes." He nervously scanned the area around the trailer. "Come quickly!"

Five minutes later, Brooke and Logan Madsen carried Daisy between them, the skeletal child cradled in their arms. The girl was dressed in a baggy sweatshirt and pants—items left behind by one of her brothers. Her head lolled back and forth as they hurried up the trailer steps.

After depositing the child on a blanket on the floor, Logan ran back to the car and returned with a diaper bag over one shoulder and a tiny six-year-old girl-child clutched to his chest. The girl sucked her thumb as tears streamed down red cheeks. She, too, was dressed in boys clothing. A small blue ball cap tilted down, shielding her face.

Logan set her gently on the floor, and immediately the child started wailing. Brooke opened her desk drawer, rummaged through a bag of Tootsie Pops, and extracted a cherry sucker. Moments later the little girl sat quietly on the blanket, licking the treat. Daisy, curled in the fetal position, snored softly, and appeared to be sleeping.

Brooke stared at Logan, who paced the small office. He cupped his face in his hands then collapsed in a desk chair.

"Your children are safe here, Mr. Madsen. Now tell me what's going on. How can I help you?"

"They've taken my wives."

"Who?"

"Eldon Higbee." Logan wiped a tear from his cheek. "I can't let him have the rest of my family. My girls. They're all I have left."

Brooke watched the two children on the blanket for a moment then turned and looked into Logan Madsen's eyes. "You have another daughter. Rose. Where is she?"

"I . . . I'm not sure. All I know is that the Pro—Higbee—intends to marry her."

Brooke stood up, every nerve and muscle in her body coiled like a spring. "What do you want to do about that, Mr. Madsen? Are you just going to let him have her?" She struggled to keep her voice even.

He leaned back in the chair and spreads his hands. "What can we do?"

109

Trak tried catching Adan, but the boy was too fast. Chase pulled up in the truck. "Get in."

"Shit!" Trak took in several big gulps of air. "There was no way to catch him. Not on my best day."

"Then hurry up and we'll find him. I don't want to think about what they might do to him."

Trak stood and shook his head. "Adan cut into the trees and went over that hill." He pointed to a low rise covered with thick foliage. "Let's hope he's smart enough to stay hidden."

"Right," Chase said as Trak climbed in and slammed the door. 'We've got two love-struck teenagers on our hands, and you're expecting the boy to use his head and be smart."

"Good point."

"What we need to do is keep tabs on the girl and get some help." Chase jammed his foot on the gas pedal.

"They'll see us."

"Yep. Maybe that'll make them think about what they're doing. And maybe we can manage to find a spot where we can get a cellphone connection. We need some help."

"Are you thinking of the marshal?" Trak asked. "He's certainly the closest. But I don't think he can be trusted. I think he's pretty much part of the program. The deputy on the other hand—"

The truck roared up the tree-lined road and rounded a bend. Trak punched at the cellphone keypad and waited. "Nothing."

"Keep trying!" Chase saw the last of the vans carrying the Prophet's wives ease through a thick metal gate that closed mechanically behind the caravan. He slowed to a stop and both men glanced up at the high, white wall with cameras balanced on top. Eldon Higbee's compound was a fortress of modern technology.

Chase hung his head. "I wish we hadn't waited so long." He slapped the steering wheel. "She's alone in there."

Trak nodded. "Hey, I think I've got a signal." He punched in another number. This time the phone rang.

110

Travis Forbush had a thick ham and cheese sandwich halfway to his mouth when the door burst open. Special Investigator Scott Parker with Logan Madsen in tow marched straight to his desk. Forbush put the sandwich down and got up. He and Parker eyed one another.

"We need to find Rose Madsen," Parker said.

Forbush was quiet for a moment.

"Brooke Neal at CPS received a call saying Rose had been removed from the clinic by a man named Oran Coombs and that he was taking the girl to marry Eldon Higbee," Parker explained.

"She's of age," Forbush said. Then he sat down and folded his hands on his desk. "Please leave. I have quite a bit of work to do."

"We can make this one stick." Parker nodded at Logan. Her father will testify against Higbee. He knows a lot, which can help us shut this down."

Forbush sighed heavily. "Then we're done after this."

111

Adan burst through the trees. He'd lost sight of the Mercedes momentarily, but had seen the vehicle carrying Rose peel off from the others, before the huge gates into the Prophet's compound had opened allowing the other cars to enter.

Now, he picked up speed, staying inside the shielded perimeter of the trees. He watched as the car turned north and drove past the front entrance to the massive estate. Then the vehicle turned again, heading west.

Adan couldn't keep pace with the car, so he decided to cut up over the hill, hoping to catch the vehicle on the other side. He leaped over a fallen log, then dodged a thick stand of young trees, tall saplings huddled close together, a natural fence too difficult to maneuver through.

His heart pounded, and—as he had often done since he'd come to the Arizona Strip—he thought of his need for water. But there was no time to stop and think when Rose had vanished up the road. He saw her face again, pleading from the other side of the dark glass, the girl he'd known on the mountain, the one he admired as she braved the frightening ledge that wended around the cliff, the girl who took a knife meant for him. When she'd seen him, she'd tried to fight back, but then, as the car drove away, her eyes had told him something horrible. She was desperate, the spark that made her special was flickering, almost ready to go out. Come on, Rose! Don't give up!

Preoccupied with his thoughts, Adan didn't see the thick root that reached out and trapped his right foot. He sprawled into a jumble of green lichen-covered rocks. His hands were bruised and cut by the sharp stones. Flat on his stomach, he raised his head. Then, he quickly ducked down. He was visible from below. In the distance, the roll of thunder echoed down from the mountain, and a fat drop of rain plopped nearby, raising a small *poof* of dirt.

The car moved past a high metal fence, hemming in a group of animals that seemed strangely out of place. Adan watched as the vehicle turned onto a dirt road and disappeared. He waited a few moments, surveying the area to make sure no one else was around. Then he got up and bolted to the bottom of the hill and across the road.

There were no houses here. Just the high fence and the menagerie it enclosed. Spotted deer rested in the shade of massive maple trees. Several shaggy bison plucked grasses, switching their tails at flies. One dark ostrich, black wings outstretched, chased a deer that scampered off into the safety of the herd.

Adan edged his way down the long fence. When he reached the dirt road, he paused and appraised the tree-lined track. Rose was here, somewhere nearby.

He had to find her.

112

Logan Madsen paced in front of the CPS trailer, where, inside, Brooke calmed the children. He'd been told by Scott Parker to sit tight, that law enforcement officers from the state were on their way, and that they'd find Rose soon.

Logan stared at Canaan Mountain, where a heavy, charcoal-colored cloud crowned the summit, and its telltale streaks formed a gossamer curtain. Would the rain make it into the valley? He'd have to wait and see. Just like everything else. His entire life had been nothing but a waiting game. He'd never done anything on his own, never made a move without considering the effect his actions or inactions would have on the ultimate prize: Celestial Paradise was all that mattered.

Had he ever behaved like a man? Or a father? What did that even mean? He hardly knew. His wives had been assigned to him. He'd stood by while the Prophet relegated his sons to the hell of the outside world for the simple crime of being boys. His daughters had been bestowed like inanimate gifts to men he barely knew, with no concern for their happiness or well-being. He'd never been consulted, never asked what he thought, or what he wanted.

A cold breeze blew in from the mountain. He could smell the rain. In that moment, Logan Madsen's world changed, though he couldn't say exactly why.

The door to the trailer opened. Brooke Neal stood atop the wooden steps. Her red hair ruffled in the wind as she glanced at the sky. A bolt of lightning shot out of the dark cloud, spidery fingers dancing on the rock face.

She turned back to Logan. "They're asleep."

"Thank you. Take care of them." He stared at the mountain for a moment, then ran to his truck.

"Wait!" Brooke yelled. A clap of thunder drowned her out.

Logan jumped in, slammed the door, put the key in the ignition. In an instant, the truck barreled away.

113

The Prophet rose when Bliss Madsen entered. He'd always had a soft spot for the woman. "You may wait outside," he said to the man who had retrieved her from her home.

"And what of the other one?"

Higbee noted Madsen's other wife. Young and afraid, but still pretty. "She can wait outside."

Bliss quickly ran her hands down the front of her skirt, smoothing the garment, and touched her hair. Then she clasped her hands and raised her head, gracing the Prophet with a smile.

Higbee offered an oily grin in return. He crossed the room and took Bliss's hand in his. "I was just remembering when we were children."

Bliss blinked, unsure of what to say. She had adored Eldon Higbee from the moment he stole a kiss from her when she was twelve. She could still feel the tingle that ran down her spine that day behind the barn when he pressed himself against her. Two of her brothers appeared and ran Higbee off. She was grateful they had not told her parents. From that moment, she had always secretly hoped to marry Eldon Higbee, but he had lost interest in her as she got older, and, at one point, had focused his attention on her younger sister. It had been an especially painful period.

And now, here she stood. Her mind raced. The fact that the Prophet intended to marry Rose did not make a possible liaison between her and Eldon Higbee out of the question. The man had, over the years, married women who were sisters, aunts and nieces, and in, one case—that was now giving Bliss hope—a mother and daughter.

Bliss flashed on her husband—no, her former husband. She knew how things worked. Those who had become apostates had their families redistributed. There was no other way.

She couldn't remember how many wives the Prophet currently had. Becoming one of so many could be problematic. The fact that she and Higbee had a past, that was as bright and shiny to Bliss today as it had been all those years ago, gave her hope that she could work her way up the hierarchy of his family. Bliss could become his partner and confidant.

She felt his moist limp hand in hers and blushed.

"I have some very exciting news for you," he said.

All Bliss could do was nod. For the first time in years, she felt a surge of happiness that threatened to overwhelm her.

"Of course, you must now remarry."

"Yes," she said softly, wanting to reach out and cradle his sallow cheeks in her hands.

He smiled. "You can come in now," he called.

The rear door to his office opened and in walked Sterling Buttars with his cowboy hat in his hands. His jaw dropped at the same moment Bliss took a step backward.

"How perfect!" The Prophet said. "I know you two will be very happy together."

114

Rose awoke in a small, but ornate room, with no memory of how she got there. Red and gold-flocked wallpaper surrounded the antique, four-poster bed that was piled high with thick down quilts. She reclined on soft pillows. A lacy, but demure, cotton nightdress reached up her neck and covered her arms. Rose peeked at the wound on her chest. Someone had replaced the bandage with a smaller one that was just big enough to cover the stitched cut in her flesh.

Rose heard a noise, perhaps the opening and closing of an outer door. A lamp by the bedside cast a low, unearthly light throughout the room. The table across the room bore a tray presenting a colorful array of foods: fruits and cheeses, and nuts and small sweet cakes, and a fresh loaf of baked bread. A sweating, silver bucket chilled a bottle of wine. Candles burned in holders mounted on the wall. The room smelled sickeningly of lilac.

"There you are!" Eldon Higbee closed the door and placed his hands on his thin hips. He wore a dark running outfit with white stripes down the legs.

Rose had never seen the man in anything but a suit and tie. She pulled the covers up to her neck. "What are you doing here?" For the first time, she noticed there were no windows in the pretty room.

"Why, I'm your husband, Rose." He plopped onto the edge of the bed, reached out, and touched the tips of her cropped blond hair.

Rose jerked away. "We are not married!"

Higbee got up and unzipped the jacket of his running suit to reveal a plain white T-shirt covering his sunken chest. "Of course we are," he said, heading for the tray of food.

"No! There was no marriage!"

"Rose. We don't need a traditional marriage. And besides, who can perform a marriage for me?"

"But—"

"If I say we're married, we are. It's as simple as that. I am the Prophet." He spread his hands and smiled. "Hungry?" He walked to the platter, lifted the tray, and ceremoniously delivered the food to Rose. "Here. Try some of the aged Camembert. It is especially delicious."

Rose reached out and upended the tray in Eldon Higbee's face. Cheese and fruits and condiments spilled onto the bedclothes and floor. Higbee was motionless for a moment. Then he slowly wiped a splash of mustard from his cheek with the back of his hand.

115

Eldon Higbee eyed his new bride. Hadn't he arranged this beautiful setting for her? Wasn't he giving the girl the opportunity of a lifetime? After all, what woman did not want to be his wife? He should be angry with the insolent child, yet somehow, her defiance added to her allure. Like the short hair. He considered again announcing that all women should wear this style, since he'd grown bored with the contrived coils and braids and ornate piles that decorated the females of his flock.

Slowly, he pushed the fallen cheeses and fruits to the floor. The Camembert stuck to the comforter, and Higbee pierced the gooey wedge with his finger then held the bony digit out to Rose. "Eat it." He tilted his head as if to watch her more intently.

Rose recoiled, sinking back into the pile of white pillows. Higbee moved closer and touched the cheese-covered finger to her lips. "I won't ask twice, Rose."

The mass of quilts had Rose pinned down. Wide-eyed, she scanned the room, looking for a way out. But there was only one door.

Higbee saw her eye the exit. "You're not going anywhere, and I am growing tired of this game." He inserted the finger into his mouth and sucked off the cheese. He squinted at Rose and smiled wanly. Then he grabbed her with both hands, tearing at the lacy cotton nightdress, ripping the high collar.

Rose gasped as the Prophet tore the bandage from her wound. A crimson flower oozed onto the pristine nightgown. Higbee didn't seem to notice. He grasped the covers and tossed them aside. Only the lower half of the girl's pale legs were exposed, but that was enough. Higbee took several quick breaths, stripped off his pants, then climbed onto the bed and straddled Rose, barely able to contain his erection. She lurched to get away, but his weight pinned her down. The sudden realization that she was too weak to fight him off made Rose sick to her stomach. Still, she balled up her fists and flailed at the Prophet as he fumbled under her nightgown.

Then Rose screamed. Tears ran down her face. "No! Don't do this!"

Rose was stunned when Higbee rocked back and wobbled. He blinked several times and reached for the back of his head. Blood streamed through his fingers.

"Papa!"

Logan Madsen still gripped the forty-eight ounce, short-handled sledgehammer. He raised the weapon and brought it down again.

Drop it!" Travis Forbush leveled his service weapon at Rose's father. Logan froze, still staring at his child, disheveled and bloody.

Eldon Higbee rolled off Rose and staggered to his feet, holding bloody fingers out before him. The sticky redness seemed to surprise The Prophet. He stared at Forbush. "Shoot him!" Higbee screamed, his voice rising to a shriek. "Shoot him now! I command you. Kill him!"

"No!" Rose screamed and scrambled toward her father.

"Stay where you are, Rose." Forbush said. He kept his eyes on Higbee. "And please put the hammer on the floor, Mr. Madsen. Nice and easy."

Madsen slowly nodded his head, bent down, and dropped the heavy tool to the polished, hardwood floor with a thud.

The Prophet took a step forward. "I ordered you to— What are you doing?" The Prophet placed his hand on his chest. He stared at the barrel of the deputy's Glock 40.

"You will step away from the girl."

"You can't do this. I'm—"

"An asshole, Higbee. And you are under arrest for kidnapping, attempted rape, and aggravated assault." Travis Forbush's grim smile hardened with each word.

"Go ahead and arrest me. I dare you!"

"I already have. Now, you have the right to remain silent. Anything you say, can and will be used against you in a court of law—"

"My lawyers will have me out in an hour," Higbee sneered.

"You have the right to an attorney," Forbush continued. "If you cannot afford an attorney, one will be appointed for you."

Higbee reached out a bloody hand as his knees buckled. He leaned on the wall and slid down to the floor. "No one will testify against me, Deputy. They will be doomed for all eternity if they do." With a weary expression, Higbee stared up at the man with the gun.

Forbush smiled. "I'll certainly testify. How about you, Mr. Madsen?"

Rose's father glared at the Prophet. "Yes. I will testify that he is an animal." Then Logan stepped to the bed and wrapped his arms around his daughter.

"I suggest, Higbee, that unless you want to be on the evening news with no pants on, you stand up and get dressed," Forbush said, still pointing the weapon at The Prophet. "Then I'm going to handcuff you and we're going to wait for state authorities to take you away."

Higbee pushed himself up and picked up his pants. He stuck one leg in and hobbled sideways, woozy from the blow to his head. The man steadied himself to try again, muttering under his breath about lawyers and legislators and how he'd make Forbush pay, when he heard a sound. In the doorway, a dark-haired young man stood watching. Higbee stared for a moment and promptly fell to the floor.

116

Adan took in the scene. Rose was bloodied but appeared to be OK. She was hugging someone. He hung back. Rose saw him and their eyes met. A tear slipped down her cheek. She smiled and buried her face in the man's shoulder.

Adan watched the deputy sheriff warily—the man who had locked him up and then let him go.

"Enough! Stand up!" Forbush pulled Higbee to his feet and pushed him against the wall. "Put your pants on." This time Higbee managed to get both legs in and his pants pulled up. Forbush grabbed his shoulder and turned him around, then cuffed his hands behind his back. Thick blood massed in the man's hair and ran in dark streaks down his neck.

Forbush turned to the boy, who backed out of the doorway, ready to flee. "It's OK, Adan. No one's going to arrest you. I'm going to take Mr. Higbee to my patrol car. An ambulance for Rose will arrive shortly. Stay here."

Adan eyed the man, unsure of what had changed. Clearly, the deputy was different.

Forbush pushed Eldon Higbee toward the door. Adan

moved aside and let the two men pass. They exited the windowless bedroom, walked through a well-appointed living room, and out the front door. The structure, built on a rocky outcrop overlooking the Short Creek riverbed, was unassuming from the outside, but, like the Prophet's manse, was usually difficult to access. Higbee, in his haste to consummate his spiritual marriage to Rose, had left the front door unlocked, allowing Logan Madsen, Travis Forbush, and Adan Reyes easy entry. That the Prophet had dismissed his bodyguards and sent them back to the main compound with his other seventy-four wives made the arrest a relatively simple matter.

Higbee ranted and railed as the deputy marched the unsteady man down to his cruiser. The dirt drive leading to the small residence that was Eldon Higbee's private getaway led down the rocky hillside and across the sandy bottom of Short Creek wash. Forbush had parked his vehicle at the bottom of the dry riverbed, not wanting to alert Higbee or any of his people to his presence. The last thing he had wanted was a shoot-out and a hostage situation.

Higbee lifted his chin. "You have no power over me."

Forbush opened the car door.

"I will bring the wrath of God down upon you!"

"You do that." Forbush grabbed Higbee by the shoulder, turned him around, unlatched the handcuffs, and reattached them, securing the man's hands in front of him. Then the deputy pushed Higbee onto the backseat and secured the cuffs to a metal bar situated behind the front passenger seat.

"I need medical attention. You cannot deny me aid, Deputy. I will say you abused me. Police brutality always makes a nice headline, don't you think? Let's see what the judge has to say about that." Higbee forced a smile.

"There's an ambulance on the way. We'll see to the victim first, of course." Forbush slammed the door.

"Victim? That's my wife! I'm the victim here," Higbee yelled as Forbush walked back toward the house.

An hour later, paramedics arrived. They examined Rose, then placed her on a stretcher, assuring her father that she would be fine. She needed a few new stitches. That was all. As they headed out to the ambulance, Deputy Forbush, whose real name was Jack Snow and who was an undercover operative working for the Mohave County Sheriff's Office, reminded the medics that there was a need for DNA evidence and that Special Investigator Scott Parker would be meeting them at the hospital.

Logan Madsen held his daughter's hand. "I'll be right behind the ambulance, honey."

Rose glanced at Adan. Logan looked from his daughter to the young man. His world had changed dramatically, so quickly. He took a deep breath and exhaled. "Come on, son, you can drive over with me."

"Thank you, Papa." Rose squeezed her father's rough hand.

"What's that?" one of the medics asked, looking toward Canaan Mountain. The dark cloud that had hovered over the summit all day had dissipated. The sun edged down the western sky bathing the rock face in red, while above the rise, a kaleidoscope of pink, purple, and peach streaked the heavens. They'd gotten only a few sprinkles down in the valley.

"Sounds like thunder," Adan said.

The noise got louder. Unlike thunder, the din was continuous.

"Shit!" Jack Snow yelled. "Everybody move up. Back to the house! Now!" The deputy turned toward his car in the wash and broke out into a sprint. But halfway down the dirt road, he stopped and stared. There was nothing he could do.

Eldon Higbee heard the thunder and believed the noise was a product of his wound. He bent forward and stuck one finger in his ear, and shook his head. He would make sure that deputy was paid back for his insolence. And Logan Madsen and the girl? He would get what he yearned for, one way or another.

The noise got louder. The earth rumbled. The Prophet looked out the window. Then his jaw dropped. A churning five-foot wall of water barreled down the wash. Coppery red, like his beloved Canaan Mountain, the stream surged with rocks, branches, and riverside refuse tumbling like children's toys. The wave rocketed toward the car as Higbee yanked at the handcuffs and kicked at the front seat.

Then he screamed.

117

The search for the Prophet continued for a week. Finally, his still-cuffed hands were found protruding from a massive heap of boulders and logs. His bloated torso had started to rot, so the smell of decaying flesh left an easily detectable trail for the dogs to follow to what remained of the man.

Higbee had been thrown clear of the cruiser. The metal bar to which he was shackled had snapped like a dry twig. Only the outer shell of the vehicle and one tire remained intact. Like Higbee, most of the bits and pieces that made up the car had been torn away and rolled into the pile of flotsam.

After the Prophet's parts were collected, however, the stench on Short Creek remained. Searchers hunted the now dry riverbed for the cause of the putrid smell, and finally found the source behind the Isaac W. Carling Memorial Cemetery. The broken patch of red earth that butted up against the fence enclosing the hallowed ground of the graveyard had been churned up by surging floodwaters. Searchers stared wide-eyed at what appeared to be hundreds of macabre dolls scattered along the ground and draped in the arms of low-hanging branches.

Workers gathered and reburied what were in reality the corpses of infants, damaged, not so much by the flash flood, but by the results of incest.

118

The loss of their beloved leader filled the residents of Colorado City with profound grief. Fear and confusion bloomed on their upturned faces at the funeral as Eldon Higbee's second-in-command, Oran Coombs, stepped to the pulpit.

"The Prophet wishes that you all rejoice." Coombs smiled at the people. "God has taken him to sit by His side." He paused and scanned the crowd. Would the parishioners be shedding their tears and nodding their heads in such absolute agreement if they had really known the man? Coombs suppressed a sudden desire to laugh out loud. "You have nothing to fear. The Prophet planned for this day."

The reality was that Coombs had been charting his own future for a long time. Later that evening, the former bodyguard turned Eldon Higbee confidant, reclined in one of the leather wingback chairs in the Prophet's office suite. He put his feet on the coffee table, placed his hands behind his head, and smiled as he stared out the window over the land called Eden.

119

After a proper period of mourning, life in Colorado City returned to its version of normal. One day, in an effort to cheer the people and divert their attention—a lesson he had learned from the Prophet—Coombs claimed to have had a revelation sent directly from Eldon Higbee himself. The rule about having no pets was lifted.

And so the deputy appeared in the marshal's office one day with a surprise for Sterling Buttars. "I found her out by the highway," he lied. Jack Snow, happy that his cover had not been blown, placed the fluffy white bundle in Buttars hands. Besides, he'd met Buttars new wife and knew the poor man needed a real friend.

A tiny pink tongue grasped at the marshal's thumb. "For me?"

Snow almost pitied the man. "I couldn't leave her out on the road. I thought you might like to keep her."

"You're a good friend, Travis. Now," he said, looking at the puppy with adoring eyes, "let's get you something to eat."

Snow shook his head as he watched Buttars trundle down the hall. The fact that he'd managed to keep his cover intact was somewhat of a miracle. He'd spoken with Scott Parker, and his boss agreed that he could stay on.

From down the hall, Buttars addressed the little dog. "You are such a sweet, sweet girl. What should we call you? Hmm? What's your name?"

Snow sighed. Having a dolt like Sterling Buttars as marshal gave him the inside access he needed. He would continue his search for the missing science teacher, Bob Wayland, and do what he could to help free those who wanted to get away from the madhouse on Short Creek.

EPILOGUE

Two weeks later, Carla Kimball sat on her sunny patio spooning chocolate pudding into Daisy's mouth.

"Wa, wa, wa!" The girl drummed her fists on the tray attached to her wheelchair. A floppy flower-covered garden hat protected the child's head.

Daisy's little sister, Iris, ran up with a bouquet of flowers.

"They're lovely, sweetie," Carla said. "Why don't you go and get a few more of the pretty purple ones?"

The child nodded her blonde head and ran back to the garden.

"How's the patient?" Chase Allred asked, taking a seat in a metal wrought-iron chair across from the Daisy.

"She loves chocolate pudding, don't you, darling?" The mayor of Hurricane offered Daisy another taste.

The girl turned her head and stared with one dark eye. "Wa, wa, wa!"

Carla wiped Daisy's chin with a cloth napkin. "We'll be seeing you at dinner, Doctor?"

"Absolutely."

Early that evening, Brooke and Rose helped Carla set the wooden picnic table on the flagstone patio with dishes sporting tiny pink flowers atop a white tablecloth. Little Iris's bouquet of flowers—placed in a white pitcher—graced the middle of the spread.

"Is there anything I can do to help?" Logan Madsen asked as he watched the women work. That Carla, a complete stranger, had insisted he and his girls move into her home until permanent arrangements were made, still shocked him. Like so many of his neighbors in Colorado City, Logan had been convinced that everyone on the outside was evil. He shook his head. How could they have been so wrong for so long?

Trak, Chase, and Adan arrived while the sun was just kissing the western horizon. Fragrant odors of baked bread and roasted turkey wafted from the kitchen.

Just before dinner was served, Brooke said, "Adan, I have a surprise for you."

The boy blinked. "A surprise?"

At that moment, the back door burst open and out stepped a huge man-child. "Andy!" Adan's jaw dropped.

"Bro! What the hell, man! You tryin' to scare me to death?"

Adan's best friend bounded down the steps with more agility than one might expect from such a large person. He grabbed his friend in a bear hug. It was then that Adan noticed Andy's parents.

"Come on, everyone! Welcome, welcome. This way. Follow me." Carla herded her guests to the patio. "Let's get situated and get to know each other."

When everyone was seated around the table, and plates of turkey and potatoes and string beans and salad and a basket of thick-cut bread were passed among them, Andy's mother spoke.

"You will come and live with us, Adan. You have to finish your senior year, and we have plenty of room. All you had to do was ask." She smiled at him.

Adan turned away and stared at his plate. Andy gave him a good-natured punch in the arm that would knock a normal person over.

Brooke watched Adan for a moment and then pulled a letter from her back pocket. "You should read this. I think it will help."

Adan took the letter and excused himself. He sat on the steps that led into the warm country kitchen, and, in the light emanating from inside the screen door, opened the envelope. The handwriting was small and neat. The words were in Spanish.

My darling boy,

I have been so worried about you. When you disappeared from foster care, I contacted Andy's parents hoping they knew where you were. They promised to find you. Though I miss you terribly, the best place for you is with them. You must finish high school and go on to college. An education is the most important thing. No one can take that from you. Only with an education can you control your future.

I will stay here on my grandfather's ranch. It is quite beautiful here and I hope that you will soon be able to visit. Please know that I am well and happy, except that I miss you terribly.

— Love, Mama

Adan wiped tears from his cheeks with the back of his hand, put the letter in his pocket, and returned to the table. He sat between Rose and Andy and across from Trak. How could he be so lucky?

Over the course of the meal, which ended with still-warm peach pie and vanilla ice cream, it was decided that Adan would spend the next month in Hurricane. Trak insisted the boy was welcome at his home and that there were a number of jobs Adan could help him with. Brooke said she'd figure out a way to make it work as far as the foster care folks were concerned. When the month was over, they would drive the boy back down to Phoenix to join Andy and his parents on a trip into Mexico, for a visit with Adan's mom.

Andy slapped his friend on the back with one giant paw. "Road trip, bro!"

After the visit, the boys would return to Phoenix, and begin their conditioning for football, and prepare for the start of the school year.

Later that night, Trak and Brooke sat in matching wicker chairs on Carla's patio. They stared into the orange flames burning inside a chiminea. The fire danced in the ceramic bowl while wisps of fragrant, white smoke traveled up the chimney and into the sky, where bright stars pierced the darkness.

Trak reached over and took her hand. "What is it, Brooke? Is there something you need to tell me?"

Despite the beautiful evening, her stomach churned. She dropped her head and closed her eyes. What would he think once he knew? The creature picked at her stomach with barbed claws. She'd counseled children to talk about their problems, explaining that keeping everything inside only caused more pain. And yet she had not been able to trust her own words.

Finally, Brooke gazed into the fire and told Trak about the child. A two year old who was under her care, a little girl the courts had taken from a loving foster care family and placed back with her mother and the boyfriend who'd hurt the child. Brooke was charged with making sure the baby remained safe. The appointment was set for 3:30 in the afternoon. Brooke had only intended on taking a short nap. Her caseload, almost twice the recommended limit, was exhausting.

"I slept through the alarm," she said. "The little girl—her name was Bella—died that day, just about the time I was scheduled to visit. He burned her with cigarettes. Then beat her. He said she was crying and he couldn't make her stop. I remember him shrugging his shoulders on the stand and holding his hands out, like what he did was completely understandable. For one sick minute I pitied him."

Trak reached over and wiped a tear from her cheek. "It wasn't your fault."

"Oh, it was."

"Then why are you still working for CPS? Wouldn't they have fired you?"

"I was reprimanded, and a letter was placed in my file. But they determined that there was probably nothing I could have done to stop it. Still—" She stared at Trak wanting to read his mind, expecting a change in his warm brown eyes, one that said she was guilty of neglecting little Bella, and so, was responsible for the baby's death.

But, instead, Trak stood and reached to her with both hands. He lifted her up and wrapped both big arms around her. He placed his lips next to her ear. "It wasn't your fault," he whispered. "And there are still so many children who need your help."

Brooke choked back a sob. She felt her whole body relax as she sank into his broad chest. After a few moments, she straightened up and kissed Trak on the mouth.

Chase leaned his shoulder into the kitchen doorway and watched his best friend. He'd promised to protect Trak from redheads. But now, Chase just smiled and headed back into the house. The big man was finally on his own

When Carla's house was finally quiet, Rose went up to her room—her very own room!—which was right next to the one where her two younger sisters slept. She was surprised to find a wrapped package resting on the bed. Before opening the gift, Rose read the card that was attached.

Dear Rose,

I made sure to ask your father if it was okay for me to buy you this gift. At first he wasn't sure if he approved, but Carla told him she thought it was a fine idea and so your dad agreed.

I'll pick you up tomorrow at 6:00 a.m.

- Adan

Trak held a cup of coffee in a white mug. The morning sun was a fiery ball on the horizon. "You be careful."

"I will," Adan called from the driver's seat of the truck. "We'll be back for dinner."

Trak waved as the boy pulled out of the drive. Holly danced in the front seat. After the vehicle disappeared down the road, Brooke appeared in one of Trak's flannel shirts. She reached out and wrapped her arms around his waist.

He smiled and kissed her on the top of her head. "Hungry?"

Brooke thought for a moment. "Starving."

Later that morning, after following Trak's directions, Rose and Adan entered Zion National Park's south entrance. Adan parked the truck at the head of the Pa'rus Trail and jumped out. Holly barked and leaped after him.

For a moment, Rose sat, riveted to the giant towers of Zion, sentinels that resembled Canaan Mountain which had loomed over her entire life. She recalled Mr. Wayland explaining how these soaring red walls had formed eons ago, buried sediments turned exceptionally hard into Navajo Sandstone that were thrust upward by the shifting of continental plates, and then subjected to millions of years of erosion.

The door opened.

"You ready?" Adan grinned. A scarlet Arizona Cardinals cap covered his dark hair.

Rose blushed. "Yes." She got out of the truck. Her feet—encased in a brand new pair of gray and teal, Saucony Peregrine 4, trail running shoes—touched the parking lot pavement.

Adan stared like he hadn't seen her before. Against the magnificent backdrop, she was even more beautiful, and she looked like she'd been wearing running clothes like the teal jacket and a matching racer-back tank and leggings all her life. And then an emerald hummingbird darted overhead, distracting them both.

"Shall we get started?" Adan asked.

"That's what we're here for," Rose said with a smile.

They began slowly, with Holly darting at their heels. They passed flowering grasses and massive jutting cliffs that resembled the naked backbones of long gone dinosaurs. Low, gray clouds floated in a cerulean blue sky and kissed the soaring summits. Finches darted by.

They took plenty of breaks for water and paused overlooking a sparkling stream overhung with cottonwoods. In the background, green clumps of foliage dotted the red-yellow slopes of the mountain called The Watchman.

Rose stretched her legs.

"You OK?" Adan asked.

"I'm fine." She grinned and raised her head. "Do you smell that?" Her eyes traveled up the cliff side.

"Rain?"

"Yes." She squinted, thinking. "Mr. Wayland called that smell petrichor: the scent of rain on the earth after a long period of dry, warm weather. Rose thought for a moment and tried to remember. "It comes from a Greek word; *petros*, meaning stone or rock. And *ichor* . . . is the fluid that flows in the veins of the Gods." She grinned.

"You're a smart girl, Rose."

She blushed. Their eyes met for a moment. Then, embarrassed, they both gazed at the stream, where several gray mule deer sipped at the rocky edge. Molly barked, impatient to get on with the run. A big buck raised its head, but had no fear of the dog, since this was the one trail in the park where canines were permitted and the deer had long ago outgrown their fear of the creatures.

"Do you want to keep going?" Adan pointed up the Pa'rus Trail. "Trak asked me to take it slow, because of your wound. If you're tired, we can head back."

Rose raised both blond eyebrows. Then she bolted up the trail, with Holly racing at her heels.

Adan grinned, counted to ten, and chased after her.

The End

ACKNOWLEGEMENTS

I must thank my agent, Donna Eastman at Parkeast Literary Agency and Amphorae Publishing Group for agreeing to take on a book with clearly difficult subject matter. Forced child marriage and child abuse often reside in the shadows. It is my hope that *The Scent of Rain* will shine a light on theses horrendous issues, specifically in the FLDS enclaves, so that the men, women, and children who are suffering at the hands of this cult can live more open and inclusive lives.

To my editors, Kristina Blank Makansi and Donna Essner, thank you for sharing your ideas and expertise, and for helping me tell Rose's story.

Many of the details depicted came directly from Flora Jessop, who allowed me to interview her at length about her experiences with the FLDS. Flora escaped twice from the cult, only to be returned by local authorities more interested in their religious beliefs than in their mandated responsibility to protect a child. Flora, who now resides in Phoenix, continues to fight to save the women and girls who are being held captive in the twin cities of Hildale, Utah and Colorado City, Arizona. Thank you, Flora, for all your help.

I would also like to thank Dr. Theodore Tarby, who treated many of the FLDS children on the Arizona Strip, and who tried to convince the cult members to marry outside their community in order to avoid the plague of birth defects caused by inbreeding. Dr. Tarby was kind enough to let me interview him about his experiences and the science behind the illnesses with which the people suffer.

When I decided to travel to the Arizona Strip to visit these polygamist enclaves for research, I knew that the local people considered outsiders a product of Satan. With that in mind, I thought going alone might be unwise, so I recruited my friend, Patty Congdon, to join me on the long, lonely drive through northern Arizona. We pretended to be totally ignorant of the area, saying we were searching for a place where she might retire. While I am not one to generally be frightened, I have to admit that wandering through the town and its market and graveyard were disconcerting. I will never forget the face of the tiny girl child standing in a shopping cart, wearing her light blue, ankle-length prairie dress, who gaped at me. She broke my heart when she turned away in fear. I'm glad Patty was with me, so we could talk through what was happening. I'm also grateful for Patty's comments, suggestions, and her ability to laugh.

I'd also like to thank my friend and fellow teacher Linda Bennett for reading the manuscript. It's not often easy to get people to take the time. So, thanks, Linda.

Finally, my appreciation to my family. To Ryan, who always has my back and who never fails to make me laugh, and to my boys, Brandon, Ziggy, and Troy. I love you all.

ABOUT THE AUTHOR

Anne Butler Montgomery has worked as a television sportscaster, newspaper and magazine writer, teacher, amateur baseball umpire, and high school football referee. Her first TV job came at WRBL-TV in Columbus, Georgia, and led to positions at WROC-TV in Rochester, New York, KTSP-TV in Phoenix, Arizona, and ESPN in Bristol, Connecticut, where she anchored the Emmy and ACE award-winning *SportsCenter*. She finished her on-camera broadcasting career with a two-year stint as the studio host for the NBA's Phoenix Suns. Montgomery was a freelance and/or staff reporter for six publications, writing sports, features, movie reviews, and archeological pieces. Her two previous novels are *A Light in the Desert* and *Nothing But Echoes*. Montgomery teaches journalism at South Mountain High School in Phoenix, is a foster mom to three sons, and is an Arizona Interscholastic Association football referee and crew chief. When she can, she indulges in her passions: rock collecting, football officiating, scuba diving, and playing her guitar.

CPSIA information can be obtained
at www.ICGtesting.com
Printed in the USA
LVOW11s0208070417
529946LV00002B/2/P